4

Flowers and Foul Play

Also available by Amanda Flower

Living History Museum Mysteries

The Final Vow

The Final Tap

The Final Reveille

Amish Candy Shop Mysteries

Lethal Licorice

Assaulted Caramel

Magical Bookshop Mysteries

Prose and Cons

Crime and Poetry

Andi Boggs Mysteries

Andi Unstoppable

Andi Under Pressure

Andi Unexpected

Appleseed Creek Mysteries

A Plain Malice

A Plain Disappearance

A Plain Scandal

A Plain Death

India Hayes Mysteries

Murder in a Basket

Maid of Murder

Flowers and Foul Play

A MAGIC GARDEN MYSTERY

Amanda Flower

CROOKED
LANE

NEW YORK

Copyright © 2018 by Amanda Flower.

Published in the United States by Crooked Lane Books, an imprint of The Quick Brown Fox & Company LLC.

Crooked Lane Books and its logo are trademarks of The Quick Brown Fox & Company LLC.

Library of Congress Catalog-in-Publication data available upon request.

ISBN (hardcover): 978-1-68331-562-9
ISBN (ePub): 978-1-68331-563-6
ISBN (ePDF): 978-1-68331-564-3

Cover illustration by Matthew Kalamidas/StoneHouse Creative Inc.
Book design by Jennifer Canzone

Printed in the United States.

www.crookedlanebooks.com

Crooked Lane Books
34 West 27th St., 10th Floor
New York, NY 10001

First edition: May 2018

10 9 8 7 6 5 4 3 2 1

For Mariellyn and Laurie Ellyn
Leave no Go-Go Girl Behind
and
David

"Magic is always pushing and drawing and making things out of nothing. Everything is made out of magic, leaves and trees, flowers and birds, badgers and foxes and squirrels and people. So it must be all around us. In this garden—in all the places."

—Frances Hodgson Burnett, *The Secret Garden*

Chapter One

I will never eat cake again. This is a vow that I can keep. Unlike my wedding vows that I will never have a chance to uphold or say because I'm not getting married—maybe ever. I'm certainly not marrying Ethan Easton, the next big thing in country music—or so I was told he would be, more times than I cared to count.

"Passport and customs form, miss!" A firm female voice broke into my muddled thoughts and, okay, the personal pity party that I was hosting inside my head. I would give anything to be able to expel the thoughts about Ethan that plagued my mind, so much so that I would even move halfway across the world.

"Passport," the voice repeated, not without a little bit of irritation. The woman behind me in line sighed loudly. I shuffled forward and blinked at the young, serious-faced woman inside the bulletproof glass booth. I handed her my passport and customs form. "Why are you entering the United Kingdom?"

I swallowed. "I'm on holiday." I didn't see any need to tell her that I planned to move there. If I said it aloud, then it would be real, and reality wasn't something I had a great handle on at the moment, right after my heart had been broken by Ethan; and then it was stomped on for good measure when my flower shop in Nashville folded because of competition from a discount flower shop that moved in across the street. Besides, I didn't have the necessary paperwork to move to the country. Paperwork and visas were the last things on my mind when I fled Nashville.

"Where are you staying?"

"Near Bellewick," I answered. "In County Aberdeen."

She raised her eyebrows but made no further comment on my lodging choice. She stamped my passport with far more force than was needed. "Welcome to Scotland," she said, sliding it back to me.

I stepped back from the window and followed the other weary travelers, like a lost lemming, through the Edinburgh Airport to ground transport.

An hour later, I had collected my suitcase and my rental car, and I was outside the city, navigating the roundabouts that opened up into the Scottish countryside, where the rolling green hills and brown mountains were shadowed in a late morning mist. Along the highway, gorse, a vibrant yellow flowering shrub, burst so brightly, I felt like I needed sunglasses to avoid the glare coming off the flowers. During the first week of May, they were in their glory. As beautiful as they were, I knew not to get too close to them. Gorse is covered in thorns that would tear your skin to shreds if you had the misfortune to land on one of the beautiful plants. Like many beautiful things, they were dangerous.

The scenery reminded me of summers gone by, when my family would come to Scotland to visit my father's old college roommate and my godfather, Ian MacCallister, whom I had always considered my uncle. Uncle Ian had been a career army man and never married. As far as I knew, my parents and my younger sister, Isla, and I were the closest to family that he had, and I loved him dearly. Dad and Uncle Ian had gone to St. Andrews together. My parents also met at St. Andrews when my American mother was there for a study-abroad program. When my mother's year in Scotland ended, my father followed her back to Tennessee and never moved back to the U.K. I was born shortly after they moved stateside. Despite the distance, they had remained close to Uncle Ian, and I, as Ian's goddaughter, was the bond that held their friendship together when distance and busyness might have otherwise torn it apart.

Although we had lived half a world away, Uncle Ian had stayed in touch and had taken his title as my godfather seriously. He never forgot a birthday or a Christmas. His presents had come from his travels all over the world as a soldier and an adventurer. He never stayed in any place for long except for his ancestral home of Duncreigan, a cottage just west of Bellewick, a tiny village tucked away in northeastern Scotland on the sloping hillside, in view of the rocky coast. It was thirty minutes south of the city of Aberdeen on the A90 and just north of the famous Dunnottar Castle. Duncreigan was a cottage that I now owned—or so Uncle Ian's attorney had told me repeatedly on the telephone. The attorney repeated it because I couldn't quite process what he said.

My father, who was Uncle Ian's best friend, hadn't even known about his friend's death until I got the first call from the attorney. We weren't family, at least not blood relations, and the British army hadn't known to notify us of Ian's passing.

The biggest shock had been that he left his cottage to me and not to my father. Maybe he had known I would need a place to escape my life. He'd seemed to be intuitive in that regard. He knew so many things and called at all the right times, like when I failed chemistry in high school, on my first day of my first real job as an adult, and when my beloved grandmother died. There had been something about Uncle Ian. He had known when I needed him. He would joke that his Gaelic ancestors whispered in his ear to tell him when I was feeling low.

Tears gathered in my eyes. There had been so much loss in my life in such a short period. However, the end of my relationship with Ethan was not nearly as great as the loss from Uncle Ian's death. When Ethan had broken off our engagement, Uncle Ian had been the first person I had wanted to call and tell about the breakup. I should have known something was wrong when I couldn't reach him after Ethan left me for the cake decorator eight days ago or when my business closed its doors for good ten days ago. Not that I was keeping track of the days or anything. The Uncle Ian that I knew would have known. I should have known then that he was dead. Maybe I had and just hadn't been able to face it. The lawyer's call had forced me to.

I wiped at my eyes with the back of my hand and took a

deep breath. Every time I thought I didn't have any more tears, another round overcame me.

*   *   *

After almost three hours of driving, Duncreigan came into view. The sun hovered just above the roof of the cottage, wrapping it in a halo of light. It was as I remembered it, with its thick stone walls cut out of the granite the region was famous for, the two chimneys on either side of the cottage, and the black slate roof. A large fir tree to the right of the house offered the cottage protection from the fierce Scottish wind that roared across the rolling glen. The cold wind could cut right through you even on the warmest of summer days. The glen itself was peppered with large rocks breaking through the thick carpet of impossibly green grass. A cobblestone path led the way from the gravel drive, speckled with weeds and grass, to the forest-green front door and its brass knocker, shaped like the head of a fox. Everything was just as I remembered it when last I was here three years ago. I found comfort in the fact that one spot in the world seemed to be caught in time, remaining as it always had been.

The tires of my rental car crunched on the gravel as I slowed the car to a stop and shifted it into park. A stout, elderly man in blue work shirt and black suspenders that held up his flannel trousers came around the side of the cottage just as I was climbing out of the car. He had a pug-like nose and bright green eyes, and wore a golf cap low on his forehead. "Hello, lass." His words rumbled in his deep Scottish accent.

"Hamish?" I blinked. The last time I'd visited, Hamish,

the caretaker of my godfather's garden when Uncle Ian was away, seemed to have been over one hundred years old. Even at his advanced age, he moved across the yard with ease. His arms and legs swung with the assurance of a man in constant motion. "Master Ian said that you would come, and you have. We will be rescued now."

I blinked at his comment. Rescued? I was the last person who was able to rescue anyone. At the moment, my life hung together by loose threads and whimpered prayer. Before I could ask him what he meant, a red squirrel catapulted from the lone tree and landed on Hamish's shoulder.

I screamed, and both Hamish and the squirrel gaped at me. The squirrel stood on his two hind legs and cocked his head.

"Something wrong, Miss Fiona?" Hamish asked.

I pointed at the animal. "Squirrel." That was all I could get out.

He glanced at the squirrel and shrugged, and I would be lying if I didn't say that the squirrel shrugged back. "Him? That's just Duncan."

"Duncan?" I squeaked.

Duncan the squirrel settled back into a more comfortable position on Hamish's shoulder.

Hamish patted the creature on the top of his head. "Aye. He's my friend. My only friend now that Master Ian has gone on to be with his Maker." His voice held a melancholy lilt to it. He shook his head as if in the process of moving on from the memory, and his face broke into a wide smile, revealing slightly crooked teeth. "My, you have grown up to be a lovely Scottish lass."

I laughed. "Can I come across as a Scottish lass with a Tennessee accent?" And I self-consciously touched my long and wavy black hair. I could only guess how tangled it must be after the transatlantic flight or how bloodshot my blue eyes might be.

"Ah, that might be true, but Scottish blood runs in your veins no matter how funny you may talk, and you are as fair as any Scottish lass I've ever seen." His grin widened. "And I bet many a young man would be proud to have you on his arm."

I winced as Ethan's face came to the forefront of my mind. "Not every young man."

Hamish and Duncan cocked both their heads to the right in unison, and I couldn't help but chuckle at the image they created.

Hamish pointed a meaty index finger at me. "There's a story there, to be sure. You will tell it when you are good and ready."

I didn't know if I would ever be ready to tell Hamish about my broken engagement or my failed business, but I nodded in any case.

Duncan jumped from Hamish's shoulder to the ground and ran to the cottage, leaping on the windowsill. He tapped on the glass with his tiny paw.

Hamish's craggy face broke into another smile, and he doffed the golf cap on his head, bowing slightly at the waist. "'Tis right, Duncan. We should show Miss Fiona her home."

My home? I took in the cottage again. Could it really be mine?

Hamish stood beside me and held out the cottage's skeleton key to me. I recognized it immediately from my time in

Scotland with Uncle Ian. "This is yours now. This is all yours now."

I hesitated for just a moment but then held out my hand. He gently laid the key on my palm, and with his other hand, curved my fingers around it. I felt the heft and weight of the old skeleton key in my hand, and reality set in that this cottage could be the setting of my new life, if I chose it.

"Now, go inside," he said gently but firmly.

I hesitated, not sure I was ready for this. "Is the cottage locked?"

"Oh, yes," he said. "No one has been in there since the memorial service."

I shuffled to the door and made eye contact with the fox knocker as I fit the key into the lock and turned it. To my surprise, the key turned easily, and the door swung inward.

Dust particles that had been thrown into the air by my entry into the room danced like woodland sprites in the light that poured through the open door. Across from me was the cottage's one massive fireplace, which heated the entire home. It was barren, with not even a speck of soot on the hearth. White sheets covered most of the furniture, creating odd ghostlike shapes.

The cottage was small, almost the size of a one-bedroom apartment. The main room served as a dining room, living room, and kitchen. The small table and chairs that constituted the dining area was to my left; the living area was straight ahead; and the kitchen was to my right. Behind the kitchen were three closed doors that I knew led to my godfather's bedroom, a bathroom, and a tiny utility closet. It was smaller than the apartment I'd left behind in Nashville.

I stepped inside and walked toward the fireplace. Memories of huddling by its warmth while Uncle Ian told stories about the Highlands washed over me like a rolling wave. For once, the memories didn't come with the tinge of sadness that I had come to expect when I thought of him, but with the warmth of the love in which he had shared those stories.

On the mantle, there was a dusty, framed photograph of Uncle Ian in his army uniform. I laid the key on the one uncovered table in the room and lifted the framed photo from its spot. In it, Ian appeared to be in his thirties. He'd only been fifty-nine when he died. He had been about to retire from the Royal Army after his last tour overseas in Afghanistan as part of the United Kingdom's forces there. He was just weeks away from flying home when he was killed.

I set the photograph back on the mantle in the exact place I had found it, which wasn't hard to find because of the thick layer of dust covering every surface. Again, I just felt warmth, not sadness, in this place. Maybe the peace I had so desperately wanted after my life fell apart in Nashville could be found right here in Duncreigan.

Hamish's voice broke into my thoughts. "Open the widows and run a broom through here, and it will be as good as new."

I smiled at him. "You might be right."

Above the mantle hung a large painting dating back to the 1700s. It was a portrait of my godfather's four-times-great-grandfather, Baird MacCallister, who was the first MacCallister to live at Duncreigan. He wore his sailor's uniform in the portrait. My godfather told me that Baird was a career merchant sailor, but when he found Duncreigan, he abandoned life at sea forever.

I moved to pick up the key from the table where I had left it, when Duncan dashed into the room, snatched the key off the table, and leaped out the cottage door.

"Duncan, you come back here, you beastie!" Hamish shook his fist in the air, looking very much like the picture of Farmer MacGregor from Beatrix Potter's *The Tale of Peter Rabbit*. Hamish ran out the door.

I joined him just in time to see Duncan dash across the green landscape with the key held between his teeth.

"We have to get it back," Hamish cried. "That's the only key."

Without a word, I took off after the squirrel.

Chapter Two

"Duncan!" I cried as I chased the squirrel across the plush green grass. Dampness soaked through my sneakers and socks.

Duncan kept going without even turning his head. I didn't know why I expected a squirrel to respond to his name when called.

The hillside pitched downward, and a stone wall came into view. It was so covered with ivy that the stones were barely visible. I slowed and caught my breath. Duncan scaled the ivy-covered wall that rose a good nine feet into the air. I placed a hand to my chest and felt the thundering of my heart. I couldn't remember the last time I'd run so fast.

From the top of the wall, the squirrel looked back at me one last time, with the key clenched in his jaws, before he leaped over the other side. I inched forward. The ivy crawled all over the face of the wall as I had remembered it, but the last time I had been there, it had been an iridescent green. Now, the leaves and vines were brown and withered. Thousands of ivy leaves lay on the ground, exposing more of the granite wall. The old dome-shaped door leading into the garden was easily found. In my memory, it had been hidden by the thick tangle of vines like a secret entrance into an enchanted world.

The door was weather-beaten and grayed with age. The black iron handle was as long as my forearm, and the black keyhole stood out on the whitened wood. I shuffled forward to the keyhole, which was an inch high and half an inch wide. Peeking through it, I gasped at what I saw. The garden, Uncle Ian's garden, was dead.

How could this be? I blinked tears from my eyes. The garden had been Uncle Ian's pride and joy. Hamish loved the garden too. How could he let it die?

I brushed away a set of dead vines and wrapped my hand around the handle, pushing in. The old hinges creaked, but the door moved enough to allow me to squeeze inside. I was surprised that the door opened at all. My godfather had always kept the garden locked when no one was inside it.

On the other side of the wall, the dead garden was even harder to bear. Brown and gray muted the vast space that had once been a kaleidoscope of color. Everything was dead—not a single blade of grass had survived. The only color that I could see was above in the blue sky.

Hamish ran into the garden and gasped for breath. "Master Ian never told me that you were a sprinter."

I turned on him. "How could you let the garden die?" I couldn't keep the accusation from my voice.

He held up his hands. "I tried to save the garden, Miss Fiona—I did try—but nothing I did helped. It began to wither up just days before I got word that Master Ian had been killed in that awful war. I should have known when the garden began to fade that he was dead. A better caretaker would have known."

I blinked at him. "Are you telling me the garden died because Uncle Ian died?"

Hamish opened his mouth as if to answer, when a spot of red dashed across my peripheral vision. Duncan. I saw the key still in his clutches.

"Duncan, stop!" I cried.

Again, the squirrel ignored me when called and raced deeper into the garden toward a large hedgerow. I followed him in hot pursuit. I came around the side of a brown hedge into the middle of the garden. A standing stone that was just a few inches taller than I was—I guessed it to be about six feet—stood in the middle of the garden. A single, bright yellow, climbing rose wrapped itself around the standing stone. Its green leaves shone in the sunlight, and its yellow petals glistened with dew, even though it was midafternoon and the dew should have burned off by now. It was the only spot in the entire garden with color.

Ian had told me once that the standing stone was called a *menhir*, a single upright stone put there thousands of years ago by long-forgotten people to mark something—to mark what exactly, we'd never know, but could only speculate on.

Duncan sat at the foot of the menhir with the key still in his mouth. He looked up at the rock as if deciding whether or not to climb it.

Behind me I heard Hamish come around the side of the hedgerow. "You're going to have to stop running off like that, Miss Fiona, if you expect me to keep up with you." He gasped. "Master Ian was right!"

I spun around to face him. "Right about what?"

"He was right that you would come here and that when you did, the garden would come back to life. You *are* the one who will save the garden. I should have never doubted Master Ian." He said Uncle Ian's name with reverence.

"But you said he died and so did the garden. How could he have told you all this, then?" I asked.

He removed his hat and scratched the top of his bald head before replacing the hat. "I got a letter, and he said in the letter that this was true. He said if anything ever happened to him, you would bring the garden back. He said he sent a letter to you as well."

"I never received any letter." I tried to keep the frustration out of my voice, but it was hard. This was all too unbelievable. I put a hand to my forehead to see if it was hot. A fever and the hallucinations that it could bring might explain my current circumstances.

Duncan dropped the key in front of the standing stone before running off and climbing a trellis covered with withered vines to my right.

I hurried forward and scooped up the key. As I did so, I noticed a black boot sticking out from behind the menhir. I peered around the side. The boot was attached to a leg, which was attached to a person, who was most certainly dead.

I must have screamed, because Hamish raced to my side. "What is it, Miss Fiona? Did Duncan do some—" He stopped mid-question because the answer as to what had made me scream lay at my feet.

Hamish muttered something in Gaelic that I didn't understand. At least I didn't understand the words. The sentiment was clear, and if I translated it into English, it would not be repeatable in polite society.

"What happened to him?" I managed to ask.

Hamish straightened and seemed to recover from the shock. At least, he recovered much more quickly than I was. "I dunno. I don't see any blood or anything. Usually there is blood at a time like this."

At a time like this? Was this not the first time that Hamish had found a dead body?

"I don't see any mark on the man," he said, inching closer. I felt sick.

"I wonder who it is," Hamish murmured.

Before I could stop him, he tapped the body with his boot, and the dead man's head lolled to the side.

The impossibly red face that I saw was of a young man not too much older than me. I guessed that he was in his mid-thirties. Even though he was dead, I could tell that he had been handsome. I looked away.

Hamish was quiet—too quiet. I peeked at him and saw him staring at the body.

"Hamish," I asked, "do you know who it is?"

"I do, Miss Fiona, I do."

I waited for a moment, and when he didn't say anything, I asked, "Well, who is it?"

He tore his eyes away from the body on the ground and met my gaze. "It's Alastair Croft, Miss Fiona."

My mouth fell open, and despite my revulsion, I looked at Alastair Croft's face again. I pointed at him. "You mean this is Uncle Ian's attorney, the man who called me just two days ago and told me that I inherited the cottage?"

He nodded. "Yes, Miss Fiona, that is who I mean."

This wasn't good. This wasn't good at all. And it was more "not good" than just finding a dead guy. I didn't know how I knew that, but I knew it down to my bones that Alastair Croft's death was going to have a major impact on my life very, very soon.

"We must call the police," Hamish said. "It might take some time for them to get here. The closest constables are in Aberdeen."

I removed my phone from my jacket pocket. "Do you know the number for the police? I can call them now. Then we can discuss what we are going to do while we wait for them."

He stared at my phone. "How does your phone work way out here?"

I smiled despite the circumstances. "I have international calling."

He shook his head. "I will never understand all these gadgets that the young people have now." He rattled off the number for the police from memory. Again, I wondered how much experience Hamish had with dead bodies, since the police's number seemed to be at the tip of his tongue.

As I explained to the dispatcher who I was, where I was, and what Hamish and I had discovered, all the peace that I had felt when I stood in my uncle's cottage floated away like one of the clouds over the snow-speckled Scottish mountains.

Chapter Three

After I made the call to the police, Hamish and I agreed that he and Duncan would stay with Alastair's body, and I would meet the constables at the cottage. Someone would need to show them how to find the garden. I was more than willing to follow that plan. I didn't want to be alone in the dead garden with the dead man, even if Duncan consented to stick around and keep me company.

I wove my way back around the hedge that hid the menhir from view, and on to the garden's door. When I was through the door, I let all semblance of dignity fall away, and I ran full tilt up the hillside toward the cottage. When I reached the top, and the cottage and my rental car came into view, I fought an overwhelming urge to jump into the car and drive away. I knew that was a bad idea. I couldn't find a dead body, report it, and think I would be let out of the U.K. without so much as a second thought. I knew what would happen. The authorities would put a hold on my passport. I would be stopped at the airport. I wasn't leaving Scotland any time soon.

All plans of fleeing the country went out of my head as I saw a forest-green jeep roll slowly up Uncle Ian's gravel driveway. It came to stop next to the giant fir tree just as I reached the cottage's cobblestone walk. A moment later, a very tall man with broad shoulders; thick, dark auburn hair; and a full, trim beard climbed out of the car. He slammed the jeep's door and walked toward me.

I adjusted my stance in case I needed to run for it. I had just found a dead body, after all, and I couldn't be too careful. "Can I help you?"

"I'm Chief Inspector Craig from County Aberdeen. I heard that someone at Duncreigan found a body." His voice was deep and had the rich Scottish brogue I'd always associated with my uncle. I wondered for a moment if he moonlighted as a singer at one of the many pubs that dotted County Aberdeen's coastline. He had the right voice for it.

"Aberdeen is a ways away," I said. "We didn't expect someone to come so quickly."

He raised one thick auburn eyebrow. "I was on my way back home from Glasgow when I got the call. Since I was the closest, I offered to come and look in."

"Oh," I said. What he said made perfect sense, but there was something about it that didn't sit well with me. It was just too pat, too easy that he happened to be in the area. I supposed finding a dead guy in a foreign country could make me question everything and everyone. Or maybe it was Ethan's calling off the engagement that made me do that. Trust in others was something I would have to work on getting back.

"May I ask who you are? Clearly, you're American. A tourist?" He looked me up and down.

I frowned. "I'm visiting the country, but I'm not a tourist."

He waited, and I wondered if I had said too much. Then again, I should be up front about things, I decided. The police wouldn't look kindly on me if it acted like I was hiding something.

"I'm Fiona Knox. I just arrived in Scotland today."

"But you're not a tourist," he said in a way that told me he wanted me to get on with my story.

"No. I'm sure you know that Ian MacCallister, who owned this cottage and land, is dead."

He nodded. "He was a war hero and will be greatly missed."

"I'm his heir, and I came to Scotland to claim my inheritance." I paused. "Or at least to look at it. I don't know for certain if I'm planning to stay. Now that I found a dead man, the temptation to stay here is far, far less than when I got off the plane just a few hours ago."

"He left Duncreigan to an American?" The eyebrow went up again, and he said it in such a way that made me think he equated Americans with Martians.

I felt my eyes narrow. "Ian MacCallister was my godfather. I'm—well, my parents, sister, and I—are the closest thing to family that he had."

He seemed to consider this. "I see. May I have your passport, Miss Knox?" He held out his hand and waited.

"My passport?" I squeaked. Anyone who travels overseas knows that your passport is your most valuable possession. To be separated from your passport at any time is a true nightmare.

He waggled his fingers. "Miss Knox?"

My passport was hidden in my money belt that I had strapped around my waist just below my bra. I had put it there for safekeeping after I'd cleared customs. There was no way that I could reach the passport without flashing the officer a view of my midsection, if not a bit more. I felt my face grow hot. "It's strapped to my body." I paused. "Under my shirt."

The corner of his mouth twitched as if he was fighting—and failing—to hide a grin. "Oh? Did you think you would get mugged out in the middle of nowhere here?"

I narrowed my eyes. "You can never be too careful, and clearly, mugging is a possibility. I think the dead man I found would agree with me."

The smile fell away from his face. "You're right, of course. My sincerest apologies." In a much more serious voice, he asked, "May I please have your passport."

I scowled. "So, if you want me to give it to you, you're going to have to turn around."

"I did not know Americans were so modest." There was humor back in his voice.

"I'm from the South, and where I'm from, all good girls are modest."

A grin spread across his broad, handsome face. "Duly noted, Miss Knox," he said. To my relief, he did as I asked, and turned around to face the fir tree.

I eyed him for a moment, just to make sure he wouldn't sneak a peek. When I was satisfied that he was staring at the tree, I took off my jacket, dropped it on the ground, and untucked my shirt. I quickly removed my passport from the money belt, dropped my shirt back over my stomach, and put my jacket back on.

"Are you getting completely undressed to do this?" Chief Inspector Craig asked.

I glared at his back. "You can turn around now."

He turned with a smile. I held the passport out to him, and he took it.

He opened the document and flipped through it. "You have quite a few stamps in here, don't you? You have traveled far and wide."

I didn't bother to respond. The stamps on my passport answered for me.

He flipped to my identification page, examined my photo, and then searched my face. He seemed satisfied that they matched, even though the photo was over six years old and had been taken on a particularly bad hair day. "I'll just keep this for now," he said.

Fear gripped my chest. "I don't think you can keep that without my permission. I'm not a suspect," I said.

He tucked my passport into the inside pocket of his jacket. "I can most certainly keep this in the middle of an investigation of a suspicious death, and if there is evidence of foul play, you, Miss Knox, are a suspect. You found the body."

My stomach clenched. Things would only become worse when he found out that I knew the dead man, and it was Uncle Ian's attorney, who had spoken to me recently. I had only talked to Alastair Croft on the phone twice before arriving in Scotland, but I would have been much better off if I had no connection to him at all.

Before I could protest more, he said, "Show me where the body is."

"It's in the garden a little ways from here. I left Hamish watching over it," I said.

Chief Inspector Craig tensed. "Hamish MacGregor? You left Hamish MacGregor with the body?"

I stepped back from him. "Yes. He is the caretaker of Duncreigan. Uncle Ian trusted him implicitly. Why wouldn't I leave him with the body? *I* didn't want to be the one left behind with it, and someone had to meet you here."

His jaw twitched. "You had better show me where it is, and quickly."

Rather than argue, I led him across the meadow and down the hillside toward the garden. I walked briskly, but I didn't sprint as I had when chasing Duncan.

Chief Inspector Craig stopped just as the stone wall covered with the dead ivy came into view. "The body was inside there? Of all places, there is a dead body inside there?"

As we stood there, the ivy turned from brown to green right before our eyes. The chief inspector stared at me and asked, "Do you know what this is?"

"A garden." It was the only answer I had to offer, and I knew it wasn't enough. A garden—a normal, everyday garden—doesn't come back to life in a matter a moments. Not like this.

When I'd boarded the flight out of Nashville, maybe for forever, I had thought I would give anything to expel my past failures from my mind. As I watched the ivy green, I realized that that wish had been granted in short order with the discovery of Alastair Croft's dead body. I should have been more specific with my wishes. Seeing the amazement and maybe just a hint of fear on Chief Inspector Craig's face, I realized it was far too late to edit my wishes now.

Chapter Four

As if it had never begun, the ivy stopped greening. Some of its pointed leaves were caught in mid-transformation. They were half withered and brown, and half lush and green. It gave the stone walls of the garden an eerie camouflage effect.

Craig turned to me. "What is going on here?"

I silently shook my head. I didn't have an answer.

"Where is the body?" he asked.

"Inside," I squeaked.

"And Hamish is in there with it?" he asked.

I nodded, still confused why he would be concerned about Hamish being with the body. My entire life, Uncle Ian had only had good things to say about the elderly caretaker. He'd even told me once he would trust Hamish with his life, and this was coming from a career soldier who faced life and death every single day when he was deployed. I tried to remember in what context Uncle Ian had made that comment, but I couldn't bring it to mind.

Craig waved me ahead as if to say "after you." Perhaps he wanted me to be the first to touch the ivy. I brushed the vines aside and pushed open the door just as I had less than an hour before. Now at least I knew what awaited me. Even with the odd coloring of the ivy, I wasn't afraid to touch or open the door to the garden. This had been my godfather's special place, his favorite place in all the world. How could I look on it with anything other than fondness? It reminded me of the dear man who I had loved and who had loved me.

The hinges on the weathered door creaked ever so slightly as I pushed in. I peeked through, half-expecting new signs of life and growth in the garden, but there were none. The grass, trees, and shrubs all appeared to be dead, as dead as Alastair Croft, esquire.

Hamish popped out from around the side of the hedgerow that hid the standing stone from view. Duncan was perched on his right shoulder, and I could be wrong, but the squirrel appeared to be smiling. I had a feeling that Duncan went through life feeling awfully pleased with himself.

"Neil," Hamish said as he brushed dead leaves off his seat, "I should have known you'd be the first one here."

"Hamish," Craig said. His voice was clipped. "Where is the body?"

Hamish pointed. "Just on the other side of the hedge."

I looked from one man to the other. What was I missing here? Clearly the two knew each other. Considering there was a dead guy on the other side of the hedgerow, I suspected that their mutual animosity was bad news for me.

Craig stepped around the hedge, and Hamish, carrying Duncan, and I followed him. By the time I cleared the side of the hedge, Craig was already bent at the waist, staring at the dead body. I grimaced as, against my will, I took another peek at it. I had to look away, but again I couldn't see any wound on the man's face or hands. Those were the only body parts that showed. He wore trousers and a wool navy coat over a white shirt and tie. His shoes were black leather loafers, and polished. He wore socks.

"Can you take a step back, Miss Knox?" Craig's deep voice interrupted my thoughts.

I blinked at him, flushed red, and mumbled an apology as I stumbled two feet back. Next to Craig's right shoulder as he leaned over the body, one of the blossoms from the yellow rose sparkled in the late afternoon sun. The dew on its petals glistened in the changing light. If Craig noticed that the rose was the only thing blooming in the garden or realized that it was May and way too early for roses to bloom this far north in Scotland, he made no comment on it.

"Hmm," Craig said as he straightened up.

"Hmm?" I asked. "What does 'hmm' mean?"

He glanced over at me. "All it means is 'hmm.'"

"We both speak English, so I'm fairly sure that *hmm* is just a sound, not a word."

He smiled. "Hmm."

I had to bite the inside of my cheek to fight a smile that was forming. I don't know why the back-and-forth with the chief inspector gave me the urge to smile. I must have been delirious. It had to be a combination of jet lag and finding the dead guy. That would take the best woman down.

"The victim is Alastair Croft," Craig said after a beat.

"It is," Hamish agreed.

Craig turned and squinted directly into the sunlight that just cleared the stone wall. It was almost like he was trying to punish himself by looking directly into the light.

"Didn't you two boys run in school together?" Hamish asked.

"We were friends once, yes," Craig said and turned back to Hamish and me.

"He's your friend?" I asked. "How terrible. I'm so sorry."

"He is not a friend. That is not the word that I would use."

I glanced back at the body. "Will another chief inspector be coming?" I asked.

"Two constables are on the way, as well as the coroner and the two crime scene techs. It will take them at least another half hour to get here. They're coming from Aberdeen. Belle-wick is the closest village, but they don't have a police force—or at least not one worth speaking of."

I knew Bellewick was close. I had been there many times when I visited my godfather. It was just a short ten-minute car ride into the village from the cottage, or a twenty-minute bike ride when the fierce Scottish wind was at your back and persistent enough to push you up the rolling road that leads into town.

"Should you be on the case if he's a friend of yours?" I asked.

He looked at me. "I don't know how they do things in the United States, but here in Aberdeenshire, I am the only one who investigates any type of murder. Whether or not I know the person, I will investigate the crime."

O-kay then, I thought. I took a step back from the police officer.

His face softened. "I do apologize if that came off a tad bit harsh. Admittedly, I'm taken aback that the victim is some-one I've known all my life."

I bit my lip to stop myself from saying, "Then maybe someone else should be on the case." Instead I asked, "Can you tell how he died?"

He shook his head. "Maybe a heart attack or a stroke. The coroner will be able to make that determination. We will have to transfer the body back to Aberdeen for the autopsy. There aren't any facilities like that in the village."

I felt a little ill at the mention of an autopsy.

"I'm more curious about how he got inside here. Isn't the garden usually locked?"

I raised my eyebrows, surprised that Craig knew this detail about my godfather's garden. Could he have been here before? "How do you know the garden is usually locked?" I asked.

He looked down at me. I was five foot nine, but the chief inspector dwarfed me with his considerable height. I guessed he had me topped by a good eight inches. I don't usually feel small, but next to Chief Inspector Craig I felt downright petite. "Everyone in the village knows this."

"The village?" I asked, looking up at him.

"Bellewick."

"I know," I said. "Are you telling me that you're from Bellewick?"

"I was. I'm not anymore." His voice was tight.

I frowned, already confused by the way everything seemed to be interconnected in Aberdeenshire. "When Hamish and I arrived at the garden earlier, right before we found poor Mr. Croft, the door was unlocked."

"Did you unlock it?"

"No. I was here for less than twenty minutes before we found the body," I said. "You can ask Hamish if you don't believe me."

He turned to Hamish. "Did you unlock the garden?"

"How could I?" Hamish asked, and crossed his arms. "Duncan had the only key."

"Duncan?" Craig rubbed the back of his head, tangled his short reddish brown curls.

Hamish pointed his thumb at the squirrel. "This is Duncan, of course."

Craig dropped his hand. "Of course he is."

"But I thought that was the key to the cottage he took," I said.

"It was," Hamish said. "It is for both."

Craig looked from Hamish to me, and back again. "Where is the key now?"

Hamish removed it from his pocket. "I have it here. The little scamp finally turned it over."

"Why is the garden always locked?" Craig asked.

My uncle had told me the answer to this question once when I was a small girl and asked the same question. "It's to keep the garden inside, *m'eudail*, my love."

When I was a child, that seemed to make sense. Now I wondered if I should have asked for clarification, but now Uncle Ian was gone, and there were no more chances to ask those unspoken questions or hear those untold stories.

"It always has been," Hamish said.

Craig sighed. "And who locks it?"

"Either Master Ian or I," Hamish said. " 'Course now, it's

just me now that Master Ian is gone. It's Miss Fiona's now, so she can lock it if she wishes. It is her right."

"When was the last time you were inside the garden?"

Hamish reached up and patted the squirrel on his shoulder. "It was two days ago. The garden has not been doing well. I peeked in to see if it had perked up at all. It didn't take a turn for the better until Miss Fiona landed in Scotland. When I left the garden, I locked it up tight."

Craig's head snapped in my direction. "What does he mean by that?"

I lifted my hands aloft. "I have no idea."

Craig backed away from the body. "There is nothing more we can do until the crime scene techs arrive. I think it would be best if all three of us step outside the garden and wait for the rest of my team and the coroner and his team to arrive."

Hamish crossed his arms. "I can't leave that man alone in Master Ian's garden. Master Ian would have never stood for it, to have a strange man in his garden."

Craig pressed his lips together, and they disappeared beneath his beard. It was as if he had no mouth all, just a beard-covered chin. He cleared his throat. "Be that as it may, we are all going to leave the garden together and wait for the other officers outside the wall. Alastair is not going to bring any harm to Ian's garden now. He can't bring harm to anything or anyone anymore."

Hamish looked as if he wanted to argue with the chief inspector, and I placed a hand on his left arm while Duncan stood perched on his right shoulder. After the "keynapping" incident, I didn't trust the squirrel not to jump on my head and tangle himself up in my long, wavy hair. If he got tangled in there, there would be no getting the snarls out. I had lost many a brush trying to untangle my thick hair. "Hamish, please. I know that you are just being protective of the garden, but we have to do what the chief inspector asks right now."

Hamish scowled. "Verra well, Miss Fiona. If that is what you wish. This is *your* garden now, and you can ask me to take care of it as you see fit."

I shook my head. "Hamish, I would never tell you how to care for the garden. You have been doing it longer than I've been alive."

"This is true, but as you can see, the garden died under my care. As Master Ian said, you are the only one who can bring it back to life."

Craig watched the exchange with interest. I would have loved to know what he made of it; I would have loved to know what to make of it myself, because I still had no clue what Hamish was talking about. How would *I* have anything to do with bringing my uncle's garden back to life?

Hamish and I followed Craig around the hedge and back through the garden door. When we were on the other side, Craig asked if he could speak to me alone.

Hamish sat just to the right of the door and leaned back against the brown-green ivy that crawled all over the stones. At least now I knew how he had gotten the leaves on his back-end, the ones he'd brushed off himself when Craig and I arrived in the garden. He had been sitting on the ground.

"Miss Knox?" Craig asked.

I followed him several yards away to the edge of the garden wall. From this angle, I could see just how big the garden was. It was the length and width of a basketball court, and now it and all of its plants were my responsibility. The weight of that knowledge felt heavy on my shoulders.

"Have you ever met him before?" Craig asked. He said this in such a way that it indicated to me that it wasn't the first time he'd asked me that question in the last few minutes.

"Who?" I asked.

He frowned. "Croft. Do you know him?"

"No," I said, happy that I could answer the question honestly. "I never laid eyes on him before."

"So, you don't know him?" His dark eyebrows knit together.

"Well, . . ."

"Well what, Miss Knox?"

I sighed and decided to come clean. It would take no time at all for Craig to learn that Alastair was my godfather's solicitor, and if it looked like I was hiding that information from him, I might never have any hope of retrieving my passport. "Alastair was my godfather's attorney. He was the one who called me and told me about my inheritance."

"I see," he said, giving nothing away with his tone.

"I had two short conversations with him. That was it. At first, he called me to tell me about my inheritance. He told me that he wanted me to come to Scotland as soon as possible so we could settle the transfer of the property into my name. He said it would be much easier for me to do in person and that my godfather's estate would cover the travel expenses for me if that was a concern. I told him that it wasn't a good time for me to come, and I would try to get away in a few months' time. He wasn't pleased to hear it. I think—just solely based on this conversation—that he was somebody who liked to take care of things quickly, someone who wanted to have all his ducks in a row all the time."

Craig nodded as if agreeing with me on that point. "But you are here," he said.

I blushed. "I called Alastair back two days later to tell him that I had changed my mind. I told him that I would be on the next plane to Edinburgh."

His bushy eyebrows shot up. "And why did you change your mind so quickly?"

"My circumstances at home changed." I faced west and shielded my eyes from the late afternoon sun as it poked through the open space between two mountains in the distance. I saw no reason to tell Craig about my broken engagement or failed business. "I prefer not to talk about it."

He frowned. "Fiona—may I call you Fiona?"

I nodded, still staring at the mountains. They weren't jagged like the Rockies in the United States or densely forested like the Appalachians, which, because I was from Tennessee, I knew even better. They were covered in pastureland, moss, and low-growing plants. Even in May, snow could be seen on the highest peaks. Like all mountains, they had a character all their own.

"Fiona, you need to tell me everything you know and the reason that you are here, because a man is dead, possibly even murdered," Craig said.

My mouth fell open. "But you said he most likely died of a stroke or a heart attack."

"Those are the first suspects for a death where there are

no obvious marks that indicate cause of death. However, Alastair was a young, healthy man. Of course, it happens that the young die suddenly in such a way, but it does give me pause, considering his good health, to assess all options. For that reason, you need to tell me why you changed your mind so quickly and came to Scotland."

I mentally kicked myself for being so open with the chief inspector. I should have said that I spoke with Alastair twice and came to Scotland to accept my inheritance, and left any mention of all my personal problems back in Nashville, where they belonged.

"I would really prefer not to speak of it," I said. "What happened back home has absolutely nothing to do with Alastair's death. How could it? I just arrived in Scotland this morning. You can check with the airport and with Customs to see when I came into the country. I got a rental car and drove straight from Edinburgh, an almost three-hour drive. There was no time for me to kill anyone. There was no time for me even to speak to anyone."

"Let me say this again. You need to tell me why you changed you mind. You might think it is irrelevant, but it's not."

"But—"

"Did Alastair know what day you would be arriving in Duncreigan?"

I nodded. "Yes, of course, I told him."

"Then, this is important. Why else do you think he was in the garden? The logical conclusion that Alastair was at Duncreigan today was to meet with you."

I gasped. "But we had a meeting planned for tomorrow, and it was to be in his office in Bellewick. We never even discussed him coming to Duncreigan."

"Maybe he meant to surprise you; maybe he was going the extra mile for his client to make sure that she settled into her new home," he suggested.

My face fell. What he was saying made sense, even if I didn't want to believe it. Had Alastair Croft come to Duncreigan because of me? Was it my fault that he was dead?

I refused to believe it. I could not take that guilt on top of the other guilt that I already suffered. I had guilt to spare between my failed flower shop and failed relationship. A man's death was more than I could bear.

"Now, will you please answer my question: Why did you suddenly change your plans and decide to come to Scotland at the last moment?"

I looked him in the eye. "My fiancé left me for our cake decorator." I said it like the fact that it was, without emotion, without tears, because if I let one ounce of emotion into that statement, I would cry. That was the very last thing I wanted to do in front of the giant, bearded chief inspector—the very last thing.

Craig winced. "Harsh."

"You're telling me," I said and turned to face the mountain again. I hoped that the tears that pooled in my eyes would be confused with sun glare, but I suspected Chief Inspector Craig was far too observant to be fooled.

Chapter Five

We returned to where Duncan and Hamish waited. As we approached the garden, a group of men in official-looking uniforms crested the hill between the cottage and the garden.

The hill was always a wonder to me. I asked my godfather once why he put his garden on the other side of the hill. Why wasn't it closer to the cottage so that he could see it from his home? He said that the garden's spot was chosen before the cottage. His ancestor Baird decided to put it there and to build the garden around the standing stone.

Even at a young age, I understood that it would have been wrong to move the stone that had been placed there thousands of years ago by unknown hands, but being an inquisitive child, I asked my godfather why the cottage wasn't built closer to the garden. He told me that his great-grandfather built the cottage and he was never told why.

"Please wait here with Hamish," Craig said to me before he went to meet with the officers.

The group of men stopped several yards away from the

walls of the garden. It wasn't lost on me that they stood far enough away to be out of earshot.

"Neil will want to talk to me next. I believe that the boy is still smarting from the time when I boxed his ears when he was just a small lad." Hamish twirled a dead ivy leaf in his hand.

I blinked at him. "You boxed his ears?"

Duncan climbed down from his master's shoulder and curled up on his lap. Although it might appear that the squirrel was taking a nap, his eyes were open and fixed on the group of officers. I wondered if Hamish had trained him to be an attack squirrel. I hoped that the little animal would never come after me.

"Americans don't have the expression 'boxing ears'?" he asked.

"I know what it means, but why would you box his ears?"

He leaned more heavily on the wall behind him that was keeping him up upright. "He and his chum tried to break into the garden there. I'd say the pair of them were fourteen at the time."

I lowered my voice. "You knew the chief inspector when he was young?"

"Oh yes, he may call the big city of Aberdeen home now." Hamish wrinkled his bulbous nose.

I suppressed a smile. By American terms, Aberdeen was not a big city. It wasn't much bigger than Akron, Ohio—and Nashville, where I was from, was much larger than Aberdeen.

"He grew up just down the road in the village of Belle-wick. He's a local as much as anyone. Neil and Alastair were as thick as thieves back in those days." He grunted. "And they *were* thieves too. On a dare, they broke into Master Ian's garden while he was away, intent on stealing the menhir. That's why I boxed their ears."

My gaze moved from Hamish's face to where the chief inspector stood with the other officers. I had an odd feeling. Disappointment, maybe. It was the closest word I had to describe it, but why would I be disappointed in the chief inspector, with this new information? The crime—or attempted crime, really—had happened well over a decade ago, but I planned to keep my distance from the chief inspector all the same.

I turned back to Hamish, trying to shake off the unease that seemed to have settled into my bones. I told myself that the bizarre world that I had stepped into, which included key-stealing squirrels, dead bodies, and gardens with secrets, wasn't completely to blame for my current feeling of being off balance. I hadn't been on balance since I'd closed the doors to my beloved flower shop back in Nashville for the last time or since my fiancé had set me down and told me that he was leaving me for our wedding cake decorator. After those two monumental, life-altering events, I should be able to take this in stride.

"Why would someone dare try to take the menhir?"

"Because of the stories surrounding it." Hamish made this statement with a completely straight face, as if he were giving me a weather update.

I blinked at him. "What stories?"

He shook his head. "Now is not the time to speak of them." He paused. "After Master Ian died, I thought the garden had died with him, but you have brought it back. You would not be able to do that without the menhir. You are connected to it."

Blink, blink went my eyes as I tried to digest what he was telling me. "Is that what you meant when you told me that Ian said the garden would come back to life when I came here?"

He nodded. "Aye. It should all be in your letter from Master Ian."

"But I'm telling you, I never got a letter. The only way that I knew he was dead was after I received a call from Alastair, telling me about my inheritance. You could have told me that he'd died. I had a right to be at his memorial service. My whole family did. He was our family." I could not keep the hurt from my voice.

Hamish's face fell. "I didn't know myself until the army told me, but by then they had already buried him. It was his wish for the army to bury him if he died in action."

I stood up. "I still deserved a call. You held a memorial service and didn't tell us."

He stared up at me. The folds and creases in his face appeared deeper, and even though he had always looked old to me, he appeared older somehow. I was afraid that was my fault. I wanted to apologize, but I couldn't yet—not just yet. What I had said was true. I did wonder why Hamish hadn't told me or my father, who was Uncle Ian's best friend in the world, that my godfather had died. I knew that he couldn't use the excuse that he wasn't able to reach us. Uncle Ian had our numbers, and Hamish could have found us even if he didn't know where Uncle Ian kept our phone numbers. The part that hurt was knowing that he hadn't even tried.

I walked away from him around the west corner of the garden walk. The ivy on this side of the garden wall was almost all green again. I stared at it. Could it be that Hamish was right, and I was bringing life back to the garden? How was that even possible? And what was this letter that Uncle Ian had supposedly left me? Where was it?

The west wall of the garden stretched before me. As I walked the length of the wall, trying desperately to control the grief that clawed at the inside of my throat, the browning ivy that was just a few steps in front of me began to green. I walked faster, trying to overcome the greening. I started to run, but the faster I moved, the faster the greening became. It was as if my forward motion was bringing the greening on. My breath caught, not so much from the exertion of running, but because of what I was seeing—if I could believe what I was seeing.

I was three-quarters of the way down the length of the wall when I abruptly stopped running. The greening of the ivy stopped just as abruptly. I bent at the waist and gasped for air. After a moment of staring at my boots and the bright green grass that surrounded them, I looked up. I still had my hands braced on my hip. Ahead, I spotted a fox peeking around the edge of the garden wall. The animal had clear blue eyes and blinked at me. My heart constricted. I felt, even though I knew it was impossible, that I had seen those eyes before. The fox blinked again. The effect was disconcerting.

I straightened up and took two steps toward that animal. I don't know what compelled me to do that. I wasn't afraid the creature had rabies or would bite me. I simply wanted to get close enough to know if I was right about those eyes. I had seen foxes many times when I visited my godfather, but they had always been skittish and afraid. The wild animals had the distinct understanding that humans were dangerous, and they fled that danger. This animal was different.

"Fiona." A deep voice behind me stopped me again. It was Craig. "We need to speak to you and Hamish together. Will you come with me, please?"

The fox didn't break eye contact with me, and I was so mesmerized by his gaze, I almost didn't notice the glint of metal in his mouth. I could be wrong, but it looked like a large key.

"Miss Knox?" Craig prompted.

I turned away from the animal to look over my shoulder at Craig. He was walking toward me. The only way that I could describe him was, he was a tower of a man. He was tall, at least six five, with muscular arms and a strong back. The sunlight reflected off his reddish-brown hair and beard, giving the skin of his face a pink overtone. The light reflection of pink didn't make his appearance any less formidable. My guard flew up, especially when I remembered that he had tried and failed to steal the standing stone from Uncle Ian's garden, no matter how long ago the attempted crime might have been committed.

"We need to speak to you and Hamish," he repeated. If he noticed that the green of the ivy had stopped exactly where I had stopped next to the wall, he made no mention of it.

I looked back to where the fox had been. He was gone. I might never know why I had seen the animal's eyes before. The key was gone as well, assuming that was what the fox had in his mouth, and was not just a trick of the light.

"Miss Knox?" the chief inspector asked. He was only a few yards away from me now. "Is something wrong?"

I turned back to him. "There are so many things wrong, Chief Inspector. That's the problem," I said, surprised by my own honest answer.

He gave me a sympathetic smile, and I appreciated that he didn't placate me and say that everything would be all right. I didn't need to hear that just then because, heaven knows, I wouldn't have believed him.

Chapter Six

I followed Craig around the side of the garden. We found Hamish still sitting against the garden wall, with Duncan curled up on his lap. As soon as I saw him, guilt washed over me. I shouldn't have taken my grief out on Hamish. He was affected as much by Uncle Ian's death as I was, if not more. I only saw my godfather a few times a year, if I was lucky. Hamish saw him whenever Uncle Ian was home at Duncreigan. I promised myself that I would apologize to him about my outburst at the first opportunity.

Craig stopped a few feet from Hamish. The door to the garden was open, and the other officers were nowhere to be seen. I could only assume that they were within the garden walls.

The fading sunlight created red, gold, and orange streaks across the sky. Craig shielded his eyes as a beam of light fought through a crack in the two mountains to the west and hit him directly in the face. He turned his back to the sunlight. "The crime scene techs will be processing the site, and the coroner will make his preliminary examination of the body. Please stay outside the garden walls while they do that."

Hamish jumped to his feet, sending an unsuspecting Duncan flying into the grass. Upon landing, the red squirrel arched his back like an irritated cat. "You can't close the garden off from Fiona! She needs to be close to the garden. It is paramount that she be able to go inside the garden. You cannot keep her from the garden, or it will die."

Craig frowned at the older man. "It looks to me like the garden is already dead. The only sign of life is that strange version of ivy that grows on the outer walls, and it's half-dead."

"But the rose is alive. The rose on the menhir is alive," Hamish said breathlessly. "The rose came back to life because she is here. You remember the menhir, don't you, Chief Inspector? You should remember it well."

The skin of the chief inspector's face turned the same color as his hair and beard. "I am not *asking* you to stay out of the garden. I am *telling* you."

Hamish opened his mouth, about to protest again, but Craig held up his hand to silence him. "I'm not saying it's forever," Craig said. "I understand that you must enter the garden to tend to it, but while my team is in there, you cannot be. We will reexamine the ban after the crime scene has been processed."

"The ban?" Hamish gasped.

I stepped over to him and placed a hand on his arm. "Hamish, there is no more that we can do here now. The garden will be fine for the time being. The temperature is dropping." As I said this, the wind picked up from the east, where it had traveled on the frigid North Sea. I shivered. "Soon it will be too cold to stand out here keeping vigil over the garden while they work. It wasn't like I was going to live inside the garden when I came here. Chief Inspector Craig will let us know when they are done processing the scene." I glanced at Craig, and he gave me a slight nod. I went on, "After he does that, we'll take it from there. Why don't we return to the cottage and warm up?"

Hamish nodded to me, but before he turned away, I caught a look of sadness in his eyes. I wasn't sure if it was over leaving the garden in the hands of the police or over my outburst earlier.

When we reached the cottage, Hamish got to work building a fire in the large hearth. "I cleaned out the chimney just as soon as you said you were coming. It may be May, but you will still need a fire to keep you warm at night. The sea may be a mile away, but the wind off the coast will cut right through you and the cottage."

"Thank you, Hamish," I said, meaning it. I took a deep breath. "And I'm sorry about my outburst earlier. It wasn't your job to tell us of Uncle Ian's passing. I know that his death has taken a toll on you just as much as it has on me. I should never have yelled at you like that." I took another breath. "You were a good friend to my godfather and took care of this place when he was away. I know that he was indebted to you, and so am I for everything that you have done."

"It is quite all right, lass. You had every right to be angry. I should have called you when I learned of Master Ian's death. I suppose that I was reeling too much from the news, m'self. Nothing has hit me that hard for such a long time. I supposed I forgot how to grieve deeply until his death reminded me of old pain."

I wrinkled my brow. I wondered what he meant by that.

What else had happened in his life that had rocked him as much as Uncle Ian's death? I could only guess that Hamish's age was something upward of eighty, so he had lived a long life with, I was sure, his share of heartbreak. But whatever the veiled reference alluded to seemed close to him somehow, regardless of how long ago it had happened.

"In any case, I'm sorry," I said.

He looked up from the fire at me with watery eyes. "It is all right, Miss Fiona. Truth be told, I was glad to hear your words because they came from love. That proved to me that you loved Master Ian, and that is important for me to know. There were not many who truly loved him in his life."

I frowned and, not for the first time, I wondered why my godfather had never married and had children of his own. I had always assumed it was his love of adventure and travel that made a long-term relationship impossible. I hoped with all my heart that he hadn't regretted choosing adventure over family. It would break my heart if I knew my godfather had died with such a painful regret. "Did Uncle Ian ever fall in love?" I heard myself ask, and was surprised that I had the courage to ask such a personal question. I would have never asked my godfather such a thing.

Hamish dropped his eyes back to the fire. "Once."

"What happened?"

"Different choices were made." He stood up. "There is a fire for ye." He stepped back from the now-roaring fire. "You will need to keep it well fed to stay warm at night. Normally, the cottage is heated with natural gas, but Master Ian would have it turned off while he was on tour. Since no one was living here, I didn't ask the gas company to turn it back on. You will want to do that soon, but the fireplace will keep you warm until then. There are two chimneys in the place. The other is the kitchen hearth, but that one has been closed for years."

I frowned, not satisfied with the answer about my god-father's lost love, but it was clear to me that Hamish was finished discussing it. I decided to drop it for the moment. Also, I was a more than a little bit concerned that I wouldn't be able to keep the fire adequately supplied during the night. Keeping a fire going to stay warm had never been a worry in my growing-up or adult years.

Duncan perched on the windowsill and seemed to be looking about for something else to steal. Well, he couldn't take the key again. Craig had that. I hoped that he would give it back to me before he left for the night, so I could lock my cottage. Like Hamish, I would like the ability to return to the garden, not to bring it back to life, but to help me figure out what on earth was happening.

I removed one of the white sheets from what I assumed was a large sofa. Months of dust particles flew into the air as the sheet broke free of the sofa. I sneezed as I folded the sheet as quickly as possible. Then I sneezed again.

By the time I finished removing sheets from all the furniture, the fire's warmth filled the small room. It wasn't until I felt its heat that I realized how cold I had actually become, standing outside in the wind. I shivered, unsure if I was chilled by the dropping temperature outside or the body in the garden.

Underneath the sheets was the simple country furniture that I remembered from my visits to Duncreigan. It was dark wood with clean lines. The sofa was a muted shade of green that almost looked like the color of moss that covered the mountains.

Hamish found a basket somewhere in the cottage and gathered the sheets into it. "I can take these into town to be washed when I leave."

I inwardly groaned as his comment reminded me that that tiny cottage didn't have a washer or a dryer. No dryer wasn't much of hardship—I could hang my clothes outside to dry. But the lack of a washer would take some getting used to. I wasn't in Nashville anymore. I decided if I were to make Duncreigan my permanent home, a washer and dryer would be on the to-buy list.

Hamish finished shoving the sheets into the basket.

"Thank you for gathering those up, Hamish, but I'll take them into the village when I go there. I need to get used to caring for myself out here, and that includes finding the laundromat."

He nodded and hurried over to the kitchen. After rooting about in one of the lower cupboards, he came up with a feather duster and set to work dusting the bare end tables.

"You don't need to do that," I said.

He continued dusting as if I hadn't said a word.

"Hamish, will you please sit down?" I sat on the moss-colored sofa.

He held the feather duster in mid-air like a maid caught in the act of cleaning by one of the nobles on Downton Abbey. The image was so comical that he made me laugh. It was the first time I had truly laughed in days. I laughed so hard that I held my middle and bent over at the waist. *This is how delirium begins,* I thought in the middle of my uncontrollable levity.

Hamish sat in one of the ladder-back chairs across from where I sat on the sofa. Through my laughter-induced tears, I saw him lean forward. "Miss Fiona, are you quite all right?"

I took several deep breaths. "I–I'm sorry, Hamish. Pl–please don't think that I was laughing at you. It wasn't that in the least. I was tickled over the situation we are in." I straightened up.

"I'm not sure I see the humor in it, lass. Is this an example of American humor, then? To laugh at such a situation?"

I shook my head. "No, no. I think I'm just tired. I think anything would make me laugh at this moment." I cleared my throat. "Well, almost anything."

He shook his head. "If you don't want me to clean, what can I do for you, lass?"

"Can you tell me about the garden?" I placed a hand to my forehead. "It's a lot to take in in a few hours. How exactly do I bring it back to life?"

"That I don't know, lass." He shook his head sadly. "You will have to learn that for yourself."

Chapter Seven

I sat on the sofa. As I did, a puff of dust rose around me, and I sneezed again. The cottage was going to wreak havoc on my allergies. "Then how do you know that I can or am supposed to do it?"

"From Master Ian's letter. That's how I know." He removed a letter from the inside pocket of his fisherman's coat. Even though we were inside the cottage now, with the fire he built nicely warming the room, he kept the coat on. He held the envelope out to me.

"My letter from Uncle Ian?" I asked. My heart was racing as I took the envelope from his wrinkled hand.

He shook his head. "It was the letter that Master Ian sent to me."

I tried to give it back to him. "I can't read that. It's your letter, not mine."

He shook his head. "Since we don't know what became of your letter, maybe reading this one will help you."

I made him take it. "I can't read your letter. That was from Uncle Ian to you. I was never meant to see it."

"Would you prefer that I read it to you, then?" he asked.

I thought about this for a moment. "I suppose that will be all right," I said. Despite my protests, I was insanely curious over what the letter said and what it would reveal to me about godfather and apparently about myself.

Carefully, he removed the letter from the envelope. I could tell by the many creases in the pages as unfolded the paper that it had been folded and refolded many times. So Hamish had read it many times. My heart ached for my letter, the lost letter. I wanted that last bit of Uncle Ian to hold. I wanted to hear his voice, if only in my head, one last time.

Hamish began to read.

Dear Hamish,

You are a good man, and I am grateful to you for our years of friendship. We have shared good times and bad times. I am happy to have you at my side and on my side through it all. I need to call on you yet again. If you are reading this, it is because one of my men in the army has mailed it to you because I have died.

I felt grief grab hold of my throat and squeeze hard. I placed my right hand there, as if there were another hand at my throat that I had to physically hold back.

Hamish continued to read.

My friend, you have taken such good care of my garden when I have been away, and I need you to tend my garden again. Do not be alarmed if the garden begins to fade. It will return when Fiona comes.

My breath caught at the mention of my name in his letter. I supposed that I half-expected it because Hamish wanted to share this letter with me, but it was still jarring.

When Fiona comes, the garden will come back to life. It might take some time as she learns how she and the garden are connected. I will explain all of this to her in her own letter. I will not put the burden on you, my friend, of telling this story. It is a story that I have owed her all her life. I only wish that I had been brave enough in life to tell her while I was living. I may be brave enough to fight in battle for Queen and country, but to tell Fiona that she is . . . well, I will not burden you, as I said, so I will leave it at that. By the time you see Fiona, she will have learned the truth, and she can tell you herself if she chooses. Now that I am gone, it will be her story to tell. It is no longer mine.

My heart hurt because my godfather was wrong. I didn't know the story—my story—this story that he had kept from me apparently all my life.

I will miss you, dear friend, but know that I will always be with you. You can reach me in other ways, and so may my darling Fiona. Please let her know how much I love her.
Ian MacCallister

My breath came in short gasps. It was the only way that I knew how to keep myself from breaking down into choking sobs. Air in and air out. *Focus, Knox,* I told myself. *Be conscious of your breath.* I had told myself the same thing when I took that first flight out of Nashville with a connection to Edinburgh, Scotland. On the plane, the panic that I'd felt course through my veins could only be held back by deep breathing exercises that my therapist back in Nashville had taught me—and Hail Mary prayers. Well, that and enough sleep tranquilizers to flatten a rhino.

Just as carefully as he'd unfolded the letter, Hamish refolded it and placed it back in its envelope. Then he tucked it into the inside pocket of his fisherman's coat. "I know you don't understand everything just yet, lass, but you are connected to the garden at Duncreigan. It needs you to survive, and I would wager to say that you need it as well. Without each other, you both could perish."

"Perish? Like die?" Now, my appetite was completely gone, and I doubted that I would ever be able eat again.

He nodded.

Okay, that's great. I'm connected to a magical garden and could die because of it. Terrific. Another thought hit me. "Was the garden why Uncle Ian died?"

Hamish blinked at me as if I had just asked the most ridiculous question he'd ever heard. "He died in battle in Afghanistan. That has nothing to do with the garden at all."

"But you said the garden died when he died."

He nodded. "Of course," he said. "The garden cannot continue if the Keeper is no more. The garden is returning to life now because you are the new Keeper. Until it is fully restored, you should stay here at Duncreigan and not travel far from it. When the garden's strength is back, you may travel far and wide like Master Ian did, but you must always come back to tend the garden."

I placed a hand to my forehead to check for any signs of fever. If I had a fever, it would prove that I was hallucinating this conversation. That would make much more sense than any of this being real. Because it couldn't be real—it just couldn't be. "The Keeper?"

"The one who is connected to the garden, the one who keeps is in bloom."

"Like a magical gardener?" I asked.

He nodded. "You can call it that. For generations, there has been a Keeper connected to this garden."

"But why keep the garden? I know it's a beautiful place and worth saving for that reason, but what is the purpose of it?"

He shook his head. "You really don't know, do you?"

I closed my eyes, trying my best not to let my frustration show. "I don't know anything."

"The Keeper's job is to use the power of the garden to help. That is the agreement that Baird struck with the sea and the one that all MacCallisters have been tied to from that moment on."

"But I'm not a MacCallister," I argued. "How can I be connected to the garden? I have visited Duncreigan before, many times when I was a child, and no one—not you, not Uncle Ian—has ever told me that I was connected to the garden. It seems like an awfully big secret to keep all these years."

"Master Ian had his reasons to keep it a secret."

I closed my eyes for a moment, telling myself to remain calm. It would do me no good to yell at Hamish. It wasn't his fault that my godfather had kept this secret from me all these years. Hamish didn't know it himself until after my godfather died and revealed it to him in his letter.

"The garden," Hamish went on, "was attached to Master Ian, and now it is attached to you, just as Master Ian said it would be."

Like that made sense. "When you say 'attached,' what do you mean? How am I *attached* to the garden?"

"It has been this way since Baird MacCallister settled this land."

Immediately at the mention of the merchant sailor's name, I glanced at the painting that hung over the mantle. "Uncle Ian's ancestor."

He nodded. "You have never been told the legend?" Hamish looked at me as if he were seeing me for the first time. "Everyone in Bellewick knows it."

"The legend about Baird?" I asked. "I know that he was in a shipwreck off the coast not far from here. I know he settled here after the shipwreck and built the garden around the menhir."

Hamish nodded. "Until Baird settled here, he was never in one place for long. He had the heart of a wanderer."

"That sounds like Uncle Ian," I said. My godfather was always on the go, and I didn't think that it was just because he was in the army. My father always said that he was running away from something. When I pressed him to ask what that something was, he would always change the subject. I never worked up the nerve to ask Uncle Ian outright about it. "As much as he loved Duncreigan, it didn't seem to me that he was here that much."

Hamish nodded. "He was much like Baird."

"What happened to Baird? I know just tidbits of the story that Uncle Ian would tell in passing."

Hamish settled back into his chair like he was prepared to tell quite the tale. "Baird was sailor, a merchant sailor from Aberdeenshire, but further north, closer to the city of Aberdeen. He became a sailor because he was the second son in his family, and he could not inherit the family land. In all honesty, that suited him just fine because he always wanted to leave Scotland. He had no love for his country. To Baird, the entire world was calling him."

"What didn't he like about Scotland?"

Hamish shrugged. "No one really knows. Some say he was running away from a broken heart. I imagine you know what that was like."

The half a granola bar I had eaten felt like a rock in the pit of my stomach. "I might have some idea."

Chapter Eight

"Baird found Duncreigan in the early spring," Hamish continued, settling into his tale. "The weather was just beginning to change, but winter, she wasn't done with the sea just yet. Baird set off on his merchant ship from Aberdeen. He wasn't a captain, merely a sailor. He wanted adventure. He had no ambition to be in charge. He wanted to escape the land, and a merchant ship was his best chance of doing that. He sailed many times but always returned to Scotland with the boat. It is told that one time he vowed never to return. He said he would build a new life in the ship's outbound destination, wherever that might be. But the fates would not have it. It wasn't long after the ship set off from the port of Aberdeen that a wild spring storm kicked up. It threw the ship to and fro and thrust it back at the jagged coast, breaking it in two. The wreck occurred on the most dangerous portion of the coast, the place where many had died before. Baird survived."

"What about the other men on the boat?" I asked. "What happened to them?"

He shook his head. "All were lost at sea. The only hope

was that they passed on quickly and didn't feel much pain while they were tossed and turned by the angry water."

I shivered.

"But Baird lived. For some reason, the sea, she chose to spare him. While he was tossed to and fro by the raging waters, he promised the sea he would never leave land again if the sea would spit him safely ashore. He promised he would never leave Scotland again and that he would change his ways and spend the rest of his days doing good deeds and helping others in trouble. Then, all was black. The morning came and Baird found himself here at Duncreigan."

I held up my hand. "Wait. How is that possible? Duncreigan is a mile inland from the coast. The sea couldn't have spit him out that far."

Hamish shook his head. "It is where the fates wanted him to be, so it is where he landed. Unlike the night before, when he'd almost died in the storm, the day was bright and clear when Baird awoke. The sky was cerulean blue and the grass emerald green. Spring had come to the land. After that storm, winter gave up her fight to spring. Although she would be back. She will always come back after her battle with autumn."

"You speak of the seasons as if they are people," I mused, enchanted by the story.

"Are they not?" he asked. "I see all things in nature as having a being."

I tried very hard not to lift my eyebrows again. I didn't know how much of Hamish's talk I should believe. I didn't know how much of it *he* actually believed. Did Hamish think Baird's tale was true, or did he just claim to believe it was true because it made a good story?

"So, Baird woke up in the middle of what would be Duncreigan? That was it?"

He shook his head as if he could not believe my impatience. "No. He woke next to the menhir, and before his very eyes, a yellow rose wound around the stone and bloomed."

"The menhir that is in the garden today?"

He nodded. "The very same."

"That can't possibly be the same rose that was there when Baird washed up. That was over three hundred years ago. A rose can't live that long."

"But it is the same rose," Hamish countered. "In these centuries, the only time that it died back was when Master Ian died, but it bloomed again when you arrived in Scotland." He took a breath. "I knew the moment your airplane landed in Scotland because the rose bloomed again. Baird knew that this was the place for him to stay, so he built the garden around the standing stone here. The place had been named centuries before as Duncreigan, which means 'high rocky place.'"

Under the guise of rubbing my forehead, I checked my head a second time for a fever, just to make sure. "None of this makes any sense."

"It will in time, and you will learn how to control the garden like Baird did and all the other MacCallisters that came after him, including Master Ian."

"Control it?" I asked. "Control it to do what? How am I supposed to use it to help people—*if* that is even what I am supposed to be doing? Who am I supposed to help?"

He smiled. "In time you will learn all you need to know."

"Did Uncle Ian tell you how I would bring the garden back to life? Supposing all of this is true and not some strange, alternative universe—"

Hamish's forehead wrinkled. "Alternative universe?"

"Yes, supposing this is real, I have no idea what I'm doing. I don't know how to bring a magical garden back to life or keep it alive."

Hamish stood by the fireplace with Duncan on his arm. "I do not know, Miss Fiona, and am truly sorry that I'm not able to answer all your questions."

All I could manage to say was, "I wish I had my letter."

"Me too, lass, me too," Hamish said with a mournful nod.

It was close to twilight outside by the time Chief Inspector Craig knocked on the cottage door. Hamish and I were sharing the potato soup from his thermos and my granola bars from my carry-on. Duncan was also a fan of the granola bars.

Hamish started to get up to answer the door, but I waved him to stay seated and answered the door myself. The wind had picked up in the time that Hamish and I had been inside the cottage, and the scent of sea and salt was heavy in the damp air as the waves crashed against the craggy cliffs just a mile away.

Behind Craig, the headlights of the police and crime scene vehicles bounced across the meadow as they drove away. Their lights reflected across the grass and rocks. I stepped back from the door to let Craig inside.

A damp chill followed the officer inside the cottage, and I rubbed my arms to warm them. The wind had mussed his curls, making strands stand up in all directions and causing his hair to resemble the fire that crackled and snapped in the hearth.

As if he caught me staring at it, he tried to smooth his hair with his large hand, but it was no use. It bounced back into its fiery shape the moment he removed his hand.

Craig nodded to Hamish and then focused his attention on me. "We're done processing the garden, and the body has been removed."

I winced when he said that last bit.

Craig noticed, because he gave me a sympathetic smile.

Hamish stood up and held his soupspoon in front of him as if it were a sword. He pointed the spoon at the chief inspector. "That's all very well, but will Fiona be able to enter the garden?"

Again, Craig patted his uncontrollable hair. "Yes." He looked at me again. "But it is very important that you stay away from the crime scene. Use the hedgerow as a guide. Don't go beyond the hedgerow around the standing stone. Don't cross the crime scene tape that surrounds it. We would like to go over the scene again tomorrow just in case anything was missed."

"That's—" Hamish started to protest, but I stopped him.

"That's fine," I said. "That seems a reasonable request."

Craig studied me with his dark eyes as if judging to see if I really meant what I said or only said what I thought he wanted to hear. In actuality, it was a little bit of both. I was relieved that I was allowed back into the garden. I knew that the garden held the answers that I was seeking. The biggest problem was, I didn't even know what questions I should be asking to find those answers. He removed from his pocket the skeleton key that worked both for the cottage and the garden. Craig nodded, satisfied with whatever it was he saw in my face, and handed me the key. "Since I don't want you sleeping with your doors unlocked tonight, I'm giving this to you. However, we left the garden unlocked, so that we, the police, can come and go."

Hamish turned red and looked as if he planned to protest again.

I was faster. "That is fair." I accepted the key from his hand, relieved to have it back. "How did Alastair die? Do you have any clue?"

The chief inspector studied me. "The coroner has not finished his investigation. I can't answer that question just yet."

"Will you tell me what the coroner says?" I asked.

He gave me a level stare. "It's not really any of your business."

I put my hands on my hips. "Of course, it's my business. His body was found in what is now my garden. I want to know how he got inside there and died. The garden is always locked, and Hamish had the only key until I arrived."

Out of the corner of my eye, I saw Hamish step away from us. He sat in one of the dining chairs at the small table. He turned and looked out the window into the inky night.

Craig peered over my head at Hamish. "Maybe you should be asking Mr. MacGregor these questions. If he was the only who could enter the garden, then he might know how Alastair got there."

Hamish glared at the chief inspector. "You are not welcome here, Neil Craig."

"I know that, Hamish," Craig said. "You've made it very clear." He turned and walked out the door.

I glanced back at Hamish, but he was glaring out the window. Before I could change my mind, I ran out of the cottage.

Chapter Nine

"Chief Inspector!" I called as the cottage door closed with a thud behind me.

Craig was just climbing into his jeep. "Miss Knox?"

I ran up to his car. The jeep's headlights were the only guide I had in the dark.

Craig climbed back out of the car and met me just halfway. "Do you have something to tell me, Miss Knox?"

I caught my breath. "You can't be implying Hamish might have—that he could have killed Alastair."

He sighed. "At this point, anyone could have killed Alastair. The investigation is only a few hours old."

"I know, but Hamish has been my godfather's trusted friend, well, forever. Hamish was caretaker to Duncreigan even before Uncle Ian was born. He would never do such a thing."

The inspector cocked his head. "So you are telling me you believe Hamish is innocent simply because he's your godfather's friend? You are going to have to give me more reason than that to remove him from my list, because as it stands now, he had the best opportunity."

"But motive," I said. "What is his motive?"

"I'll find it," Craig said with determination, which convinced me that Hamish was his number-one suspect.

My stomach drew into a knot. I knew how upset my godfather would be if he knew Hamish was in trouble. He would have dropped everything to save his friend. Uncle Ian wasn't here, so it was left up to me to do that. I shivered.

In the dim light, Craig's expression softened just a tad. "You should go in. It's cold out here, and your thin Tennessee blood isn't used to this kind of cold."

"I'm fine," I said.

He grinned and opened his mouth to say something, but then he closed it again as if he thought better of it. He gave his head a little shake. "I'll be back tomorrow."

"When?" I asked. "I'd like to go into the village in the morning."

"I don't know the time exactly, but you don't have to be here when I return," he said.

I may not have to be here, but I wanted to be here so that I knew what was going on. I didn't want Craig or any of the other officers to take something from the garden without my knowledge. Which made me ask, "Did you take anything from the garden?"

Craig raised his eyebrows. "What do you mean?"

I wrapped my arms a little more tightly around my waist to fight the cold. "Well, you were gathering evidence from the scene of the crime. Did you find any clues? And did you remove those clues from the scene?"

Craig pursed his lips together, and I had a suspicion that he was fighting a smile. "Clues?"

"Aren't you supposed to give me a list or something that tells me what you took from the scene? The garden is my property," I said.

Craig managed to suppress the smile that threatened to appear. "All that we took from the scene was the body, and leaves and soil samples from around the body, so we can run our forensic tests back in Aberdeen. However, if you would like a proper list detailing all of those things, I can bring it to you tomorrow."

I lifted my chin just a hair. "I would like a list. Thank you."

Craig nodded. "Now, I must head back to Aberdeen." He walked back to the driver's side of his jeep. "I'll see you tomorrow, Fiona Knox."

I couldn't decide whether that was a promise or a threat, or whether I wanted it to be one thing more than the other.

"Drive safely, Chief Inspector," I called after him.

He turned toward me. The jeep's headlights lit him from behind so that his face, turned toward me, was in shadow. He raised a hand in farewell. I turned and walked back inside the cottage as he drove away.

Back inside, I found Hamish standing beside the sofa. He lifted Duncan off the pillow where the little animal had been sleeping, and tucked him inside his coat. Duncan didn't as much as twitch as he was moved. I could see that he had complete trust in the elderly caretaker. Somehow, seeing how Hamish was so kind and caring to such a small creature put me at ease. I knew I had to be right that he couldn't have killed Alastair. My godfather had trusted him. As a career soldier, Ian MacCallister had not given his trust lightly.

But still I had to ask. "Hamish?"

He looked up at me. I was a few inches taller than the elderly caretaker. Once upon a time, I guessed, he had been my height or taller. His back was bent from hours of bending over and working in the garden. This man had given his life and health in the service of my godfather's family, but still I had to ask.

"Hamish, do you know how Alastair might have ended up in the garden when you had the only key?"

He looked me square in the eye. "I do not, Miss Fiona."

I swallowed. I wanted to believe him.

"I should be off too, lass," Hamish said and gently patted the coat pocket where he had placed the red squirrel.

I wanted to ask more questions, but it was clear that Hamish was tired. The skin of his face appeared to sag more than it had a few hours ago, and his eyes drooped. Perhaps I would find more answers in the village the next day. I was certainly going to try.

"Can I give you a ride home? It's dark outside."

"Oh, I walked. I have a cottage about a half mile from here myself. Master Ian gave it to me when he said it was too far for me to walk from my little flat in Bellewick any longer. He was good man, Master Ian was." He blinked away the moisture in his eyes.

"You can't walk that far on a night like this," I said. "The wind is howling."

He laughed. "If you think this is a rough night in Scotland, you are in for a rude awakening, my lass, a very rude awakening indeed. We have storms that come off the sea that will curl your toes and make seasoned Highlanders hide under their beds."

"But—"

He crossed the room and opened the door that I had just closed, then held it just like I had against the howling wind. "I will see you on the morrow, lass." He turned and went.

After Hamish left, I paced the cottage, opening doors and drawers every few steps. Everything in the place had the mark of my godfather. I found his pipe, tobacco pouch, a few of his medals from the army, and the usual implements of everyday life too: bills, pens, half-written notes. I finally forced myself to stop searching. I didn't even know what I was searching for. I didn't know if I was looking for clues to Uncle Ian's death, Alastair's death, or my lost letter from Uncle Ian. I supposed of the three, it was the letter that I wanted the very most. I didn't find it, but I promised myself that I would start looking the next day when the light was better.

Before I got too carried away with searching, I would have to go into Bellewick the next morning; that was certain. The remaining two crushed granola bars at the bottom of my carry-on bag wouldn't carry me very far, and I thought as I looked down at the basket of sheets, I could take the laundry in as well.

I went into my godfather's bedroom and found a freshly made bed. I knew I had Hamish to thank for that, and I was grateful. I didn't think I would have had the energy to change the sheets myself. The comforter on top of the bed was brown and masculine. As was everything else in the room. It was clear that this was the home of a bachelor. It would take some work to make it my own, if I was willing to do it. I wasn't decided on that point. It had been a bumpy start to my life in Scotland so far. I curled up on the bed and went to sleep, or tried to. I succeeded hours later.

Chapter Ten

When I woke up the next morning, light streamed in through my godfather's bedroom and fell directly on my eyes. I groaned and rubbed those eyes, and a loose spring in the old bed dug into my side. I reached for the nightstand and grabbed my cell phone to see what time it was. My cell had caught up with the time change the moment I set foot in the Edinburgh Airport. I, on the other hand, had not.

It read noon. I groaned and sat up on the lumpy bed. I knew that it was only six in the morning back home, but still I felt like I had wasted half the day, even if I had desperately needed the sleep after my rude welcome to Scotland.

I stretched and sat up in bed. Then, after a lot of yawning and grumbling to myself about jet lag, I got up and went to the window. My breath caught as I looked out.

The sky was a color of blue that I can't even attempt to describe. White puffy clouds bounced through like sheep on a blue field. The green meadow rolled out in front of me in a wave, only occasionally interrupted by granite rocks that forced their way through the surface of the earth.

I realized Ian's bedroom faced the direction of the garden, and I could see the top edge of the garden wall above one of the green rolling hills.

I had never noticed that before, but perhaps that was because I had never before slept in my godfather's room. Any time that I came with my family, we always stayed at a little B&B in the village, and when I came alone, I slept on the sofa in front of the fireplace.

Even though my godfather's cottage didn't have a washer or a dryer, I was thrilled that it had a full bathroom with a bathtub and a shower. The tub was the old-fashioned, claw-foot kind, and I could imagine myself taking many bubble baths there while reading a book. The tub would have to wait since I was starving. The granola bars were long gone. I needed to make a trip to the village to buy food so I could keep myself functioning to find out who killed Alastair Croft and protect Hamish's good name. I wasn't so much worried about protecting my own name. I knew that as soon as Craig spoke with the airline, I would be in the clear, but Hamish was a different story.

I took a quick shower, and as I dried my hair, I decided that I would stop by the local pub for lunch when I got into Bellewick. My mind might say it was breakfast time, but the sooner I adjusted to the time difference—and that included mealtimes—the better off I would be.

I gathered up my leather tote bag and the basket of white sheets, and went out the door. I stood there for a moment, looking in the direction of my godfather's garden. I wanted to see what state the police had left it in the evening before. Chief Inspector Craig had said that I was allowed in the garden, but I could not touch anything within the crime scene tape.

My stomach rumbled. I hadn't eaten a proper meal since I was on the plane, and truthfully no one in their right mind would consider airplane food a proper meal, not even the airline companies. Curiosity won out. I locked the cottage door with the skeleton key and tucked it into my jacket pocket. I was going to have to think of a better way to carry or hide the giant key. It was a bit cumbersome to carry around, and I always ran the risk of Duncan stealing it again.

I walked the same way that I had the day before with Hamish and Duncan. Since it was midday and not late afternoon, the light was different now, and the green of the land had somehow ever so slightly changed. People said that Ireland was green, and that was true; I had been to Ireland on a few occasions. But Scotland was green too. It was just a different kind of green, a little more intense and dark.

I had never known there were so many variations of green until I went to Scotland for the first time with my family as a child, when I was nine. Before that, Uncle Ian had always come to see us in the States. I think I fell in love with this land on the very first visit, but even so, I never ever thought that I would one day live here.

As I walked over the half-grassy, half-rocky earth, I felt off-kilter from the ever-changing topography. Someone, especially someone as clumsy as myself, could easily roll an ankle. I hadn't noticed it that day before because I had been too intent on chasing Duncan on the run to the garden, and then so shocked by the dead man in the garden on the walk back to the cottage.

When I reached the garden, I noticed that the ivy on the outer wall was all but green, and I could only count a handful of dry and wrinkled leaves withering on the vine. In less than twenty-four hours, the ivy had come back to life, and Hamish would have me believe it was because of me.

I pushed my way through the ivy and walked through the garden door. By the way Hamish had talked, I half-expected the garden would be in full bloom when I reentered it, but it wasn't like that. The garden was as dead as it had been the day before.

The willow tree I'd swung from as a child looked like a skeleton petitioning the heavens for some sort of relief, but it need much more than rain to bud again.

There were withered daffodil blossoms languishing on their stalks. I touched the dry and wrinkled flower petals, and nothing happened. I blew on the withered flower. Again, nothing happened. "Huh," I said, and I couldn't help but feel disappointed. When you are told that you have the power to bring a garden back to life, it would be a cool trick to blow on a flower to make it bloom—one that I would have loved as a child because I had always been fascinated with flowers and other plants, not just for their beauty, but for their resilience. They died but always came back, be it through a bulb, a cutting, or a seed. They always found a way to go on. I wanted that kind of resilience in my own life. Unfortunately, being as resilient as a flower wasn't that easy, which was a bummer, as Isla would say.

I thought that out of the corner of my eye I saw a spot of red. I turned but there was nothing there. Duncan was red, so the blur I had seen could have been him or one of his cousins, of whom I was sure there were many, but it had seemed too large to be a squirrel. What had I seen out of the corner of my eye? I wondered if it was the fox that I had seen the day before outside the garden.

Whatever it was had gone around the side of the hedgerow. The hedgerow that the chief inspector had explicitly told me to stay clear of. I glanced around as if Craig were somewhere in the garden, even though I knew that he wasn't.

On the other side of the hedgerow, yellow crime scene tape was tethered to the hedgerow; from there it ran to a wooden peg to the north of the standing stone, then back to the hedgerow, making a large triangle.

The rose that had been blooming beautifully around the menhir the day before was wilting. My heart constricted at seeing the flower languish, but I couldn't bring myself to cross the crime scene tape, and I already knew that blowing on the flower wouldn't bring it back to life. Maybe the rose had bloomed on a fluke when I arrived, and Hamish was wrong about my strange ability. Not that I believed in that sort of thing. The rose's blooming had been merely coincidental with my arrival. Maybe the greening ivy was another fluke. I shifted back and forth on my feet. The ivy was much more difficult to discount because I had seen it green before my own eyes.

I ran the sole of my boot over the dead grass outside the crime scene tape, as if I were looking for something. What? I still didn't know, and I knew if there had been anything there, Craig and the other officers would have found it the evening before.

When I looked up from my search, the yellow rose was lush and blooming again. The sight of it caused me to jump back. My head hurt. I didn't understand a single thing that had happened since I had arrived in Scotland. I backed away from the standing stone, and my heel caught on a root. I fell hard on my back end.

As I braced my left hand on the ground, it touched something long and metal. I wrapped my fingers around it and brought the object into view. It was a key, identical to the skeleton key I had for the cottage. Unless, I had dropped it. I shoved my hand into my coat pocket and came up with a matching key. Hadn't Hamish told me that the key I had was the only key to the cottage? Had Alastair had a second key and dropped it when he died?

The image of the fox with the blue eyes and the glint of metal in his mouth—perhaps the key—came to mind. Could that be the key in my hand? If it was, that might explain why the police hadn't found it on a thorough search, but it would also mean that the fox had dropped it here by the menhir, either on purpose or by accident. It just didn't make any sense. And did finding another key make it better or worse for Hamish? I suspected the latter because he had been so emphatic that there was just one key to the cottage and the garden. If anyone knew there was a second key to Duncreigan floating about, it would be Hamish. I would have to ask him, and I hoped that I would like his answer, whatever it might be.

Unsure what to do, I shoved both keys into my coat pocket. I wasn't going to leave the key there for Craig to find. He would surely wonder why his constables hadn't found it the day before, just like I did.

I stood and brushed dead grass off my backside. There might be something more that I could learn from the garden, but I needed to head into the village. I wanted to be home when the chief inspector returned to revisit the scene.

I hurried back through the garden and over the field to the cottage. I stopped at the front door and collected the basket of sheets.

Shoving the basket into the car's trunk, or "boot" as my godfather would have called it, I slammed it closed. I would have to take the rental car back to Edinburgh soon. I'd only rented it for my first week in Scotland, because I had moved across the world with no plan in place.

Having no plan was very unlike me. My wedding, for example, had been planned down to the minutest detail. The only thing that I hadn't accounted for was Ethan's wandering eye.

I turned the car around and headed down the long gravel driveway to the road. I hoped the village could answer at least some of my questions.

Chapter Eleven

The drive into Bellewick, through the Scottish countryside, was quick since the village was only three miles away. The short drive took my breath away. Sheep with spray-painted patches dotting their coats grazed along the hillside. My godfather had told me that the shepherds spray-painted their sheep so they knew which ones were theirs. All the sheep in the area comingled on the mountainside together, and each shepherd had an assigned color to avoid any confusion as to which sheep belonged to whom. Bellewick came into view from the country road in the valley, between two large, green mountains.

A huge stone arch marked the entrance into the village proper. The road curved around a roundabout where a seven-foot-tall bronze unicorn overlooked all who entered the village. One of the arms of the roundabout went to the right, into the shopping district of the village. Another arm crossed a stone bridge that looked as if it had been pulled directly from the story of the *Three Billy Goats Gruff*. I drove over the bridge and parked in the first metered spot that I could find along the street.

I climbed out of the rental car and found myself on the

corner of two cobblestone streets. The laundromat was to my left, but the chance to find something to eat was to my right. I decided that the sheets could wait. The first thing I needed to do was find some food. I was already getting lightheaded from eating hardly anything the day before. I dropped a pound coin in the meter and left my parking ticket on the car's dash, as instructed.

It was midafternoon on a Tuesday, and the streets were nearly empty of any foot traffic. A few older women walked down the street with shopping bags swinging from their arms. Meanwhile, the working-age folks were at their jobs, and the children were at school.

One woman smiled at me as she passed.

I smiled back and asked, "Can you tell me the way to the Twisted Fox? Is it far?" I asked because I had remembered the name of the pub that my godfather had frequented when he was home. I had even gone there a few times with him, but I couldn't remember exactly where it was located in the village. I was easily turned around in the narrow streets, and I was reluctant to use the GPS on my phone because it would cost me a fortune. Although it did work internationally, it wasn't cheap to use data on this side of the pond. If I planned to stay, I knew I would have to invest in a phone that worked in Scotland, another big decision and purchase that I should make very soon.

The woman adjusted the shopping bag on her left arm and pointed down the street with her right. "It's just at the end of the street there. It's on the left on the corner. You can't miss it." She smiled.

"Thank you," I said, returning her smile.

She examined my face. "You're American." It was a statement, not a question.

I nodded. There was absolutely nothing I could do to hide my Tennessee accent, so I didn't even attempt to. "I just moved here."

She blinked at me. "You moved here. No one moves to Bellewick, especially not Americans." She said this with such certainty, I wondered if it was somehow written into the village charter.

"I haven't moved to Bellewick exactly," I said. "I live a few miles away at Duncreigan."

"Duncreigan." She stepped away from me.

"Do you know it?

She backed away further from me and moved her shopping bag in front of her body like it was some kind of shield. "Everyone knows Duncreigan, but you can't live there. Only MacCallisters live at Duncreigan. Are you a MacCallister?"

I shook my head.

She nodded. "Then, you won't be there long." She gave me a finger wave and hurried down the street, moving much more quickly than I would have expected for a woman of her age.

I stared after her and caught my reflection in the window of the shop next to me. I had long, wavy black hair and blue eyes. A decent nose, I thought. I had always liked it, and I had a nice smile. But I wasn't smiling at the moment. I shook off the odd feeling her reaction gave me and continued down the street to the Twisted Fox.

In truth, I didn't even have to ask the woman where the Twisted Fox was. Like she'd said, if I'd just kept walking down the street, I'd have run right into it. A circular sign jutted out from the side of the brick building at the corner. In the middle was a fox's face; below it were the words "Twisted Fox Pub, established 1799."

Two laughing men walked out of the pub. It was midday, and I could tell that they'd already had a wee bit too much to drink. A small, wiry man in a T-shirt and jeans followed them out. "Don't you come back, the lot of you, until you sober up, or you won't be welcome here again. You have my word on that."

Even though the man in the T-shirt was half the size of either of the drunken men, they sidled away from him. One of them bumped into my shoulder as he passed me.

The wiry man looked at me. "Sorry you had to see that, miss."

I shook my head. "It's okay. No worries."

"You're American," he said.

Internally, I sighed. I suspected that I would be hearing that a lot until the villagers got used to me. If I was here long enough to get used to, that is.

He wore a golf hat tilted at a jaunty angle on the top of his head. "We don't get many Americans in Bellewick. We don't get much of anyone other than villagers and their relatives in Bellewick. It's not the place the tourists come to. Most spend more time in Stonehaven and the others like that."

"I don't know why Bellewick would be overlooked by travelers," I said. "It's such a charming village. I've always thought so."

He looked me up and down, but it wasn't in a way that a

man usually appraised a woman. He looked at me like he was trying to piece something together, not like he was scoping out what might be hiding beneath my clothing. "You've been here before?"

I nodded. "Many times, but not for several years."

"You hungry?" he asked.

"Starving," I admitted.

"Why don't you come inside, and I'll fix you up. Then you can tell me why you have been to Bellewick before. I always love to hear a good story, and I'm thinking that you have one of the best."

I wasn't sure my story was one of the best, but it was certainly strange. Maybe it would earn me a free pint. I could use it.

I followed him into the pub. The room was dark, and it took a little longer than usual for my eyes to adjust. When they did, my vision took in the very Scottish bar. Tartan covered all the seat cushions on the dark wooden chairs that sat around equally dark wooden tables, and clans' coats of arms hung on the wall. The bar itself was long, running the entire length of the pub, and mahogany in color. Backless stools lined its long counter. Behind the bar, a wall-sized mirror reflected the many bottles of liquor available, and it looked like the Twisted Fox offered all the local scotches.

Pipe smoke floated across the room to me. Apparently, the country's no-smoking rule didn't apply to pipe smokers in Scottish pubs. Three elderly men sat around the large hearth on the north wall of the pub, smoking their pipes and laughing. From where I stood, it appeared that one of them was squinting like Popeye while he puffed away. I wouldn't be the least bit surprised if he had an anchor tattoo on his arm.

There were two more men, who were younger than the first three, sitting at the bar. I was the only woman in the place.

The wiry man stepped around the side of the bar and waved me over. I slipped onto one of the cracked leather stools at the bar, one spot down from my closest neighbor, who, I guessed, was in his forties. I smiled at him. He didn't smile back, so I turned away.

The bartender held out his hand to me. "I'm Lee Mac-Gill, and this is my place."

I shook his hand. "It's nice to meet you, Lee. I'm Fiona Knox."

"Fiona Knox? Now there is a strong Scottish name if I ever heard one, but don't mind me, miss—you don't sound Scottish in the least. To me, you sound like you are ready to belt out a classic country western song about how you lost your man, truck, and dog—not necessarily in that order."

I laughed. Even with all the less welcoming eyes in the room on me, he had somehow found a way to put me at ease.

"My father is Scottish. He grew up not that far from here. Although he lives in the States now and has since before I was born."

Lee nodded knowingly. "Fell in love with an American, did he?"

I nodded. "My mother."

He shook his head and moved on to wiping the next glass. "You American girls have a way of getting the best of us. You're hard to resist."

I couldn't help but wonder if he said this from experience.

"So, you have come on a visit to our little village. Do you have a place to stay? I could put in a good word for you at the B&B. The owner there was a friend of my grandmother. She's a grumpy old bird just like my grandmother was—I think that's why they got along so well—but I am always sending business her way. She would take you in on my recommendation."

I shook my head. "Thank you, but I have a place to stay."

"Oh?" He picked up another stout glass from the rack in front of him and began to polish it. "And where might that be?"

"Duncreigan," I said.

There was silence. All the chatter in the pub ceased when I answered his question. I looked around the room and found that all the men, even the old men smoking their pipes, were staring at me.

I glanced back at Lee. "Is it something I said?" I tried and failed to make a joke of it.

Lee resumed polishing his glass. "Nay, it wasn't anything that you said, miss." He laughed. "The whole village is still reeling over Ian MacCallister's death. He was a hero to us, you know."

My heart constricted. "He was a hero to me as well."

Lee cocked his head. "You don't say."

"Ian was a hero. Died for Queen and country, but there have always been rumors about the MacCallisters," the old man who looked like Popeye called from his post by the fireplace.

I glanced back at Lee, feeling like he was the only friend I might have in the room. "What kind of rumors?"

Before Lee could answer, the man one stool down from me spoke. "About his garden."

The garden where I had found the dead body less than twenty-four hours before.

Chapter Twelve

"What about the garden?" I asked again, looking to Lee for the answer.

Once more, my neighbor on the barstool beat him to it. "About his garden? People say the garden blooms in all weather and all seasons. I've heard that roses were known to bloom there even when we're a foot deep in snow."

"I heard," the man next to him said, "they bloom in up to *three* feet of snow."

Lee replaced the glass back on the rack. "That is crazy talk. Nothing could bloom in snow like that. You just ignore them, lass. The MacCallisters have always been well liked in this village."

The first man at the bar snorted into his beer.

"Jock McBride, you don't care for a single living soul," Lee said. He turned back to me. "Jock is just grumpy from pulling a double shift in the harbor."

I noticed for the first time that Jock's hair was damp. "What do you do?"

He eyed me. "I clean the bottom of boats. Someone has to scrape the barnacles off them."

"Underwater?" I asked. "Sounds like a dangerous job."

"It has its moments," Jock said. "I have the best scuba gear to do it. I never skimp on equipment." He raised his glass. "Or on my beer."

"It's a good job for you, Jock!" Popeye shouted.

Jock scowled. "It's a living."

"It's a good living," Lee said. "Don't let those old codgers make you think any different on that." He turned to me. "What is that you do, Fiona?" Lee asked.

"Well, I owned a flower shop back in Nashville, but it recently closed."

"We used to have a flower shop here in Bellewick until the widow Clooney died. It was right next door. Place has been empty for going on three years now." He paused. "It's hard to keep a business afloat in a village this small."

"Your pub seems to be doing well," I commented.

"It's the best pub in County Aberdeen," Popeye declared.

Lee tipped his hat to the man.

"Why are you staying at Duncreigan?" Jock asked. "Ian MacCallister is dead." He said this with no remorse or sadness. It was clear to me that this man, Jock McBride, had not cared for my godfather in the least. He eyed me. "Are you a MacCallister? I thought Ian was the end of the line."

I swallowed but refused to look away. "I'm not a Mac-Callister. I'm Ian's goddaughter."

Lee raised the glass that he was polishing to me. "No wonder you saw him as your hero." He eyed the gossips. "Any man who died defending our country and freedoms deserves our utmost respect."

One of the men spat. "Our freedoms? Those are the

freedoms of the English that Ian was fighting for on the other side of the world. It has nothing to do with the Scottish people. Parliament would do much better to concentrate on the problems at home than to send men overseas."

"Men and women," Lee corrected.

"Makes me wonder if Ian MacCallister cared about Scotland one whit," Jock said. "He kept running off to do good in other parts of the world. It would have spoken much more highly of him if he'd been willing to stay around here a bit more and impact change in his homeland."

I opened my mouth to defend my godfather again, but the bartender beat me to it. "You shut your mouth if you ever want another drink from me again. I have thrown you out of the Twisted Fox before, Jock, and I will do it again. Don't you try me on that!"

Lee was half Jock's size. Given his many years as the proprietor of the Twisted Fox, and after watching him throw those two drunken young men out when I first arrived, I believed he was more than able to throw any man out of his bar.

Jock turned away. I supposed the threat of not being able to drink a pint at the Twisted Fox again was enough to keep him silent. At the fireplace, Popeye and his two friends turned back to their pipes and their own conversation.

Lee set a pint of beer in front me. I had no idea what variety. "I'm sorry about that, miss. Jock is just in a bad mood. I'm sorry to say, he's always in a bad mood, so don't pay him any mind. Drink up. You'll need it."

I curved my hands around the pint of beer that he insisted I drink. The glass was cold and damp.

"Can I get you something to eat?" Lee asked. Before I could answer, he pointed at me. "What you need is a shepherd's pie. That will fix you right up. It's my late mother's recipe and always does the trick."

The shepherd's pie sounded way too heavy for me. I knew that I wouldn't be able to get more than three bites down before I would be done with it. But I couldn't see how I could refuse his suggestion, considering it was his late mother's recipe. Before I could decide one way or another, Lee disappeared through the swinging door to the left of the bar. When the door swung inward, I caught a glimpse of a large gas range. While he was gone, the men in the pub ignored me. After the welcome I'd received, I was happy to be ignored. I removed my cell phone from my pocket and opened the notes app. I scrolled through until I found where I was to meet Alastair that day to talk over the estate. That had been the original plan: I was to arrive at Duncreigan on Monday, and on Tuesday meet with Alastair to go over my uncle's affairs. Now, that was never going to happen.

I zoomed the screen out to enlarge the notes. There was an address where we were to have met. It was Alastair's law office, and if my memory of Bellewick served me right, the address was only a block away from the pub.

Lee reappeared through the swinging door with a steaming shepherd's pie in his hand. "Fresh from the oven," he declared and set it down in front of me. "I hope you like it piping hot."

Gravy oozed out of cracks in the piecrust, all over the plate, and the smell made my mouth water. It turned out I was hungry after all. I picked up my fork and dove in.

Lee laughed. "That's a girl. It's good, isn't it?"

I nodded between bites. You would have thought that this was the first time that I had seen food in weeks by the way I devoured it. "I'm so embarrassed. I've been living on granola bars for the last day. There's no food at Duncreigan."

Lee grinned. "This meal will stick to your ribs until you find some. Do you know where the market is?"

I nodded. "I saw it on the way to your pub."

"Ah, so you came into town to do a little shopping, did you?"

"Actually, I came to the village about Alastair Croft."

"Alastair? What does a nice girl like you want to have to do with him?"

Before I could reply, he said, "I haven't seen him yet today. Alastair is usually here in the evening for his supper. Although now that you mention him, I don't remember seeing him here last night."

A bite of shepherd's pie caught in my throat. Lee didn't know Alastair was dead, and if Lee didn't know as the owner of the village pub, it was very likely that no one in the village knew.

I took a gulp from my pint to force the food down and immediately regretted it as the inside of my throat burned.

Lee eyed me. "You okay?"

I nodded and took a more tentative sip of beer. "Alastair is my godfather's attorney, and I have a meeting scheduled with him today to go over some things. I thought I would pop into his office today to say hello," I said, choosing my words very carefully.

"Ahh," Lee said, relaxing a bit. "You're looking for Croft and Beckleberry then."

"Beckleberry?" I asked.

"That is Alastair's law partner, Cally Beckleberry." His voice rose just a tad as he said the lawyer's name.

"I hope your chat with Alastair goes well. He can be . . ."—Lee searched for the right word—"disagreeable at times."

"You seemed to have an odd reaction when I mentioned his name."

"Odd how?" Lee asked.

"Like you thought it was strange that I was looking for him."

"It's not strange if it has something to do with your godfather's estate, but you don't look like a rich developer to me, so I was surprised that you were looking for him. That's what the majority of strangers coming in here looking for Alastair are."

"Why are developers looking for Alastair?" I asked.

"Long story. If I told you, I would be keeping you here all day."

I started to say that I wanted to hear the long story, when he said, "When you see Alastair, he might be a wee bit hung over from the last time he was here." He rubbed his chin. "I would hope that he's recovered from his bender by now. It has been a couple of days, but he drank so heavily that I wouldn't be surprised if he found some rock to hide under somewhere and doesn't plan to come out for a week. I didn't see him at all yesterday, and he comes to the pub for most of his meals."

I squirmed on my barstool. I knew why Lee hadn't seen Alastair the day before. It was because Alastair had been dead in my godfather's garden. I'd been right when I arrived at the pub and first assumed that no one knew about Alastair's death. I wondered when Craig and the rest of the police planned to tell the villagers what happened.

Lee didn't seem to notice my discomfort with the conversation and went on to say, "If he is hiding under some rock somewhere with a bloody hangover, he more than deserves it."

I took a sip from my beer to give myself a moment to think. "Was it normal for him to drink so much?"

Lee shook his head. "No, Alastair is a two-pint man. He came in after his law office closed for the day, drank several pints, and ate. I had never seen him drink so much or come in so early. He was three sheets to the wind and then some."

"When did he come in that day?" I asked, trying to sound casual. I didn't want Lee to think that I was fishing for information when he heard what happened to Alastair, even though that was exactly what I was doing.

"I'd say that he came in around two in the afternoon. Right after his big win."

"His big win?" I asked.

"The Bellewick coast land deal. Alastair has been working on that for years. The village and a group of environmentalists have been fighting him tooth and nail the entire time, but in the end, he and the developer came out on top." Lee tossed his cloth onto the bar in frustration. "It just goes to show that if you have enough money and stubbornness, there is very little in the world that can stop you. Even if most of the world despises you and wishes you dead."

The last bite of pie lodged in my throat. *Wishes you dead.* People had wished Alastair Croft dead, and now he was.

Chapter Thirteen

"The villagers despised Alastair?" I asked.

Lee went back to wiping down the counter, moving the white cloth in a circular motion around the bar. The circle became progressively larger, like the rings in a pool of water after a stone hits its surface. "The village had a conflicted feeling about Alastair."

"Why's that?"

"Why are you so interested in Ian MacCallister's attorney?"

"I–I will be working with him to settle my godfather's estate. It would be helpful to have a mental picture of the man who I'm working with."

Lee was quiet for a few beats. "We were proud of him. He grew up here and is one of our own, but then he had to get tangled up in the sale of the coast."

I took another bite of my shepherd's pie and thought this over. The warm vegetables, pastry, and beef warmed me all the way through. After I swallowed, I asked, "Can you tell me about the Bellewick coastal land deal? What is it exactly?"

"It's a plan to sell the village access to the prettiest bit of coastline. Access that we've had for centuries."

"The harbor?" I asked. Bellewick was a fishing village, and loss of access to the harbor could ruin the village financially. Most of the villagers in some way or another made their livelihood off the bounty of the North Sea.

He shook his head. "No, the harbor belongs to the village, but there is a mile of coast just north of the harbor that has been up for sale. There is finally a buyer."

"Who is the buyer?"

Lee shook his head. "I don't remember; he's not from the area."

"Since Alastair was a villager, I would have thought that he would be more interested in arguing for the side of Bellewick," I said.

Lee snorted. "All he cared about was his commission from the sale. He made it clear the other night that it would be handsome."

"So, Alastair came directly to the Twisted Fox? For what reason?" I asked.

Lee nodded. "To gloat."

"How did the villagers take his gloating?"

"Everyone in the pub was glaring daggers at him," Lee went on. "But he didn't seem to notice. He was jubilant. There is no other way to describe his mood that night."

It sounded to me like the pub had been full of a bunch of angry murder suspects that night. I sipped my beer again. This time the bitter taste was somehow soothing. Or maybe just the hot meal had mellowed me out. "When will construction begin on the land?"

"Not long after the sale is final is my guess," Lee said as he folded his rag after wiping down the bar.

I put my sweaty pint back on top of the bar. "Wait. Are you saying the sale isn't final?" I felt my heart quicken. If everyone in the village was against the sale, and the deal wasn't final, maybe whoever put Alastair in the garden thought that by killing him, the project could be stopped altogether, and as far as I could tell, this was a motive—a good motive—that had nothing to do with Hamish.

"No, the sale wasn't final. According to Alastair, he and the developer and buyer only shook on their plan. No contracts had been filled out just yet. Last I saw him, it was little more than a verbal agreement."

I swallowed. Perhaps that was no longer true. Perhaps now that Alastair was dead, the sale wouldn't go through at all. And perhaps whoever was against the sale was now a murderer.

"This doesn't make sense. Alastair was—is an attorney," I said quickly, hoping that he didn't notice I had slipped up and used the past tense for Alastair Croft. "It sounds to me like he's acting as a real estate agent here."

"He is, in a way. When the last earl who owned that land died with no heirs, he made Croft and Beckleberry executors of the estate."

"Who gets all the money from the sale? I mean other than Alastair's commission."

He shrugged. "Don't know." He stopped polishing the glass in his hand. "I can't say I've ever met anyone so interested in their barrister's back history before meeting him."

I forced a laugh. "Naturally curious, I guess."

Lee studied me for a moment. His eyes were a startlingly shade of blue, much brighter than my own.

I looked away. "I do have one last question."

"I have a feeling you have more than one, but go ahead."

"You said that pretty much everyone in the village dislikes Alastair because he's greedy."

He nodded.

"Does anyone in particular dislike him?"

He thought about this for a moment as his resumed polishing his glass. "Raj Kapoor comes to mind. He's spearheading the fight against the sale of the land to a developer."

I sat up a little straighter. Raj Kapoor sounded like someone I needed to speak to soon.

"The only other name that comes to mind is Hamish MacGregor. You must know the old man if you're staying at Duncreigan."

My shoulders drooped. That was exactly the name that I didn't want him to say. "I know him."

He set the thoroughly polished glass on the counter and picked up another to work on.

"I can see why Raj wouldn't care for Alastair, but why do you say that about Hamish?" I asked.

He opened his mouth like he was going to answer my question, when the pub door opened, letting bright sunlight into the dimly lit room. A young man in uniform came through the door. He removed his hat and tucked it under his right arm, then stood in the open doorway for a long minute, looking around, as if he wanted everyone in the place to see that he had finally arrived.

It was apparent that no one cared about or was impressed with his triumphal entry into the pub. The three old men by the fireplace didn't so much as turn the page of their newspapers, and it looked as if two out of the three, including Popeye, were sleeping.

"Kipling, for God's sake, would you let the door close. A whole village of flies could swarm the place in the amount of time that you have been standing there," Lee snapped.

Kipling let the door slam behind him, and he marched across the room with his chin jutted out. It sort of reminded me of those old videos that I had seen in school of women balancing books on the top of their heads to perfect their posture. I had always thought they looked ridiculous, and Kipling looked just as ridiculous.

Clearly by his uniform, he was some type of law enforcement officer. Chief Inspector Craig had not been wearing a uniform when I met him, but the officers under him had, and their dress was very different from the one this man wore. Theirs had been navy and trimmed with their name embroidered over the pockets. Kipling's uniform was covered with shiny pins and buttons that looked as if they were polished on a regular basis. I had not seen him at the scene in the garden, where I had discovered the dead body of Alastair Croft. If he had been there, I was sure that I would have remembered seeing him—even though I was dealing with the shock of the evening's events as they unfolded around me.

"Kipling is the volunteer police in Bellewick," Lee said, as if he could read my mind.

"The chief of police," Kipling corrected.

Lee snorted. "If you being the only one makes you the chief, then I suppose that is true."

So, this explained why I hadn't seen Kipling at the crime scene. I didn't know much about Chief Inspector Craig, but from what I did know, he took his job very seriously. He wouldn't have wanted a self-proclaimed volunteer police chief messing with his murder investigation, and Craig had made it abundantly clear that this was *his* investigation.

Kipling slid onto the barstool next to me, and although there were a good nine inches of space between us, it felt like he was far too close as he leaned in my direction.

A shiny badge was pinned to his flannel-covered chest. "Can I buy you a pint, miss?"

I blinked at the short man. "A pint?"

The bartender laughed. "Leave her alone, Kip. She's way too far out of your league."

I looked to Lee for an explanation. He grinned from ear to ear. "Old Kip here has been looking for a wife since the day he finished upper school. Since every woman in the village knows him, he's been shot down more times than anyone can count."

Kipling frowned and sipped from his pint of beer.

I took one last swallow of my own beer. It was very good when I got used to the overly bitter taste. Then I stood up. I had no interest in listening to Kipling's romantic history. "I should be off to my appointment. It was very nice to meet you both, but I really must be going."

Kipling stood up from his stool. "I didn't mean to run you off, miss."

"You—"

"Her name is Fiona." Lee interrupted. "And of course you've run her off. You run all women off, Kip. That's what I keep trying to tell you."

"No, really," I said, trying to salvage the awkward situation. "I really do have an appointment that I must get to." I turned to Lee. "How much do I own you for my meal and beer? Can I start a tab or something? I think I will be here a lot until I can find some time to grocery shop and cook."

Lee shook his head. "It's on the house."

I began to protest.

He wagged his finger at me. "Ian MacCallister never paid for a pint in my pub, and neither will you."

I opened my mouth, but he was faster. "It's not up for debate, Fiona. Are you off to meet with Alastair?" he asked.

I glanced at Kipling, unsure that I wanted to say anything about Alastair around this would-be cop. It was clear that, just like everyone else I had met in the village, he was clueless about the murder. I found this surprising. Although I hadn't discovered the body until late afternoon of the day before, I would have sworn that everyone would have known about it by now, especially in such a small community. Clearly, Craig had his reasons to keep a lid on the murder, and I wasn't going to get on his bad side by spoiling that, especially as, for all intents and purposes, Hamish was a perfect murder suspect, if not the prime suspect.

"I'll meet with Alastair or his partner. What was her name again?"

"Cally Beckleberry," Lee said. "And if you ever have a need to look for Cally, look no farther than the law office on Queen Street. She's there day and night. As far as I can tell, all she ever does is work, and Alastair, not her, is the one who reaps the rewards from that."

I thanked him again for the meal and turned to go.

"Fiona," Lee called after me.

I looked over my shoulder at him just as my hand settled on the doorknob.

"Don't worry about the rumors swirling around about Ian and the MacCallisters. In a village the size of Bellewick, there will be enough rumors circulating about you yourself in no time at all. That's just the price of living in such a tiny village."

I nodded and went out the door into the sunlight, thinking that he had no idea how right he was. As soon as the village learned that Alastair had died in my godfather's garden and I was the one who'd found the body, I would have more than my fair share of rumors to contend with, without the help of anyone else.

Chapter Fourteen

Queen Street was on the other side of the troll bridge. When I crossed it this time on foot, I peered over the side of it, just as I had as a little girl, for a chance to see the troll who lived underneath and gave billy goats such a hard time. But just as had happened when I was a child, the troll did not show himself.

The law office was on the edge of a residential neighborhood, the only neighborhood in the historic part of the village. The streets were cobblestoned and narrow like those around the Twisted Fox. I tried to imagine two cars passing each other in such a tight space without scraping the paint off each other's fenders, but it was hard to do. At present, there was no true way to tell because the street was empty.

At the beginning of the neighborhood, the stone and brick townhouses that lined either side of the street had been converted from homes to businesses. There was a barber, a dentist, an accountant, and the law office for the firm of Croft and Beckleberry.

Croft and Beckleberry's was on the corner, and a metal

sign with its name jutted out from the gray stone building. There was also a second sign over the door and one beside the window. Bellewick was such a small place that I wondered what was up with the excessive signage for the law office. Lee had said it was the only law office in the village, and every villager could have told me with little thought where it was located.

Three steps led to the front door. I could tell they were the original steps to the building, constructed of stone hewn from the earth and not poured into a concrete mold. They were also uneven with age, where countless people had walked upon them. It reminded me again how old everything in Scotland was. In Nashville, the city practically builds a force field around a house that was built in the 1800s, to protect it from wear and tear. But the 1800s weren't even a blip on the timeline in a place like Bellewick, where most of the buildings dated back to the thirteenth and fourteenth centuries.

There didn't appear to be a doorbell on the house, so I grabbed the anchor-shaped knocker and banged hard. Then I stood on the top step and waited. There was no answer. I knocked again. Still no answer. I knocked a third time with the same result. Instead of knocking a fourth time—because I could see that would be pointless—I placed my hand on the long handle and pushed. Much to my surprise, the door gave way easily, as if it were well oiled and like someone was expecting me.

The door opened into a narrow vestibule that led directly into a staircase, at the top of which was another door, dark wood with a golden plaque on which the law firm's name was engraved. I hesitated before I went up the stairs. I felt like I was in this place without permission, and I knew that Alastair was dead, very dead. I had seen his body with my own eyes. The plan had been that I would meet him today in his office to go over my godfather's estate, so now that he was dead, it seemed wrong, somehow, that I was there to take care of everyday business, but he was not.

I shook off the feeling and climbed the narrow stairs, which had been made in a time when a person's feet were much smaller than my size nine boots.

When I reached the dark wood door, I tried the antique doorknob instead of knocking. The knob didn't turn easily, but it turned. It creaked and groaned in its socket as I rotated it.

I pushed inward on the door and found myself in a sitting room that was decorated with all the charm of Scotland gone by. The furnishings were sparse, but it was clear they were antique and expensive. It was as though the owner of the space was saying, "I have money, so much money that I don't have to show off." It remained to be seen if that was true or just a carefully calculated front for the owner; but then I remembered that this space, at least in part, belonged to Alastair, and Lee had given me the impression that he would have come into a lot of money in the very near future.

There was a crash deeper in the building, followed by a woman's voice swearing. "Bloody hell!" rang out from the back of the office.

I hesitated, wondering if I should call out and make myself known, but before I could, a heavy door, identical to the one that I had walked through to enter the sitting room, opened. A woman stomped out, carrying a cardboard box full to bursting with manila file folders and loose papers.

Her strawberry-blond hair was cut asymmetrically so that her bangs angled across her face from the top of her right eyebrow to the bottom of her left earlobe. However, the severity of the haircut could not hide her pretty and delicate features or her complexion, which my mother would have called an "English rose" coloring.

Dark brown eyes glared at me from under the heavy red-blond bangs. "Who are you?" she asked bluntly in an English accent.

"I'm sorry. I—I knocked and no one answered. I'm sorry if it looks like I'm pushing in."

She dropped the box unceremoniously on a settee below the window. "It doesn't *look* like you're pushing in; you *are* pushing in."

I squinted. "I suppose that's tentatively true. I'm so sorry to drop in on you like this, but I have an appointment this morning with Alastair Croft—"

"You don't have a meeting with Alastair today. No one does. All meetings with Alastair are canceled. He's dead." She said this without emotion, but as she spoke, I saw that her eyes were red. She clapped a hand over her mouth. "I'm sorry. I shouldn't have blurted all that out."

"I already knew Alastair was dead, and I'm sorry for your loss," I said.

She blinked at me. "How?"

"I'm Fiona Knox. Alastair was settling my godfather Ian MacCallister's estate . . ."

"Of course!" She waved her hand. "Say no more. I should have known when I heard you speak that you were the

American girl coming in today because you inherited Duncreigan. I have to tell you the office is a bit of a mess today because . . ."

"I understand." I walked over to the settee. "Mind if I sit?"

She shook her head.

"I hate to be a bother at such a difficult time, but I wonder if you have a few minutes to talk to me about Duncreigan?"

She frowned, and I thought for a moment that she was going to kick me out of the office altogether. Then she plastered a smile on her face. "Yes, of course. Ian was a longtime client of ours, and I do have a few minutes before—well—before the next thing."

I so wanted to ask her what the "next thing" was, but was afraid if I did, I might push my luck too far. I guessed Cally was looking for any excuse to kick me out of the office.

I scooted forward on the settee. It was a lovely red velvet, soft to the touch, but slippery to move around on when you were wearing jeans. I had to remind myself that when the settee was constructed, denim hadn't even been invented yet, so it wasn't a concern at the time.

Suddenly she covered her mouth again. "Alastair was found at Duncreigan, or at least that was what Neil told me."

Neil? It took me a moment to realize that she was talking about Chief Inspector Craig. Hamish had mentioned that his first name was Neil. I squirmed in my seat. There was something about Cally saying his given name in such a casual way that made me uncomfortable. It reminded me that everyone in the village knew one another, knew one another's past histories too. I was the outsider.

I cleared my throat. "Yes, I found the body."

She placed her hand to her cheek. "You poor thing." Some of the frostiness that I had gotten from her earlier melted away. "If I remember correctly, you were supposed to arrive yesterday."

"I did."

"What a horrible welcome to our country."

My mind's eye went back to the moment when I saw Alastair dead on the ground. In truth, the discovery, although very upsetting, hadn't been horrible. There was no blood, no wound that I was forced to see. The only disturbing thing about it had been Alastair's eyes, which had been half-opened, half-closed, frozen in an unlifelike position. I swallowed as I saw his eyes again in my mind. "It was difficult. Definitely not the welcome that I had expected when I came to Scotland."

She nodded. "No, of course it wasn't." She stood. "Why don't you stay right there, and I will make us some tea. I'm English, and that's how we cope with things. It seems to me that we are going to need some tea for this conversation, but I assure you it won't be long. Ian was meticulous about his affairs. Everything should be an easy transfer to you."

When she left the room through the door in the back, I was tempted to jump out of my seat to see what was in that box. I was just about to get up from my seat to do that, when a large, gray, striped cat with folded-down ears and a pushed-in face—the Scottish Fold breed—jumped into my lap. "Well, hello there."

The cat looked up at me with perfectly round yellow eyes and began to purr.

A moment later, Cally came back into the room with the tea tray. She must have been out of the room for less than five minutes. I looked down at the cat. Had the animal known that she would be back so quickly and stopped me from being caught in the act of rifling through Cally's box?

Chapter Fifteen

"I see Ivanhoe found you," she said as she set the tea tray on the empty end table beside the settee.

"Ivanhoe?" I asked.

The cat looked up at me with imploring yellow eyes. It appeared that Ivanhoe was in fact his name. He certainly recognized it when it was said aloud.

"That's Alastair's cat. Alastair was a very proud Scotsman and *Ivanhoe* is the best-known work of Sir Walter Scott. It seemed the natural name for the cat, or at least it did to Alastair. Honestly, I don't know how the cat got here. He lives in Alastair's house just a block from here. I came into work yesterday morning, and there he was on the doorstep, meowing away to me to be let in. I planned to have Alastair take him home when he was in again, but as you know Alastair never came back to work after brokering the land deal on the coast. Now, I don't have the heart to take the cat back to his little house. I'm not sure what to do. He's a sweet and gorgeous cat."

Ivanhoe nestled down lower into my lap as if the compliments made him feel all snuggly.

"But I can't take him," she went on. "I'm allergic to cats. Severely allergic, actually. I have to keep him in the sitting room here and not let him into the rest of the building. If I did, I wouldn't be able to breathe after a few hours." She looked at him in my lap. "He seems to have taken a shine to you."

I already saw where she was going with this. I held up my hand like a traffic cop. "I can't adopt a cat. I just arrived here to Scotland, and I don't know what I am doing."

"That's why you need a companion to come home to. He could help you adjust to life in a new place. It must be kind of frightening sleeping out in Duncreigan all by yourself."

It hadn't been scary in the least until she'd said that. I hadn't been afraid last night, when it was my first night alone in the cottage and I'd found a dead body in my godfather's garden only a few hours before. Even so, Cally made it sound ominous to sleep there.

I had a feeling that Cally was very good at talking people into things. I had a feeling it wouldn't be too long before I had a cat named Ivanhoe, but I was going to hold out just as long as I could.

I wondered why I hadn't seen the cat when I'd first arrived in the room. If he had been there, although I might not have seen him, I was certain that he'd seen me. From the looks of how comfortable he was on my lap, it seemed to me that he'd come to the conclusion that I was harmless.

Cally sneezed as if to make her point. She removed a tissue from the pocket of her trousers and rubbed the end of her nose. "I don't know what is going to happen to the poor creature now. I can't take him, and Alastair doesn't have any family to take him. I asked Neil to take him, but he said he couldn't."

I ran my hand down along the cat's back. "You asked the chief inspector to adopt Alastair's cat?"

She nodded. "They were close friends once."

"What happened?"

She pursed her lips together. "Alastair never said."

I held my cup just below my lips, blowing on the hot tea, and asked, "Have you known Alastair a long time?

She leaned back on the settee. "Since law school. We went to the same one just outside London." She swallowed. "I wanted to live and work in London and make my mark there."

"How did you end up in Bellewick?" I asked. I couldn't think of a place in the whole country more unlike London than this little fishing village. I nodded in what I hoped was an encouraging way and sipped my tea, taking care not to spill it on the cat.

"I was in a rut in London and looking for a way out." She peered into her tea.

"I can understand that." I sipped from my cup. "It's very hard when everything you've dreamed of and worked for turns out to be not what you wanted."

"Yes, well." She cleared her throat "Alastair called. We had remained in touch with each other over the years, and he knew I wasn't happy in London. He offered me this partnership, and the rest is history. But I know you didn't come all the way here to hear about me or Alastair."

She was wrong. I very much wanted to hear more about Alastair and her.

"It must have come as a shock to hear he was murdered."

She gave me a level stare. "It was."

"Do you have any idea who might have done it?"

Her brow wrinkled. "No."

"Perhaps it's related to the sale of the coastline?"

Her eyebrows rose as she picked up her teacup again. "My, you are well informed, aren't you?"

"I just came from the Twisted Fox Pub."

"Ahh," she said knowingly. "Lee would have gotten you up to date with all the news, and I'm sure those old grumps that hang out in there threw in their two cents for good measure."

I laughed. "They certainly did."

She waved at me unconcernedly. "Don't pay any mind to them. They have nothing better to do. I have to remind myself of that from time to time because they crawl under my skin, but I still want to go to the Twisted Fox because Lee makes the best shepherd's pie north of London."

I grinned. "I had it today; it was very good."

She smiled. "He always breaks out the pie when he's trying to impress a pretty lady. It's one of his standard moves. He's tried it on me more times that I can count—to no avail."

Her comment brought to mind that wistful look that had been on Lee's face when he spoke of Cally. I suspected that there was an unrequited crush there, and from the looks of Cally's expression, it was completely one-sided. I set my teacup on the end table next to my chair and rested both hands on top of the cat, who was purring with the ferocity of a steamboat.

"Were many villagers upset over the potential sale?"

She smiled. "If you've spoken to Lee, I assume you already know the answer to that."

"He said they were," I admitted.

She nodded. "Everyone in the village has been up in arms over it. It's one of the last pristine areas in the county. It overlooks the sea. It would be a terrible shame to lose it to a bunch of vacation condominiums, which is the plan. It will be summer homes for Londoners and people from the continent to spend their summers off the coast of Scotland. Scotland is a very popular summer getaway because the Queen spends as much of summertime in Balmoral as she can. I can't say I blame the villagers for being upset."

"It sounds to me like you weren't enthusiastic about the sale either."

She set her teacup on the side table next to her chair. "I hated the idea. I told Alastair that there were other options we could explore for the land and still do well for the late earl's estate." She shook her head. "He wouldn't hear of it. Alastair was my partner, but we didn't always see eye to eye. I never thought about leaving because I fell in love with this little village and its people. I even care about gossips like Lee MacGill."

"Could you have opened up your own practice here?" I asked.

She shook her head. "No. First of all, Bellewick is far too small for two law offices, and second, I would never have been able to compete with Alastair."

"But if he was so . . ." I trailed off.

She shook her head sadly. "That doesn't matter. He was the local boy, and that's what comes first. The Scottish people, especially up here this close to the Highlands, are very loyal to one another. It wouldn't have mattered if I was the better lawyer or the more compassionate person; he was born and raised in the village, and that was all there was to it."

I glanced at the box. "You were doing some organizing when I arrived?"

She gestured to the box next to her. "I was gathering up documents for Neil. He wanted every case that Alastair worked on in the last year. Most of our files are on the computer. Neil already took that back to his station in Aberdeen, but I promised him that I would look through the paper files for anything that might be helpful in giving him a clue as to who could have done this to poor Alastair." She gave a half laugh. "Poor Alastair, indeed. Never in his life would anyone have said, 'Poor Alastair.'"

"The police didn't want to look through the papers themselves?" I scratched the cat behind his folded right ear. He was as soft as velvet. I imagined this was what the Velveteen Rabbit from the children's story felt like. The cat kept on purring.

She frowned as if I'd suggested something that she didn't like. Perhaps I had. I'd suggested that she might have had time to hide or remove some of the papers that she was giving to the police. I didn't say it aloud, as I suspected Cally was a sharp woman and understood the implications.

"Why do you think he was killed?" I asked.

"If I were putting my money on it, his death has something to do with the land sale. There was nothing else that he was working on at the moment that was so contentious or worth so much money," she said.

"How much money are we talking?" I asked and then sipped my tea. For some reason, tea in Great Britain always tasted better to me than it ever did back in the States. I didn't know if it was the water or how the British made it, but I could never replicate it back home, even if I did everything exactly as I had learned to do it in Scotland.

"Millions of pounds." She paused. "I think, if I'm not mistaken, it would have been Alastair's last case here. He had been talking about moving the firm to Edinburgh. If he brokered this deal, he'd have indelibly made his mark here, and he said he was ready to move onto more challenging and competitive waters. I doubt that he would ever have left Scotland again—at least not permanently—so Edinburgh would have been the place for him to be. He'd been talking about it over the last several months. To be honest, he was driving me crazy with all the talk about his grand plan."

"Would you have gone with him to the capital as his law partner if that had come about?"

She shook her head. "I told him that if he did that, I was out. He didn't care and made no secret of the fact that he would have more than enough money to buy out my half of the firm. From there, he could go to Edinburgh alone and even hire a new partner. He would have had plenty of money to attract both up-and-coming and established attorneys to his firm. I supposed that the only thing that might have worked against him was that all his law experience was in rural law up here in Aberdeenshire."

I picked up my teacup and held it in front of me, partly to hide my expression. Cally Beckleberry might not realize it now, but she was a smart woman who would come to the same conclusion that I had soon enough. Which was that she had just given me her motive to murder Alastair. She didn't want to leave Bellewick, but had no chance of starting her own law firm while Alastair was here. Now that he was gone, the firm and all the clients in the town were hers. But then why kill him when she believed that he would leave on his own accord?

Ivanhoe purred in my lap.

After hearing about Alastair's plan to make that terrible land deal on the coast, I was all ready to write him off as just another money-hungry lawyer, but the cat gave me pause as he curled up on my lap in a gray and white striped ball of fluff.

Cally set her teacup down. "I'm sorry if I am boring you with all this. I'm sure you just wanted to find out about Ian MacCallister's estate and be on your way. Let me see if I can find the file." She pulled the large cardboard box toward her.

"Ian's file is in that box?"

She nodded. "Of course, it is. Neil wanted to know about all Alastair's cases in the last year, and Ian's case would have been the most recent, other than the land deal, of course. I believe those were the two largest cases that Alastair was working on when he died, and Ian's case was a very distant second to the Bellewick coastline sale."

She continued to rifle through the folders, the tip of her tongue in her teeth, looking like a little kid concentrating hard on a school spelling test. As she sorted through the files, one that she passed over caught my eye. I saw the name Twisted Fox on the edge of one of the folders. Lee was getting legal advice from Alastair, and according to what Cally had shared with me about the box's contents, he'd been getting that advice in the last year. It seemed funny to me that the personable bartender hadn't mentioned that when I'd told him that I had a meeting with Alastair that day. Then again, I was practically a stranger to him. There was no reason for him to confide his legal troubles, if there were any at all, to me.

"Ah-ha!" Cally proclaimed, holding the folder aloft triumphantly. "Here it is." In her hand, she held a folder with my godfather's name on the tab.

I dug my trembling fingers into the cat's velvety fur. "May I see it?"

She opened the folder and removed a folded sheaf of papers. "Here is Ian's will. Have you seen it yet?" She held it out to me.

I leaned forward and took it from her hand. "No."

She released it. "Alastair should have emailed you a copy, but you can take a look at this one, and I can make you another copy now."

"Thank you." I unfolded the legal-sized paper on the cat's back. My hands shook a little as I did so. I scanned the document, and my eyes landed on the following sentence: *And my entire estate and land, including the garden, the cottage, and all other buildings found on the premises, I leave to my one sole heiress, Fiona Knox.*

I was his heiress. I was an heiress. Perhaps not in the royal sense, but what I was getting from Ian at the time of his death was worth more than I had made in my entire adult life. "Was there perhaps a letter that was left with the law office? A letter from my godfather to me?"

She looked through the other papers in the folder but didn't offer any of them to me. "Not that I see. Were you expecting one?" she asked.

. I looked over the will again. "I was. Hamish MacGregor—do you know him?" I lifted my eyes from the document that lay across the cat's back.

"The caretaker at Duncreigan? Yes, I know him." She said this in a neutral voice without judgment.

"He received a letter from my godfather after Uncle Ian died. In that letter, it said I would be receiving a letter too after my godfather died, but I never got it."

"Perhaps it got lost in the mail," she offered.

"That's what I'm afraid of. Like it was on its way to the States and got misplaced."

"Maybe it's in America by now. If it was on the way to your home and got delayed because of overseas mail or because you aren't there anymore."

I stared at her. She could be right. Maybe that was exactly where my letter from Ian was. Before I left for Scotland, I had left my forwarding address as my parents' house because I didn't know how long I would be gone. My mother promised to send anything of importance on to me. I didn't get much snail mail anymore, as it was. I paid all my bills and took care of all my business online. Sometimes I would get junk mail, but I couldn't remember the last time I got a real letter. For that matter, I couldn't remember the last time I had gotten a chatty email from a friend. It seemed that all communication now was through some social media outlet or text message.

I smiled at her. "That's a really good suggestion. I'll ask my family to check."

She smiled. "I'm glad I could be of help to someone today. That's more than I expected would happen."

"What other cases do you think could have be controversial enough to put Alastair in danger?" I asked, not sure that she would answer my question. There was no real reason for her to respond.

"There's one—"

Sirens broke through our conversation. Ivanhoe jumped off my lap and ran to the window that overlooked Queen Street. Cally also raced to the window, leaving whatever she was about to tell me hanging in the air.

"What's going on?" I asked.

"Two fire trucks and an ambulance went flying down the street. That never happens in Bellewick. We don't even have a volunteer fire department. Those must have been from Aberdeen, and they were headed to St. Charles Street." She spun away from the window. "I have to go."

"Why?" I jumped out of my seat.

"Alastair's house is on St. Charles."

The implications hit me as she flew out the door without another word.

Chapter Sixteen

I followed Cally out, but by the time I reached the street, she was gone. All I had to do to know where she had gone was to follow the sirens, which led me a block away, onto St. Charles Street.

The scene on St. Charles Street was chaotic. Two fire trucks, an ambulance, and three police vehicles crowded the narrow lane that back in Nashville would have been seen as little more than a wide sidewalk. A throng of villagers stood between me and wherever the police were. I searched the crowd for Cally but didn't see her.

I didn't see Chief Inspector Craig either, but I knew he was there because I heard his voice come over a bullhorn. "Please, we need all of you to clear the area. Get off this street!"

The crowd collectively shifted from foot to foot, but no one made a move to leave. Although I still had no idea where Cally was, I recognized the old man I had named Popeye at the pub, and I saw Lee there as well. I had to believe something big was going on if Lee had left his pub. I got the impression that his whole life revolved around the Twisted Fox Pub.

"Leave the area," Craig said again, making another attempt to control the crowd, "or you will be arrested for disobeying a police order!"

The villagers held their ground. There were a lot of people crammed around the emergency vehicles on the narrow street. If I were to guess, I would say that the entire village of Belle-wick was there and ignoring Craig's instructions. He might be a chief inspector, but he was still a child of the village and therefore didn't get much respect from his fellow citizens.

"Leave the area!" Craig shouted into the bullhorn. "It is for your own safety. We have discovered a natural gas leak on this street, and it's far too dangerous for you to be here."

A natural gas leak? I had a sinking feeling. Cally had said that Alastair's house was on St. Charles Street. I didn't think that I was jumping too far in thinking that the gas leak was at Alastair's home.

"I repeat," Craig bellowed into the bullhorn, "there is a gas leak. If you do not leave the area, one of my officers will arrest you and take you to the county jail for putting yourself and others in danger. Am I understood?" He was so loud that he didn't need the bullhorn to make himself heard.

In a flurry of fierce whispering, the crowd began to disperse. As the villagers, following the chief inspector's directions, hurried past me, I continued to move in the direction of Craig's voice.

I stopped a woman in a long woolen dress. "Where is the gas leak?" I asked her.

She looked up at me, slightly irritated. "Pardon me?" she barked.

"The gas leak," I said. "Does anyone know where it origi- nated? From a home or a business?"

"Alastair Croft's place," she replied. "I'm not surprised. I bet he left the stove on in the kitchen. He can be mighty irre- sponsible. I always thought so. I taught him in school. He's lucky that the place didn't blow sky high. He could have taken out half the houses on the street with an explosion like that."

"So, it was a gas stove that caused the problem?" I asked.

"Don't know," she said sounding annoyed, and then she looked me up and down. "You aren't from around here are you? You're not Scottish, I can tell that much."

"I'm half Scottish," I replied.

"Hmm . . ." she said, as if she found that distinctly suspicious.

The woman left me then and rejoined the flow of villagers who were now in a big hurry to get as far away from St. Charles Street as possible. Finally, I spotted Cally's red hair bobbing in the crowded street. Like me, she was going against the grain of traffic as she was desperate to reach the source of the commotion.

The villagers made way for me as I walked against the tide as quickly as I dared. I took care not to knock into any of them in my haste.

Finally, enough villagers had passed me by that I could see the building that everyone was running from. It was a free- standing, red-brick townhouse with purple ivy crawling up the side of it. Two firemen in full fire gear came out of the build- ing. Craig was waiting for them at the bottom of the steps.

The first fireman removed his helmet. Sweat matted his

hair to his head. "It was the gas fireplace. It looks to me like the pilot light was blown out."

"Accidentally?" Craig asked.

The fireman ran a hand over his sweaty hair. "That's always possible. We've had some high winds over the last few days, and it's always possible that a draft could've come down the chimney and blown the light out, but that's not what I think happened."

Craig folded his arms. "What do you think happened?"

"Someone blew out the pilot light on purpose, hoping to blow the entire townhouse up." He said this statement with no inflection, as though he were talking about the day's football scores or the weather.

I shivered at the idea of it and knew I shouldn't even be there. Other than Cally and myself, the only people who remained on the street were law enforcement and emergency personnel. They ran from place to place and spoke in tightly gathered groups of four or five. None of them paid Cally or me any mind, but I knew that it was just a matter of moments before Craig took notice of me. Then, I would be sunk.

Cally was only a few yards away from me. She was staring at the townhouse. Her hand covered her mouth.

I was about to go to her, when I heard Craig say, "What makes you think it was intentional?"

"The gas was turned up much higher than it needed to be for a normal cozy fire. I can say that for sure. The valve was all the way open. My guess is, someone went in there, blew out the pilot light, and turned the gas all the way up. One electrical spark was all it would take to blow up half the street."

Craig whistled. "After we get the all-clear, I'll have my guys going in there to dust the gas valve for prints."

"Why would anyone want to blow up the townhouse?" the second, much younger fireman asked.

The first fireman grunted. "This is exactly why I can tell you haven't read the police blotter, Samuels." He pointed behind himself with his thumb. "This is Alastair Croft's place."

"The lawyer?" Samuels asked.

"The dead lawyer," the first, nameless fireman corrected.

"How long until it will be safe to go into the building?" Craig interjected.

"I'd give it a couple of hours just to be safe. I wouldn't so much as flip a light switch on in there right now. If you do, it might go up. We're lucky that the place wasn't blown sky high."

I felt a knot form in the pit of my stomach.

"As soon as we don't smell gas any longer, it should be clear, but it doesn't hurt to give it a little extra time," the first fireman said. "We have all the windows and doors open so the place can air out quickly and naturally. It's the best way. Using an electric fan or anything with a motor to hurry the process along is too risky and might cause a spark. Until the gas is completely dissipated, a spark is all it will take to blow the place. There is little more than that we can do now."

"The gas is off?" Craig asked.

The first fireman pursed his lips together as if he was insulted by the question. "Yes. We turned the gas off to the entire building. The gas company turned it off at the street."

Samuels scratched at the beard at the very bottom of his

chin. "Do you think whoever killed Croft is the one who turned up the natural gas in his fireplace? How did he die anyway?"

"It fits," Craig sighed. "The coroner just said to me this morning that Croft died by natural gas asphyxiation. My theory is, he was murdered here and then the body was moved."

"Moved where?" Samuels asked.

"The garden at Duncreigan."

Samuels pulled his head in, giving himself a double chin. "Ian MacCallister's garden?"

Craig nodded. He opened his mouth to say something more, when a high-pitched voice interrupted him. "Chief Inspector Craig! Chief Inspector Craig! I am here to help!"

Craig spun around and his eyes fell directly on me. His brown eyes narrowed. I swallowed hard, afraid that I might melt under his penetrating stare, until his gaze moved over my head.

"Chief Inspector, I'm here!" the voice came again.

I looked over my shoulder and spotted gawky Kipling with his police jacket half on, half off, tripping over himself to reach the scene. Kipling came to a wobbly stop in front of the Chief Inspector and panted. Although he was thin—almost painfully so—I didn't think it came from running or working out.

The volunteer police officer didn't so much as glance in my direction. I was grateful for that. I didn't want him to recognize me from the Twisted Fox Pub. Craig knew that I was here. That was more than enough.

Kipling doubled over, clutching his knees and gulping down air.

The two firemen who had been talking to Craig collectively took a step back, afraid the panting man might throw up from the overexertion of running up St. Charles Street.

"What do you need me to do?" Kipling asked between gulps of air.

Craig rubbed his forehead. "We have everything well under control, Kipling."

Kipling straightened up. "I'm the law in the village. Why hasn't someone called me to tell me what's going on? I didn't know a thing was wrong until a slew of villagers came into the Twisted Fox talking about a gas leak. Where is the leak? I demand to be informed about the situation."

Craig dropped his hand. "This isn't a jaywalking violation, Kipling. I don't have to inform you about anything, especially not a murder."

"Murder?" Kipling gasped. "What are you talking about? No one is ever murdered in Bellewick. If they were, I would know about it. I am the law in the village," he said, repeating his earlier declaration.

Craig squinted at the younger man as if he was fighting a headache. At six five, Craig was a good foot taller than Kipling, and the volunteer police officer was well aware of his size disadvantage because he straightened his back, rising to his full height, to take advantage of every last centimeter that he might gain from good posture. "Fill me in on what happened."

That sounded a lot like an order to me. Craig winced as if he recognized the same tone in the smaller man's voice. "This is the county investigation. You do not handle murder cases."

The smaller man jabbed his fists into his hips. "I may not be in charge of the case, but I have every right to know.

I need to be able to do my duty and protect the village from wrongdoing." He stuck his chest out in a superhero pose. "And if that includes protecting them from murderers, then so be it."

Craig rubbed his eyebrows. "When the scene is secure, I will let the village know what's going on. We'll hold a village meeting in the Twisted Fox."

"I should know before the rest of village knows." Kipling still had his chest out. I feared if he held that pose much longer, he was at risk of throwing out his back. "It is professional courtesy to tell me first." Kipling shook a little bit as he spoke, and this stance reminded me of the mallard that returned to the pond on my parents' farm back in Tennessee every year. He always seemed to have his feathers ruffled, just like Kipling, and he wasn't well liked by the other ducks. I suspected the same was true for the volunteer police officer.

"Kipling," Craig began. It was clear that the younger man was trying his patience. "You're welcome to stay and observe, but please stay out of the way. Also, if you stay, it is at your own risk. There was a natural gas leak here. There is a real risk of explosion."

Kipling took a step back. All the bravado that he'd had a moment ago ebbed away. "Is it dangerous to be here?"

"I wouldn't light a cigarette," Craig said.

Kipling took two more steps back. "Maybe it would be better if I left." He snapped his fingers as if suddenly he'd gotten a brilliant idea. "I know. I'll run ahead to the Twisted Fox. I'll tell the villagers that you'll be there soon to share news with them about what's going on. Someone needs to handle crowd control."

The corners of Craig's wide mouth twitched. "You're the best man for that job, Kipling. In fact, I think it's a fine idea."

Kipling glanced at Alastair's townhouse again as if he were afraid it would blow up at any moment. "Good, good. You know my motto has always been to protect and serve, serve and protect."

Craig folded his arms over his broad chest. "I didn't know that, but I will certainly make a mental note about it for the future."

Kipling took one more step back and said, "You do that." With those words, he spun on his heel and ran back down the street in the direction he'd come from.

Kipling's choice to remove himself meant that there was no one standing between Chief Inspector Craig and me. The large chief inspector narrowed his dark eyes and crooked his finger at me to indicate I should approach.

I narrowed my eyes in return. I was not the kind of girl who came when beckoned, and Craig should have known that from having met me the day before.

Chapter Seventeen

When I didn't approach as he wanted me too, Craig walked over to me. He loomed head and shoulders above me, but I refused to make myself taller like Kipling had. I wanted him to know that his height had no effect on me, even if that was a lie.

"Fiona Knox, what are you doing here?" he asked.

Before I could answer, he added, "You shouldn't be here. How did you get here?"

"If you give me a chance, I'm happy to answer your questions," I said.

He frowned, and it could just be my perception, but his frown appeared a little more menacing when directed at me than it had been when he'd pointed it at Kipling.

"I was meeting with Cally."

"Alastair's law partner?" he asked.

I nodded.

He frowned. "Why were you meeting with Cally Beckleberry?"

"She my attorney now that Alastair is dead, and I needed to talk to her about my godfather's estate. I might have inherited it,

126

but there are documents that need to be signed and forms that need to be completed. The estate won't be settled overnight."

"Ahh," he said, somewhat appeased by my answer. "I thought I saw her here a moment ago, before Kipling showed up." He grimaced when he said Kipling's name.

"She is right over there." I pointed to the end of the street. Cally was speaking to another officer and gesturing wildly as she spoke.

Craig shook his head as he spotted Cally with one of his officers. "Better him than me," he muttered.

"Why do you say that?" I asked.

"Say what?" he asked, as if he were trying to play dumb. I knew it was an act. I hadn't known Chief Inspector Craig for long, but I knew he was far from dumb.

I decided to let it go. "I assume this is Alastair Croft's house. Cally said as much when she ran from the legal office. There was a gas leak?"

He studied me with his dark eyes. Even though he was a seasoned cop, his eyes somehow conveyed an inner kindness that I found appealing. They were so different from Ethan's eyes, which were startling green. When Ethan had looked at me, I'd thought I was under some type of bright light, and felt like I should be grateful he'd paused his pursuit of country music greatness to turn his attention on me. Craig's gaze couldn't have been more different. It was intelligent but gentle. He held my gaze for a long moment, so long that I finally had to look away. I pretended to examine Alastair's townhouse, but I don't think I did a good job at covering because out of the corner of my eye I spotted a small smile curving on the chief inspector's lips. My cheeks grew hot.

"I'm sure you heard that there was a natural gas leak when I told the crowd that just a moment ago," he said, seemingly taking pity on me in my embarrassment.

"I did." I paused. "Accidental?"

"Possibly, but I don't think so. I assume that you overheard my conversation with the firemen too."

"I did." There was no point in denying it. "Why would someone move the body to Duncreigan? Why not just blow up the house to hide the evidence? In that case, the murder could have been blamed as an accident, an unfortunate gas leak. The person who did this would have never been caught because no one would have suspected foul play."

"That's a good point," Craig conceded.

"And why are you just finding the gas leak now? If the body was found yesterday, didn't an officer come here to check the victim's house? I thought that was standard procedure when someone was murdered."

He frowned.

I held up my hands. "I'm not passing any judgment here on your policing; I'm just asking a question."

His frown deepened.

When he didn't answer me, I gave up on that question for the moment and asked, "You can't possibly think Hamish is responsible for Alastair's death now, can you?"

Craig shook his head. "A man should be so lucky as to have a champion as fierce as you, Fiona Knox. You do not give up when you are presenting your case."

"Hamish couldn't have done this."

He sighed. "I know you believe that, but right now I have another problem."

"What's that?" I looked up at him.

His dark brown eyes clouded with concern. "We haven't found Alastair's cat yet." He pressed his lips together for a moment. "I hope nothing happened to the poor creature. Alastair doted on that little animal. I would hate for anything to have happened to him, but if he's been in the townhouse all this time, it's likely that he's no longer alive. He would have suffocated with the amount of gas in the air. If it was enough to kill Alastair, it was more than enough to kill a cat."

My heart softened toward the chief inspector just a little, knowing that he was concerned about Alastair's cat. "Do you mean Ivanhoe?" I asked.

He blinked at me. "You know the name of Alastair's cat? I thought you said you hardly knew Alastair."

"That's true. I do know of Ivanhoe because I met him earlier today at Croft and Beckleberry."

"How did he get there?"

"You will have to ask Cally for the particulars," I said. "But she told me that he just showed up yesterday morning. She had planned to have Alastair take the cat back to his house, but as you know, Alastair never showed up for work yesterday."

His shoulders sagged. "Well, that's a relief." He tapped his chin with his index finger. "Cally didn't want the cat at the office?"

I nodded. "She's terribly allergic of cats."

"I didn't know the cat was there at the same time I was. I saw no sign of him."

"He must have been hiding," I said. "He was probably a little afraid of you. You're a big guy."

Craig laughed then, and it was deep laugh coming from his chest. "That I am, but most animals like me. Most people do too—except the ones I put in prison. They aren't that fond of me."

"Cally tried to talk me into adopting Ivanhoe." I frowned. "It seemed like an odd concern to have so soon after she learned Alastair had been killed."

He watched me for a moment. "I think so too."

I lowered my voice. "Is Cally a suspect?"

"What do you think?" he asked in an equally low voice.

I swallowed.

Craig looked over his shoulder at Cally, who had seemed to calm down in whatever she was telling the other police officer. Even though she was no long gesturing wildly, by the way her lips were moving, it seemed she was still talking a mile a minute. Because of the distance between her and where Craig and I stood, we couldn't hear what she was saying, but just recognized her insistent tone. I shuffled from foot to foot. "It seems to me that Cally is the only villager who knows Alastair is dead."

He raised his eyebrows.

I decided to answer the unspoken question. "I was in the pub earlier today, and it seemed that no one knew that Alastair was dead."

Craig pursed his lips again. "The Twisted Fox is the place to go for gossip in Bellewick. The men that frequent that pub are chattier than the women in any beauty parlor."

I nodded, happy that he didn't press me to find out what the gossip was. I wouldn't have told him if he had, and I didn't want to lie.

"You're right, the rest of the village hasn't been informed yet. I told Cally because she and Craig were business partners, and she would be the most likely to report him missing if he didn't show up at the office after some time. However, I didn't tell the rest of the village because we were having trouble finding Alastair's next of kin."

"Oh, who is that?" I asked.

He scowled. "His sister. We were finally able to track her down in Wales. Now that she's been notified, we can inform the village."

"Is she coming here?"

He nodded. "She should be here later today." He paused. "There is much to do when someone dies," he said, sounding as if he spoke from experience.

"What's his sister's name?"

He looked at me for a long moment. "Aileen Croft."

"She's not married?" I asked.

"Divorced." His voice was clipped when he said this.

I found myself frowning. There was something more to that answer than Craig was letting on.

Cally stomped over to us. "Neil, you have to tell me what's going on here."

"Cally." Craig nodded.

"I want to know what you are doing to find Alastair's killer. I hope that your past history with him won't make you brush off his case," she snapped at the chief inspector.

My eyebrows went up. Past history? Was she talking about Craig and Alastair's childhood friendship that Hamish had told me about—or something more?

"Please calm down," Craig said to the attorney.

She glared at him. I would have done the same if I had been in her position. I don't think there is a woman on the planet who likes to be told to calm down, and it might just have the opposite effect on someone than the person saying it wants to achieve.

"Calm down? Calm down? I don't have to tell you that Alastair is dead. Alastair and I were partners. He was . . ." Cally trailed off and took a deep breath. "He was my friend."

Not for the first time did I wonder if Cally had wanted to be more than just friends with Alastair. She claimed that he'd been greedy and hadn't treated her well, but she wouldn't be the first woman to be attracted to the wrong guy. I was speaking from my own painful experience.

"And then there is the cat," Cally went on. "I don't know what to do with the cat. I'm allergic. He's a sweet animal, but every time I'm around the creature, I start sneezing. I was trying to convince your officer to let me put him back in the townhouse until Aileen arrives, but he refuses." She held up her hand. "Of course, I would wait until after the townhouse was safe again—I just can't have the animal in the office or in my home."

"We can't let you put the cat back in the townhouse. Even after it's safe," Craig said. "It's a crime scene. Investigators will be going in and out of the townhouse for some time to figure out what exactly happened."

Cally threw up her hands. "Then, what do I do with the cat?"

"I'll take him." The words popped out of my mouth before I even had a chance to consider them.

Cally clasped her hands together. "You will?"

"Umm . . . yeah. I mean," I hedged, "I don't know how long I will be at Duncreigan, but as long as I'm there, he can stay with me. It will give you some time to make more permanent arrangements for him."

Cally beamed at me. "Thank you so much! Thank you! I hate the idea of the cat going to a shelter or somewhere else. He was important to Alastair, but I didn't know what I was going to do. I hope it won't be much trouble."

I shook my head. "He's a nice cat, and he won't be any trouble. It might be nice to have some company while I'm here."

Craig looked at me. "I thought you had plans to stay here permanently."

I raised my eyebrows in surprise, wondering why he would even care. "I'm trying not to make plans anymore. They rarely work out."

Craig looked as if he wanted to ask me what I meant by that, and I wished I could grab the words out of the air and shove them back into my mouth, even though they might be true.

My sister Isla's voice rang in my ear: "Fi, you are too honest. You need to learn to hide your feelings. If you can do that, I think you will be way happier." Maybe she was right.

Thankfully, Cally, who was so relieved over me solving her cat dilemma, wrapped her arm around my shoulders and saved me from answering Craig's unspoken questions about my disbelief in plans. "Let's go to the office now, so you can get the cat."

I slipped out from under her arm. "I have some errands to run in the village before I go to Duncreigan. Can I stop by your office later to pick him up when I'm ready to head back?"

She smiled. "Of course, but don't forget, and if you do, I will drive Ivanhoe up to Duncreigan myself."

I had little doubt that she would do just that.

Craig looked from Cally to me and then back again. "I think you both should leave now. It's much safer here than it was a few minutes ago, but I still can't have any citizens this close to Alastair's townhouse."

Cally dropped her arm from my shoulder. "Very well, Neil, but as soon as Alastair's home is cleared, I want to get in there. As Alastair's executrix, I should give everything a once-over."

"You are Alastair's executrix?" Craig asked. "Not Aileen?"

"Of course I was. We were business partners. I don't think anyone in their right mind would put Aileen in charge of their estate, do you?"

"No." Craig said the word in the clipped voice that he had used just a few minutes ago when Aileen's name came up. "I should be at the pub within the hour. I assume that you want to be there when I talk to the village?" He directed this statement at Cally, but I included myself in it. I definitely wanted to be there to see Craig tell the villagers about the murder. It might be my best chance to see their honest reactions to the news.

"I'll be there," Cally promised.

As Cally and I turned to go, Craig called, "Miss Knox! Wait! I have something for you."

I turned back to face him.

He held a piece of paper out to me "Your list."

"My list?" I asked.

He smiled and extended the white paper to me. Our fingers

brushed as I took it from his hand. I unfolded the paper, which was a typed form with the Aberdeen Police Department insignia on it. It listed everything that Craig and his team had removed from the garden the day before. True to his word, besides the body itself, they had taken only plants, grass, and soil samples.

I met his eyes. "Thank you." A part of me was startled that he'd actually given me the list.

He smiled. "I keep my promises, Miss Knox."

I couldn't think of anything to say in return.

He nodded to us both before heading back to his officers standing just outside the townhouse.

Cally and I wove around the police cars and emergency vehicles parked in the street. We walked together until we made it to the corner. Cally went toward the law office, but I was headed in the opposite direction. I stopped her. "Cally, what's going on with Chief Inspector Craig and Alastair's sister? Every time her name came up, he looked upset." I paused. "I don't know if 'upset' is the right word. Maybe it would be better to say that he looked guarded."

She studied me before answering. "That's because Aileen Croft is Neil's ex-wife. It was not an amicable divorce. Aileen moved away right after they broke up and hasn't been back. I'm certain Neil didn't want to make that call informing her of her brother's death. And I'm even more certain that he doesn't want to see her when she arrives."

Chapter Eighteen

At the corner, Cally and I parted ways after I promised yet again, for a third time, that I would stop by the law office to pick up the cat before I left the village . She headed in the direction of her office, and I hesitated on the corner, unsure of what to do.

Everything in me wanted to go back to Alastair's townhouse and watch the police, with the hope that I would learn something new, like why they had waited until the next day to enter his home. It was a very good question that the fireman had asked, but Craig had never answered it. However, I knew hanging around St. Charles Street was a terrible idea. First of all, it was dangerous to be there, as Craig had said, and second of all, I had to be careful with the chief inspector. Up to this point, he had shared a bit of the investigation with me. If I irritated him too much, the little bit he was willing to share with me would dry up. I couldn't let that happen, for Hamish's sake.

A fiftyish man with a priest collar walked up to me. "You should be ashamed of yourself. You're the one who has brought all this heartbreak to our little village."

I blinked at him. "Excuse me?"

"Don't play dumb with me," the man spat. "You know exactly what I mean. I hoped and prayed that it would be over when Ian MacCallister passed on, but now here you are, bringing the same disgrace on the village of Bellewick."

"I have no idea what you are talking about. Who are you?" I asked.

His gaze narrowed. "Minister Quaid MacCullen, and Bellewick is my parish. There is no place for you in it. I insist that you leave."

I opened and closed my mouth, unsure of what to say. How did this man know me? And how on earth was I bringing heartbreak to Bellewick?

I backed away from the minister. "I'm sorry, but I have to go." I turned to leave.

"You must really be a MacCallister if you are running away."

I spun around. "I'm not a MacCallister, but I would be proud to call myself one. They were brave men and women."

The minister pointed a long, wrinkled finger at me. "Know that I will be watching you just as I have watched everyone from Duncreigan since I took over this parish. I know what goes on there. I may not have been able to in the past, but this time I will put a stop to it."

I swallowed. "I don't have to listen to this." Without another word, I hurried to the corner and turned. On the next street, I ran into the first shop that I could find.

I just made it too. As I peeked out the front window of the shop, the minister came around the corner. He looked up and down the street, apparently searching for me. When he didn't see me, he threw up his hands and went back in the direction from which he'd come.

I slumped against the window frame.

"Hiding from an ex-boyfriend?" a voice with a deep, female, East Indian accent asked from behind me. I turned to face her. An Indian woman about my mother's age, in jeans and a flannel shirt, held a brightly pink and bejeweled scarf around her shoulders.

My face flushed. "I'm so sorry to come bursting in here like this. I'm so embarrassed."

"We've all run away from ex-boyfriends, my dear, even if we aren't willing to admit it."

"I wasn't running away from an ex-boyfriend," I said.

All around me I saw tables and tea sets. Above the counter in the back of the room, an antique sign read "Presha's Teas." The room was decorated in purple tartan and thistle. The only nod to Presha's own culture was a small shrine to Ganesh, the elephant god in the corner of the teashop near the door that I assumed led to the kitchen.

"If not an ex, then who?" She asked.

"He said his name was Minister MacCullen, and he doesn't like me at all."

"Ahh," she said. "I should make some tea so that you can tell me all about your encounter." She gracefully turned and beads of her scarf clinked together. "I am Presha Kapoor," she said before disappearing into the kitchen.

Kapoor? I couldn't believe my good fortune. Hadn't Lee said that the person—other than Hamish—who disliked Alastair the most was Raj Kapoor, the leader of those opposed to selling the coast? Presha had to be related to him in some way in a village as small as Bellewick.

While I waited for Presha to return with the tea, with my hand I smoothed a tiny wrinkle out of the tartan tablecloth in front of me. As soon as I removed my hand from the cloth, the wrinkle reappeared. It reminded me of everything that had happened since I'd arrived in Scotland. As much as I tried to fix things to prove Hamish was innocent, the chance that he might not be came back.

Presha returned with the tea tray filled with Scottish short-bread cookies, scones, butter, and jam. My mouth watered as soon as I saw it. Even though Lee had said the shepherd's pie I'd eaten at the Twisted Fox would stick to my ribs, I was hungry again. I never ate this much in Nashville. Investigating a murder seemed to make me work up an appetite.

She poured from the teapot, which was unlike any that I had ever seen. The strong scent of the chai permeated the air. She nodded at the scones. "Go ahead. Take one, Fiona."

My hand froze on the way to the plate. How did she know my name? I'd never introduced myself.

She laughed. "You must be wondering how I know your name. It's well known in the village that Ian's goddaughter is here. You stopped at the Twisted Fox, did you not? You might as well have taken an ad out in the village paper to notify everyone of your presence. News travels fast out of the pub. Ian was my friend, and he spoke of you often. I knew your name was Fiona, and when you opened your mouth and spoke in an unmistakable American accent, I just used my little gray cells, as Hercule Poirot would say."

I smiled and took a scone from the plate. "Oh. I guess I am a little paranoid. It's been a weird couple of days."

"I can imagine."

The scone was as large as my fist, and I placed it on the fragile bread plate in front me. A delicately painted purple thistle decorated the edge of the plate. It was clearly fine bone china and the type of plate that my mother would have kept in her china cabinet back on the farm but would never have used, not even for a special occasion, for fear it might break. I had never much seen the point of having dishes that weren't used. Dishes, to my mind, should be used, not stored so that someone else could store them later, which I'm sure was my mother's plan for those dishes. I hoped Isla would volunteer to take them so I wouldn't have to deal with them someday.

I broke the scone in half longways and liberally topped both halves with butter and strawberry jam. The first bite was like heaven. I was embarrassed to think that I might even have moaned a little when I bit into the fluffy pastry. It was the absolute perfect consistency. Try as any baker back in Nashville might, none would never be able to reach this level of scone perfection. It must be something in the air of the British Isles that made them so good.

Presha smiled when she saw my expression. "I might not be Scottish by blood, but I am in my baking."

I dabbed at the corner of my mouth, where jam had unattractively collected. "You are. These are some of the best scones I have ever had, and I used to visit my godfather here in Scotland a lot more regularly."

She looked at me over her teacup. "When was the last time that you were here?"

"It was three years ago." I looked down at my scones. "But it was a short trip. I wish I could have come more often."

It wasn't until I came up for air after inhaling the rest my scone that I realized we were the only ones in the teashop. I commented on it.

"Usually this place is full of customers, but everyone is over at the Twisted Fox, waiting to hear the news about Alastair Croft's murder," she said before taking a sip of tea.

I stared at her. "You know Alastair was murdered?"

"I do." She nodded. "And I know that you found his body in Ian's garden."

"But how?" I asked.

She shook her head, and I knew I might never know the answer to that question. In any case, now I knew that Cally wasn't the only citizen in Bellewick aware of Alastair's murder. There were others, but with the meeting in the pub planned, everyone in the village would know soon. I was trying to decide if it really mattered that Presha knew beforehand. It felt important, but I wasn't certain why that was the case.

I picked up the cup of tea that she had poured for me. Even before I drank from it, I could tell that the chai was strong, much stronger than the chai that I was used to back in the States. I sipped the tea, and the cardamom bit back at me. I did my best to keep my face neutral, but I must have failed miserably because Presha laughed. "You will get used to it, I dare say. When I first opened the shop forty years ago, the villagers took some time getting used to my strong chai. Now, it is the most popular drink on my menu."

"Are you related to Raj Kapoor?"

She raised her eyebrows. "You know my brother?"

I shook my head. "His name came up in the pub. I was asking about Alastair . . ."

She sat a little straighter in her chair. "I see. My brother was not a fan of Alastair Croft. Anyone in the village can and probably will tell you that."

"Because he was at odds with Alastair over the land deal?" I curved my hands around the warm teacup. Although it was May, it was still damp and cold along the Scottish coast, and the damp cold seemed to have seeped into my bones. I was grateful for the tea, even if it was a bit too strong for my tastes.

"You are well informed, young Fiona," she said. "Very well informed."

Chapter Nineteen

"Your godfather was a good friend to my brother, Raj, and me," Presha said. "He was the first one in the village to make us feel welcome. In fact, he was the first one to try my chai. After Ian pronounced it as good, the rest of the villagers were willing to give it a try."

"That does sound like Uncle Ian," I said. "Does your brother work for some type of environmental group in his protest against the land sale?" I asked, trying to get the conversation back on track.

She sat back in her chair. "He belongs to many such groups but doesn't have any official title."

"What else does he do then?"

"He runs the laundromat on St. Mary's Street."

I straightened up in my seat. "I was planning to take some sheets there today. I haven't been there yet. The day went a little haywire."

"Death will do that." She said this as if she was speaking from experience. "There is nothing like a death to make life go astray. Any death has a ripple effect on the earth and the life inhabiting it. It changes those left behind—some for the better, some for the worse."

I thought about this for a moment. How had Uncle Ian's death changed me? Potentially, it had changed my entire life.

"Do you plan to go to the Twisted Fox when the police speak to the village?" I asked.

She sipped her tea. "I will. I don't like the circus that Alastair's death has created, but I have found that even though I don't like what may be going on, it's better to be informed."

"If you like to stay informed, didn't you know about Alastair's land deal?"

She pursed her lip. "I did." She peered into her teacup as if she no longer wanted to meet my gaze.

"What did you think of it?"

She looked up from her tea. "I hated it like most of the village does, but not as much as my brother. He was obsessed with it."

Raj Kapoor's obsession promoted him to my number-one suspect for Alastair's murder.

"You can drop off whatever you need to have washed with my brother, and he will see to it," Presha said. "You can pick it up later. That was always Raj's arrangement with Ian, so I don't see why that would have to change with you."

"I'll talk to your brother. What was his relationship with Alastair?" I hoped my question seemed much more casual than it sounded to me. "I know that they were on opposite sides about the coast sale, but how was their relationship other than that?"

Presha studied me for a moment. "I think that's a question you should ask my brother. I can't speak for him."

I changed tactics. "Did my godfather ever talk about the coast sale?"

She relaxed. "He did. Ian gave my brother his full support. He was against it just as much as the rest of the village was."

It was the answer I expected to hear, but I had to ask, "If Uncle Ian was opposed to the land deal, then why did he use Alastair as his lawyer?"

"Alastair's firm was the only one in town, and I would wager a guess that Ian wrote that will many years ago, before the sale of the coastline was even an issue. I bet everyone in the village who has written a will in the last ten years used Alastair's firm. He might have been an unpleasant young man, but he was a good lawyer." She straightened her colorful scarf on her shoulders. "Also, Cally Beckleberry was in the firm. No one in town has anything bad to say about her."

I sipped the tea again. This time it didn't taste quite as jarringly strong. Maybe I was just becoming accustomed to the strong taste, or maybe some of my taste buds had burned off.

I was about to ask her more about Cally, when she said, "But enough about that. How is the magical garden?" Presha studied me with bright eyes.

I choked on my tea, and a bit spurted out before I managed to force out the words "The magical garden?"

She smiled encouragingly. "Has it returned to life like Ian said it would when you came to Scotland?"

"How did you know that?" I set my teacup on the purple tartan tablecloth.

"Ian told me years ago, that's what would happen."

I frowned. If Uncle Ian had told Presha this, why hadn't

he told Hamish until it was revealed in that letter? Why hadn't he told *me*?

"Actually, it has started to—or at least according to Hamish it has. A few things like the ivy on the walls are greening again, but most of the garden is still very much dead." The withered willow tree came to mind.

"You must bring it all the way back to life. It will take some time for you to learn, but Ian had every confidence in you, and so do I." She gave me a wide smile.

"I don't understand. How do I do that?" I asked.

"Didn't Ian explain?" she asked. Her dark brows knit together.

"No. I know nothing about all of this. I mean, I knew there was a garden, yes. Uncle Ian would take me there many times during our visits, but I don't know anything about what I need to do with it. And I didn't know that it had some kind of mystical history that I am also apparently connected to. I don't know how it can have anything to do with me at all."

"It has everything to do with you." Her tone was matter-of-fact.

"Then tell me what because no one else has," I pleaded. "It seems to me that Hamish and now you know what is going on, but I am clueless to all of it. All I know is, I inherited Duncreigan. I came to Scotland to claim that inheritance and found a dead man in my godfather's garden. Can you please tell me what is going on? Hamish won't. I think you might be the only other person who knows."

"Hamish won't tell you and neither can I because it is Ian's place to tell you." The sequins on her scarf reflected on the tablecloth the light coming in from the window, creating pinpricks that glowed on the purple tartan.

"Ian's dead." I let those words hang in the air between us for a few minutes. "But he left me a letter."

"And what did the letter say?" she asked eagerly.

"I don't know. It must have been mailed back home, and I haven't had a chance yet to call my sister and ask her to find it. I'm almost afraid to read it," I admitted.

I was staring into my teacup, but I could feel her studying me. "Why?"

"Because Hamish said that there was supposed to be a letter from my godfather explaining whatever it is that's going on. Hamish received a letter too and read it to me. It was clear from Hamish's letter that my godfather at least intended to tell me something. We don't know for sure that he ever did."

She stared at me for a long moment. "In all your life, did Ian MacCallister ever say he was going to do something and not actually do it?"

I shook my head. "No."

"Then, there is a letter." Her voice was straightforward. She rose. "Are you ready to see the commotion at the pub?"

I took one more sip of my chai and gave the scones still on the plate a forlorn look. "I'm as ready as I'll ever be."

"Good, because we need to go so we can grab a good spot. The entire village will be there." She headed for the door. "It promises to be quite a show."

Chapter Twenty

Presha had been right that the entire village was at the Twisted Fox Pub to hear what Chief Inspector Craig had to say about the gas leak on St. Charles Street. Most of them didn't know the real bombshell that was coming. They didn't know that one of their own was dead, murdered. I bit the inside of my lip and wondered if Craig would reveal where Alastair's body had been found. If he did, it would only add to the MacCallister family's poor reputation with some of the villagers.

Even at his height, Craig had to stand on a chair at the front of the bar to be seen by all the villagers crowding the pub and spilling out onto the street. I guessed that the pub was in serious violation of fire codes with so many people crammed inside it, but since I saw two of the Aberdeen firemen standing nearby, seemingly unconcerned, I didn't see any reason for me to be worried.

Craig stood on the chair and surveyed the packed space. I stepped behind a large man in a thick denim coat when the chief inspector's eyes slid over to where I stood. Craig's gaze moved on. "Thank you all for coming," he said in his booming voice, the same one that he had used with the bull-horn on St. Charles Street.

The crowd didn't even pause in their gossiping to acknowledge that the chief inspector had spoken.

A sharp whistle rang out, piercing the chatter in the room, and the villagers fell silent.

Craig glanced down at someone I couldn't see because of the crush of bodies. "Thank you, Lee." He turned back to the villagers. "Let me start again. Thank you all for coming. I called this meeting because I know many of you have been wondering what's happening over on St. Charles Street."

"It's Alastair Croft's house, isn't it?" a male voice called from somewhere in the pub. "The only thing that Croft does for Bellewick is cause problems."

Several other voices chimed in in agreement.

Craig held his hand up in the air in the universal sign that means "stop."

"Please, let us not jump to conclusions," he said. "Yes, a gas leak was discovered at Alastair Croft's townhouse. The area has been secured, and the threat to the neighborhood has been removed. If you live near St. Charles, you can return to your homes now. The fire department has declared it safe."

"What happened? Is there something wrong with the gas line?" Someone shouted the question.

Not being able to see where the question came from was a tad disorienting for me. I felt like I was trapped in some sort of alternative funhouse, but I couldn't say it was much fun to be there.

Craig shook his head. "No. This was strictly an issue in Croft's home. There is no reason for any of you to be concerned about your own homes. The gas company was out early today and checked the entire area."

"Of course, we're concerned!" another voice chided. "We all could have been killed!"

Other voices agreed. Before Craig could respond to that outburst, someone said, "Has anyone seen Alastair lately?"

"No," a voice murmured.

"Haven't seen him for a couple of days," another voice added.

"He's probably down in Edinburgh celebrating his big win," someone said scornfully.

"Maybe he was in the house!" a fourth person called out.

There was an audible gasp as the villagers began to realize that Alastair wasn't among them.

Craig shook his head. "No one was in the house when the leak was discovered."

I couldn't help but take note of the fact that Craig chose his words very carefully. He had said that no one was in the house when the leak was discovered. He didn't say no one was in the house when the leak had *occurred*. I suspected that it was a calculated decision. I didn't think the chief inspector was someone who used his words without consideration.

"Then where's Croft?" the angry male voice rang out again. Now that I had heard it a second time, I thought I recognized it as my friend from the pub earlier that day, the one Lee had called Jock.

Craig cleared his throat. "That brings us to the second reason that I have called this meeting. I am very sorry to report that Alastair Croft has died." He paused. "And it appears that his death was the result of foul play."

A collective gasp traveled through the room, and then everyone started talking at once.

Lee let out another whistle, and they settled down again.

"How did he die?" someone asked.

Craig held up his hands. "Please, quiet down."

"Are we in danger?"

"Was it a serial killer?"

"There is no serial killer in Bellewick," Craig said in an even tone.

"It's because of the land deal. Someone offed him because of that," a voice said, leaving no room for argument.

"Not that he didn't deserve it," another disembodied voice replied.

"Please," Craig said, "I am not telling you this for speculation, but because Alastair Croft is a native of our little village. He came back to live here when, with his impressive credentials, he could have lived anywhere else in the world. He has done a lot of good for everyone in this room."

I glanced around the room as the chief inspector said this. Some of the villagers nodded in agreement. Others shook their heads. There didn't seem to be a general consensus about how good the attorney had been for Bellewick.

"The land deal isn't good for the village," someone cried out.

Craig held his hands aloft. "You and I both know that is not the only thing that Alastair has done. Now, I called this meeting today to ask you to come forward if you know anything at all about how Alastair died or who might be responsible for his death. We need your help to find out who did this to one of our own."

I let out a deep breath, relieved that he made no mention of my godfather or his garden. This relief was short-lived, as another man asked, "How can we tell you anything when we don't know where or how he died?"

"I would prefer to share that information privately with anyone who comes forward," Craig replied evenly.

A frustrated murmur ran through the Twisted Fox Pub. There was no way that Chief Inspector Craig would be able, for very long, to keep a lid on where Alastair had been found. However, the time for that information to remain secret ran out much more quickly than I could have expected.

"I know where he was found," a scratchy and angry voice called out. I turned to see the minister standing in the door, and my heart sank. The bright sunlight backlit him, giving a heavenly or hellish glow. The exact type of glow it was would depend on the person you asked. If you asked me, I would have said the latter.

I ducked my head so that Minister MacCullen couldn't see me. Then I sidled behind the large man in the denim jacket again. I might start asking the man to follow me wherever I go so I'd have a body to hide behind.

"Alastair Croft was found dead in the garden at Duncreigan," the minister declared like he was making a statement of damnation. "I have been telling you for years that that place was no good. Finally, you will all have to listen to me."

Craig glared at him. "Minister MacCullen, if there is

something that you want to speak to me about concerning this case, I must ask that we discuss it in private."

"In private?" the minister countered. "So that you can hide the MacCallisters' involvement? I always thought you turned a blind eye to what was going on at Duncreigan, and now I am sure of it."

"The MacCallisters are all dead," Lee said. I couldn't see him, but I recognized his booming voice. "They can't do any harm to anyone now that they are all dead."

"What about the girl?" the minister shot back.

There was a murmuring in the pub. "What girl?" someone asked.

"Who's the girl?" came another voice.

"The one living at Duncreigan now." Minister MacCullen was victorious now, as though he had some great secret to share. Unfortunately, it seemed that I was that secret.

It was time to make my exit. I inched toward the door. It was only a few feet away, but there were half a dozen people between me and escape. They were packed together tightly as if each one wanted a better view of the front of the bar and as if each wanted to find the girl living in Duncreigan—me. I very much wanted to avoid that at all costs.

There was an opening in the crowd as it surged forward in the direction of the bar. I spotted daylight between two villagers and lunged for it, only to be jerked backward like a puppet on tangled strings.

The man in the denim jacket held me fast by the arm and pushed me forward. "She's right here."

That's when I realized a moment too late that it was Jock,

who had tormented me at the bar earlier that day, the man saying all those awful things about Uncle Ian and his family.

Everyone in the room stared open-mouthed when he pushed them aside as he frog-marched me to the bar at the front of the room. The phrase "all eyes on me" had a brand new meaning for me, a very literal meaning.

Chapter
Twenty-One

Jock stopped just shy of Chief Inspector Craig's barstool.

The giant chief inspector jumped off the stool and hit the scarred wooden floor with a resounding thud. "Let her go, Jock." His voice could only be described as menacing, and Jock dropped my arm like he'd received an electric shock.

Jock glared at me. "She's been here the whole time, listening to the meeting. Never coming forward and telling her part in it."

"I attended the meeting as a concerned citizen, the same as everyone else," I snapped.

"How can you say that?" Jock glowered at me. "You aren't a citizen of Bellewick, and don't pretend that you are."

"I own the property at Duncreigan," I shot back. "I deserve to know what is going on."

The minister appeared at my elbow, and space was so tight I was literally wedged between the minister and the chief inspector. I tried to take a step away from Jock toward the chief inspector and brushed up against his middle. It was an awkward place to be, but I felt much better about taking my chances with him than with the minister.

Minister MacCullen pointed a bony finger at me. "She is behind all of this trouble."

I looked behind me, searching the crowd for a friendly face. Presha's or even Cally's would have been welcome, but I didn't see either of them anywhere.

"The MacCallisters are behind this all of this," the minister said. "No one is safe from them. Even those who work for them aren't safe."

I held up my hands and, not for the first time, said, "Wait. How many times do I have to say that I'm not a MacCallister? Ian MacCallister was my godfather. We aren't actually related in any way."

"He left you his land, and a man died in that garden of his," the minister hissed.

Several voices in the crowd murmured in agreement.

"Settle down. Settle down." Craig climbed back onto the chair. As he did, he squeezed the top of my right shoulder on the pretense that he needed support to climb back onto the chair. I knew that he didn't. I could be wrong—part of me *hoped* that I was wrong—but I got the distinct impression that the chief inspector was trying to comfort me with his touch.

Back on the barstool, Craig clapped his hand. "Listen! Listen everyone. Yes, Alastair's body was found at Duncreigan, but I do not—I repeat, I do *not*—think that Fiona Knox, his heiress and goddaughter, was responsible for his death. At the time of Alastair's murder, she was on a plane flying to Scotland. There is no way that she could have killed him."

A whoosh of air escaped my lips when I heard it; even though it had been the outcome I had expected, it still was a great relief to hear him say it. I didn't know if Craig really believed it or said it only in order to calm the crowd, but I was happy to hear it all the same.

"But someone is behind this, and I will find out who." The chief inspector's voice was firm.

My momentary relief was gone. I might be in the clear, but Hamish most certainly was not. I knew that my godfather's dear friend could not have murdered anyone. Maybe he disliked Alastair—maybe he'd even had the opportunity—but I knew he would never have put Alastair's body in Uncle Ian's garden. The garden was too important to him to be dishonored in such a way.

"How did he die?" someone asked.

"I heard there were no marks on the body," the minister said. He glared at me as if that told him something about me.

The chief inspector scowled down at him from his height advantage. "Where did you hear that?"

The minister gave him a cold smile in reply.

Craig ground his teeth before redirecting his attention back to the crowd. "Now, you have the basics, and that is all I have to share with you. Yes, Alastair Croft is dead. Yes, his body was found at Duncreigan, although I do not personally believe that's where he died. Yes, a gas leak was discovered at his home late this morning. The leak has been stopped, and for those of you who live on that side of the village, it is safe for you to return to your homes. You are dismissed."

There was a pause, but no one moved.

"Now, please go about your day!" He said this with a little more force than the words warranted.

There was another pause and then a little grumbling ran throughout the pub as people started to shuffle toward the door and outside. I sighed with of relief when more space appeared around me. I no longer felt that crushing feeling like the room was closing in on me.

As the crowd thinned, Craig climbed down from his chair again. He put his large hand on my shoulder and squeezed. He did it to lend me support—there was no question about that this time. He squeezed my shoulder ever so slightly again before letting go.

The minister folded his arms. "You may not think she's innocent, but are you taking her to the station in Aberdeen for questioning? I think we can all agree that she's closely tied to this case, and you should take a cold, hard look at her."

Over Minister MacCullen's shoulder, Jock narrowed his eyes at me. I looked away. I decided Jock was the very last man I would want to meet in an alley at night.

Craig straightened his tweed sport jacket, and I caught sight of the gun holstered under his arm.

"I am the investigating officer on this case," Craig said. "So I, not you, will decide who I will take a cold, hard look at."

I glared at the minister. "You have no right to judge me. You don't even know me," I said. Maybe—and I will admit this only to myself—I had the gumption to say that because I had the tall chief inspector to back me up.

Minister MacCullen sniffed. "I know what you people are like."

"*You people?*" I asked.

Lee appeared on the other side of the bar. "Minister Mac-Cullen, can I get you anything? A nice malt Scotch perhaps?"

Minister MacCullen turned up his nose at the other man.

"I would not eat or drink in such a disgraceful place, and you know that I don't partake of spirits."

Lee shook his head, as if what the minister said saddened him somehow. "Then, I'm going to have to ask you to leave the Twisted Fox. This public house is for customers only, and if you aren't a customer, I'm afraid that you'll have to go."

"The whole village was inside here just moments ago. You can't tell me that they *all* are customers," Minister MacCullen protested.

"Oh, but I can." Lee removed the tea towel from where he kept it on his shoulder and picked up one of the glasses from the drying rack. It seemed to me that it was impossible for him to remain still. He always had to be doing something and was constantly in motion. There was a very good chance that the Twisted Fox Pub had the cleanest glasses in Scotland, judging by the number of times he polished them.

"You are the only one in Bellewick that refuses to eat or drink at the Twisted Fox, which is why you are the only one who has to leave." Lee smiled at him. His bright blue eyes crinkled at the corners as if he were sharing some sort of joke with the minister.

The minister wasn't laughing. "You will see me again, Miss Knox. That is a promise." He pushed his way past me and out the door.

Despite myself, I shivered. That wasn't a promise. It was a threat. I knew it, and everyone who heard it knew it.

"Fiona, there you are. I've been looking for you." Presha's voice floated over to us.

I glanced in the direction of the pub's front door, where

the minister had just exited, and saw Presha gliding toward us. The stones on the edge of her pink scarf clinked together and sounded like bells. I blinked at her. I had no idea where she'd come from, and I wondered where she had gone when she and I had entered the pub. I had gotten stuck in the back until Jock had thrust me into the limelight, but when we entered the pub, Presha seemed to effortlessly melt into the crowd. "I just saw Minister MacCullen leaving."

I made a face.

Presha wrapped her arm around my shoulders. "Don't you worry about him, Fiona. The minister's bark is much worse than his bite."

"I don't know," Lee said from his spot behind the bar. "Have you seen those false chompers? If pressed, he could do some real damage with those."

Presha and Lee shared a laugh. I knew they were trying to cheer me up by joking over the situation, but I couldn't say it helped.

"Neil Craig, as I live and breathe," Presha said, turning her attention to the chief inspector. "What are you doing getting the village all worked up like this by having a meeting?"

I thought Craig would scowl like he did at everyone else who dared to question him about almost anything, but to my surprise, he smiled. "I'm just trying to keep it interesting in the village."

Presha laughed again. "It's always interesting in the village." She turned me toward the door. "Now if you'll excuse us, Fiona and I have some business we need to attend to." She guided me to the door and out the pub.

Chapter Twenty-Two

O utside, I blinked against the bright sunlight. The pub hadn't seemed to be that dark when I was inside it, but when I was outdoors again, the bright light certainly was a big change. The crowd that had been inside the pub was still milling along St. Mary's Street. Maybe they weren't all present, but it seemed to me that a lot of the people who had been inside the pub were now on the street. I knew that the village had just received a shock, but I couldn't help wondering who was running the village today. Didn't these villagers have to work? It was a weekday.

Presha touched my arm. "Fiona, I'd like you to meet someone."

I turned around to see an Indian man standing next to Presha.

"This is my brother, Raj," she said.

Raj gave me wide grin. "It is so very nice to meet you." Like Presha, he had a slight Indian accent. However, their speech wasn't the only resemblance between the siblings. "We're twins," Raj said with a grin on his face. "Can't you tell?"

"There is a strong family resemblance," I said. They both had the same high cheekbones and deep-set brown eyes.

"Raj!"

Two young women and one young man, all about my sister's age, jogged across the street toward us. They carried big sheets of poster board.

"Raj," the young man said again. "We got the poster board we need to make signs. Blackwell doesn't stand a chance against us now."

"Blackwell?" I asked.

Raj beamed at the trio. "Good, good. Students, this is my new friend, Fiona Knox, from Duncreigan."

I frowned, unsure whether Raj had ignored my question about Blackwell or if he was just trying to be polite by making introductions.

"Duncreigan. You know my uncle then," said the broad-chested young man, who looked strong and athletic.

I blinked. But I had always known Uncle Ian not to have any relatives. I'd thought my own family was the closest to a family he'd had. "I–I—"

"I'm Seth MacGregor. Hamish is my uncle—great-uncle, actually."

"Oh yes, of course, I know Hamish."

Seth grinned. "Well, do me a favor and don't tell him that you saw me here today. He thinks I'm at medical school right now."

I studied Seth. "Should you be?"

He laughed. "Probably, but I realized that this fight we are having for the land is much more important."

"Fiona, this is Seth, the man you just met, and Cara and Kay Govern," Raj said, pointing to them each in turn. "They are helping with the protest against the land sale."

The girls were identical blond twins with bright smiles.

"We're students at the University of Aberdeen," Kay—or maybe Cara—said. It was truly impossible to tell them apart.

"When we heard about Raj's protest, we knew we had to get involved. It's such a horrible thing that is happening," Cara—or Kay—added.

"I would have thought when Alastair got killed, it would all be over, but Blackwell, the developer, plans to go through with it. At least that's what his latest press release states," Seth said. He shook slightly, as if even getting out the words was a challenge for him.

"Killing is never the answer," one of the twins said with a nod.

Seth pursed his lips as if he didn't quite agree with her on that point but knew enough not to voice it. I would have to keep my eye on the young protestor.

I still wanted to know who Blackwell was, and I was about to open my mouth to ask the question again, when a commotion outside the Twisted Fox distracted me.

"Where is he? Where is my brother? I want to see him now!" The words came in a screeching yell.

The woman, tall and willowy, with the most striking red hair that I had ever seen, marched up Queen Street like she owned it. Her translucent milk-white skin was only more enhanced by the bright red lipstick on her full lips. Despite the color, the lipstick wasn't garish, and somehow the color suited her just fine and looked almost refined. If I had worn such a color, with my black hair, I would have looked like a Goth.

The crowd parted and let the woman forward.

Out of the corner of my eye, Craig appeared in the doorway of the pub. He froze when he caught sight of the woman.

She pointed at him. "You!"

A low murmur ran through the crowd. I glanced at Presha for some type of explanation, but she only shook her head as if to tell me not to ask any of the questions swirling around in my mind.

"What have you done to my brother this time, Neil?" The redheaded woman glared at him. Now, that sultry look that she had appraised him with when she first arrived on the scene was gone.

The change in tone seemed to be good for the chief inspector and shook him out of whatever stupor the woman's presence had caused by saying his name the first time. "Aileen," Craig said. "I think you and I need to discuss in private what happened to your brother."

"In private?" she scoffed. "That sounds like a proposition to me. We aren't married anymore, Neil; you can't tell me what to do. You can't make any suggestions about how I should live my life. That's why I left you, remember? Because I couldn't live your way."

There was an audible gasp on the street, and I thought I heard a muffled laugh. I wouldn't be surprised if it was from Popeye and his friends, who found this humorous. I couldn't see the humor in any of it.

"Tell me what's going on with my brother, here and now," Aileen said, and she was right in front of him now. "I won't let you keep this secret from me. I won't let that happen to me again."

Craig's ruddy face turned that same shade as his full reddish-brown beard, which was trimmed close to his skin. His face was so red, it was impossible from where I stood, a short distance away from him, to know where his beard even began. "I will not discuss this with you here, Aileen."

"This sounds all too familiar to me," she said.

Craig touched her elbow. "Let's at least go inside the pub to talk. We can't discuss this out in the middle of the street."

She jerked her elbow away from him as if his touch had burned her skin through her black leather jacket. "Don't put your hands on me," she hissed. "You lost that privilege the moment I threw your ring into the ocean."

I grimaced.

"Heavens knows, you don't want to make a scene here." She tossed her hair over her shoulder. "You never wanted to deal with anything, Neil. You were far too busy trying to pretend everything was fine. Well, it wasn't. It was never fine. You can't sweep this under the rug."

"I'm not sweeping your brother's murder under the rug. I want to catch whoever did this more than anyone—even more than you. Now, will you please come inside the pub so that we can talk?" he asked.

She lifted her chin in the air so high to look him in the eye that her neck bent back slightly. I don't know what she must have seen, but her posture changed and her shoulders drooped. She simply nodded and stepped around the chief inspector into the pub.

Before he followed his ex-wife into the pub, Craig glanced in my direction. Our eyes made contact for the briefest moment. And then, he was gone, back inside the Twisted Fox to deal with the beautiful woman who was both Alastair's sister and his ex-wife. Something told me that the relationships in Bellewick were a tad complicated, but what had I expected in a place so small?

The students seemed unconcerned with the scene that Alastair's sister had caused. "We're going to work on the posters now," Cara said. "We'll bring them by the laundromat so you'll have a chance to see them before the protest tomorrow."

Raj grinned at his protégés.

After the students left, Raj clicked his tongue. "I didn't expect to see Aileen Croft back in Bellewick, well, ever."

His sister raised her eyebrows at him. "She had to come back after Alastair died. She's his only living relative, as far as I know."

Her brother nodded and then turned to me. "Presha said that you were interested in the land deal," he said, changing the subject abruptly.

I nodded slowly. My brain was still processing what I had just witnessed. "I am."

Raj folded his arm. "Why would you get involved?"

"Because I found Alastair in my godfather's garden," I answered. "I want to know what happened to him and how it might be related to the land sale. I would like to start off my life in Scotland on the right foot with everyone. The minister and some others would be pleased if I turned around and flew back to Tennessee."

"You shouldn't waste any time thinking about the minister," Raj said, reiterating his sister's sentiments from earlier.

"No one who matters in Bellewick wastes any time on him at all," Presha chimed in.

"I certainly don't," Raj said with a big smile. "But if you want to see the land that is in dispute, I would be happy to take you there. I think it's important for you to see it—not because of the murder; I don't care a wit that Alastair Croft is dead. He was a greedy man, who only looked out for himself. His death, although any loss of life may be sad, is not going to break anyone's heart."

"What about his sister?" I asked.

"You saw her. Her heart is not broken—no one would think that—but she will be very happy to learn what her brother left her. It's likely that's the only reason that she is here," Raj said in a quiet voice.

I paused, considering my next question, and decided to go for it. "What about Cally Beckleberry?"

Presha smiled. "I see you are as observant as Ian was. Yes, if anyone is going to mourn the death of Alastair, it will be Cally. I'm sure the girl is hurting. I plan to go visit her later today. Some tea and scones might soothe her."

Raj wrinkled his small nose, which was identical to his twin sister's. "I don't see why she should miss him. With Alastair dead, the law firm will be hers. She can finally run the place just as she would like to. It was no secret that Cally was frustrated by the way that Alastair ran the business."

Presha shook her head and chuckled. "So like a man."

Raj folded his arms. "What do you mean, my sister?"

She grinned. "I mean it is so like a man to miss the signals that Cally is in love with her law partner. I saw it, and Fiona, who just met her, saw it."

"That's ridiculous," her brother argued. "How could a smart woman like Cally Beckleberry fall for such a terrible and greedy man as Alastair Croft? That just doesn't make any sense."

"Who a person falls in love with doesn't have to make sense," I said quietly. My own experience was proof of that.

Presha cocked her head and studied me. After a moment, she nodded to herself as if she had learned something important about me in that moment.

Raj rolled his eyes. "Women are crazy. This is exactly why I have remained a bachelor all these years."

Presha chuckled in a way that told me this wasn't the first time that she had heard this line from her twin brother.

Raj turned back to me. "I am happy you would like to see that land. It's important that people living in this area, and that includes you now, know what is at stake if the land deal goes through."

"I thought the deal came to a complete halt because of Alastair's death," I said.

He shook his head deliberately. "It's only slowed down. If Cally won't sell it to the buyer Alastair arranged with the developer, the developer will find someone who will." My suggestion, which Alastair ignored, is to turn the land into a park. It would be a beautiful spot and has plenty of green space. It would also preserve the Scottish coast for future generations. If we don't do it, no one will. Too many people are worried about the here and now. They don't care that this decision will have a lasting impact on the environment and children for generations to come. The village even offered to pay for it."

"Why didn't Alastair take that offer then?"

"Greed. As the executor, he will get a percentage of the sale. Of course, a big developer like Clyde Blackwell can pay much more than our tiny village. The more money Alastair got for the land, the more money he would make in commission."

"I would like to see it," I said, meaning it.

He nodded. "I have something to do today, but I can take you out there bright and early in the morning. It might be the best time too. It's less likely that we'll run into anyone who might claim that we are trespassing."

"That works for me," I said.

Raj nodded. "I'll pick you up at Duncreigan in the morning."

Chapter
Twenty-Three

With our plans for the next morning set, Presha touched her brother's arm. "Fiona has something that needs to be laundered."

Raj grinned. "Of course. Washing and drying is what I do best. There is no stain that I can't get out. What do you need cleaned?" he asked me.

"They're old sheets that were covering the furniture at Duncreigan. They're in my rental car," I explained. "It's parked not far from the laundromat."

He waved his hand. "That is all? That is easy."

"Then, I will leave you two to it," Presha said. "My guess is that the teashop will be busy this afternoon because everyone will want to talk about what happened to Alastair." She reached over and gave me a warm hug, and I was enveloped in the smell of a jasmine and something sharp like cloves. The combination was both pleasant and distinctive. She let me go. "I am glad that I met you, Fiona. I know we will learn much more about each other in the coming days as our friendship grows."

I blinked back tears in my eyes. This woman, who I had

only met an hour ago, was offering friendship. It was a welcome gift in what could be my brand-new life if I ultimately decided to stay.

Presha headed down the cobblestone street, her dazzling bright-pink scarf trailing after her. She moved with such elegance that I stopped and stared at her for a moment. I realized, looking up and down the street that I wasn't the only one. Presha was the type of woman who garnered attention wherever she went, and I don't mean from men only. She was a beautiful woman, but her greater attraction lay in her elegant presence and the way that she moved.

"Where are those sheets?" Raj asked.

Raj and I walked together back to Queen Street, where I had parked the rental car. It was good that I had returned, because I needed to put more coins in the meter. I'd been in the village much longer than I'd expected. After feeding the meter, I opened the car's trunk and retrieved the basket of sheets.

Raj took it from my arms. "Aw, this is nothing at all. I won't even have to bleach them." He sounded somewhat disappointed when he said this.

"You can bleach them if you like," I said.

He grinned. "I'll do just that. A white sheet can never be too white."

"Can you bring them tomorrow when you pick me up to check out the cliff?" I asked as I closed the trunk.

"Not a problem at all," Raj said. "I will have them clean and pressed for you."

"You really don't have to iron them," I said, because I personally hated ironing and would make my shopping choices based on whether the clothing would require ironing. One hundred percent cotton was my own nightmare.

He gasped. "Of course I do. Any and all things coming out of my shop are ironed. I can't have my reputation ruined by wrinkles."

I smiled. "All right. If it's that important to you."

"Believe me when I say that it is. Very important." He nodded emphatically.

I hesitated for a moment and then asked, "When was the last time you saw Alastair?"

He frowned. "I don't know exactly."

"I just thought you might have seen him the day that he died since the two of you were at odds over the land sale. Were you there when he met with the developer?"

Raj gave a short laugh. "No, I wasn't there. All of that was done behind closed doors. It's how shifty men like Alastair do business."

"Other than the land issue, did you have any other disputes with Alastair?"

He eyed me. "The land issue was enough, I'd say."

"Maybe—"

He held up the basket of sheets. "I'll have this as good as new."

My shoulders drooped. "Just let me know how much I owe you when you come to Duncreigan tomorrow morning. I can pay you then."

He laughed and tucked the basket under his left arm in a practiced move. "You are not paying for this. Ian Mac-Callister was a good friend of mine. It's the least I can do, to clean these for you. They signify that life has returned to

Duncreigan, and that is a beautiful thing. There is no cost for this."

I hadn't looked at the sheets in the same way, but I realized that he was right. By washing the sheets and putting them away, I was saying in part that I was in Scotland to stay. The question was, Was that really true? Did I mean to stay in Scotland permanently? Is that what I wanted to do? It was too early for me to answer those questions for Raj, for anyone else, or even for myself.

"Thanks Raj," I said and stepped onto the sidewalk. "That's really kind of you, and I could use the help. The sheets will be one less thing for me to worry about."

"I'm happy to do it, and if you find something with a more serious stain, send it my way. I'm always up for a challenge."

I shook my head as I watched him walk away in the direction of his laundromat.

Before going to the law office to retrieve Ivanhoe, I popped into the small Tesco and filled up my tiny shopping cart with groceries, buying enough to get me through the next couple of days. I hoped that after that I would have a better idea of how long I planned to stay in Scotland. Happily, I managed to do my shopping without incident, other than the clerk who was ringing me up giving me the once-over when she saw my name on the credit card I'd used to pay for the groceries. I had a feeling that she'd heard about me or had been at the pub when Jock had forced me in front of the entire village.

Back at the car, I put my groceries in the trunk and then decided to walk to the law office to collect Ivanhoe. I didn't know what I'd been thinking when I'd agreed to take Alastair's cat off Cally's hands. He seemed to be a very sweet animal, but I wasn't in a place where I could take care of a cat. I wasn't in a place where I could take care of anyone, including myself.

After all the commotion outside the Twisted Fox Pub over the news that Chief Inspector Craig had revealed, I decided to walk a different way to the law office. I didn't want to run into Popeye or his cronies or Jock. I didn't even want to run into the chief inspector.

I walked along a street that ran parallel to Queen through the village. This cobblestone street appeared to be deserted. Perhaps all the villagers were still outside the pub, gossiping about everything that had happened in the village that day. The homes were flat-face stone houses with double chimneys. Each was identical to the next, and they were built three feet apart. I had grown up on a farm where my closest neighbor had been half a mile away. I wondered what it would be like to grow up in such a place, where you were practically on top of your next-door neighbor. It wouldn't give you or your family much privacy—I knew that. The only difference between the identical homes was the color of their front doors. Some were bright purple, others green, and I even spotted a dark pink one.

I almost came to the end of the street, where I was to turn onto St. Charles Street, when I heard men speaking on the corner. Rounding the corner, I spotted Jock speaking with a man in a tweed suit. Neither of them looked happy.

"You can't play both sides, Jock!" the man in the tweed suit said. "That's not fair to anyone, and it will cost you in the end."

"Is that a threat?" Jock snarled back.

I shivered, and I was glad that Jock's back was to me so he

didn't know I was there. The other man seemed to take no notice of me.

"I don't make threats, Jock. I have enough money that I don't have to stoop to your level. Now, that we understand each other, I have nothing more to say to you."

"Just because you got what you wanted doesn't mean you can forget how I helped you."

The man in tweed crossed his arms. "I didn't get what I want yet, and I won't until the deed is final. I never assume everything will go as planned. Alastair's death is proof of that."

I felt my pulse speed up. Jock and this other man were talking about Alastair's murder. Could they have had something to do with it?

The man in tweed started walking toward me, and I hopped into a doorway of one of the houses close to the street and pressed my back against the door. The man walked by me without giving me a second glance. Jock stormed off in the opposite direction.

I moved out of the doorway, wondering which way to go. Finally, I broke into a jog in the same direction that Jock had gone. I hoped following cranky Jock would not be a decision that I'd come to regret.

Chapter
Twenty-Four

Jock was easy to follow. He was a big man and angry at the moment. He stomped through the cobblestone streets, past squat stone homes with window baskets bursting with vining ivy, geraniums, and petunias; past small shops selling everything from soap to fishing gear tucked into narrow alleys. I could have walked the streets of Bellewick for days, and they would never lose their charm. Jock had no interest in his surroundings as he stomped along. I promised myself a long walk through the quaint village after all this murder business was over, so I could really take it all in.

Before we reached the sea, I could smell it. It was the overpowering combination of salt water and dead fish. I heard it too. There was the clank of buoys hitting the docks and lines knocking against boat masts in the wind.

We came around the side of a large stone building, and the view opened up onto the harbor. Old white and rusty fishing boats with nets tethered to their sides bobbed in the harbor. Weathered fishermen sat on old oil barrels and chewed on tobacco or on the end of cigars. Occasionally, there was a burst of laughter from these men. Other shipyard workers used cranes and pulleys to unload fish or load cargo onto the ships' hulls. I couldn't see Jock among any of the men.

There wasn't much beach to speak of. Stones ranging from the size of my thumb to the size of my fist peppered the water's edge. I could imagine sitting on those hard stones on a warm summer day—not that the North Sea was much of a beach destination.

Since Jock was nowhere in sight, I walked down the main dock on the pretense that I was taking in the view. To my right, a black harbor seal poked his head out of the water and then disappeared again underneath the inky water.

Near the entrance to the dock, there was a wooden building with a peeling slate roof. Large scuba diving tanks sat outside the building, as well as diver flippers in various sizes.

The screen door to the building banged against the outer wall as Jock, now wearing a black wetsuit, stomped out. He was very good at stomping.

Instinctively, I turned around and took cover behind the edge of one of the empty, docked fishing boats.

Jock leaned over, picked up a pair of flippers that leaned against the building, and tucked them under his arm.

One of the men on the barrel called out to Jock. "Going to scrape the boat bottoms again, Jock, my boy?"

Jock glared at him.

"It's good work for you. No one is better at removing barnacles."

The old man and his friends laughed.

Jock's face morphed to the color of a plum. I winced. Jock had not exactly been friendly to me, but I couldn't help feeling some sympathy for him as these other men teased him.

"How many barnacles are you going to get today, Jock?" This from the same man, who seemed to be the ringleader of the retired fishermen hanging out on the dock.

"Probably only a handful because I'm not cleaning the hull of your boat, Ewan."

Ewan sneered at Jock, but his friends laughed.

"And it won't be long before I don't have to clean anyone's boats. Others will have to clean *my* boats, and they will have to sparkle. I can tell you that."

"How will you manage that?" Ewan asked. "Gonna win the lottery?"

Jock only smiled in return. He walked around the men, carrying his scuba gear.

I peeked around the boat, wondering if I should follow him, but I didn't know how I could do that without walking around the old men sitting on the oil barrels. I was almost certain they would call my presence to Jock's attention.

"What are you looking at?" a voice asked in my ear.

I yelped and bumped my shoulder against the boat. It bounced away from me, and I would have fallen off the dock if a small but strong hand hadn't grabbed me by the wrist, pulling me back to safety.

Seth and one of the blond twins stood looking at me as I caught my breath.

"Are you okay?" Kay or Cara. I had no idea which of the twins was standing next to Seth.

"You shouldn't scare someone like that!" I placed a hand on my heart and felt it thundering against my sternum.

Seth looked sheepish. "Sorry. You were just concentrating so hard, I didn't know how to get your attention."

"So whispering in my ear like a serial killer seemed like the best option?"

I smiled at the twin. "Thanks for saving me."

"No problem," she said cheerfully.

"What got your attention so much that you didn't hear us coming?" Seth asked.

I ignored his question and asked one of my own. "What are you two doing down at the docks?" There was a large camera in Seth's hand.

"We're taking photographs for Raj so he can use them in his case."

"His case to who?" I asked.

"Anyone who will listen about the land. Just because Alastair is dead, it doesn't mean that we can stop fighting. And that is what we are fighting for." He pointed to the north, and there was a large fishing boat cruising around the corner of a large black cliff. Blotches of green and yellow vegetation dotted the rocks. The black rock jutted out from the coast. At the very top, there was a blanket of green, where anyone standing on that spot would have a clear view of the harbor or the boats coming in, just like the fishing boat that was pulling in now, with large seagulls circling its masts.

"That's what we are fighting for," Seth repeated. "Can you imagine if there were a dozen condos sitting on the top of that peak overlooking the harbor? Think how they would ruin that picturesque view for everyone in the village and how they would block off access to that place for the people living here."

"Plus the environmental impact," Kay or Cara said. "A large structure like that would definitely lead to some coast erosion, not to mention the impact on all the plants and animals that live up there. Did you think Blackwell would let them remain?"

"No," I said because I knew it was true and also knew that it was the answer they wanted to hear.

Seth beamed at me like I was an exceptional student. "Exactly."

A thought struck me. "What does your uncle Hamish think of your involvement in all this?"

Seth frowned. "Did you say anything about this to him?"

I shook my head. "I haven't seen him since I saw you earlier today."

He gave a sigh of relief. "Good. Good."

"Why don't you want me to mention it?"

Seth frowned and gave his head the tiniest shake "no."

"I can't keep a promise to you to stay silent if I don't know why, and even when I do find out, I can't guarantee that I won't say anything to Hamish."

Seth scowled. "I don't see it as your place to say anything at all about me to my uncle."

The blond twin touched his arm. "Oh, Seth, Fiona is on our side. Don't you see that? Go ahead and tell her."

I liked Kay or Cara for backing me up on this.

Seth looked at the girl, and the pair seemed to have a conversation without speaking a word. Finally he nodded, and she patted his arm again, which convinced me that this twin had won the staring competition they were having.

"My uncle thinks that I am still attending medical school, but I dropped out to help with this cause. Saving this coastline and other places like it—that's my cause for life, not saving lives."

"I see, and you think that he would be disappointed in you if he found out?"

"I know he would."

My brow wrinkled. I couldn't remember a time that my godfather, or Hamish for that matter, had mentioned that Hamish had any relatives. I had always thought that Hamish was a lonely bachelor with no family. "I'm certain that Hamish would be sympathetic to your cause. Why don't you tell him what you've decided to do? I'm sure he would be understanding."

"It's not that simple," Seth murmured. "Cara and I had better get back. Kay is painting the posters for out protest tomorrow, and she always gets a little cranky when she is left to that task alone for too long."

Ahh, so the twin in front of me was Cara. That was good to know.

"It was nice to see you again Fiona," Cara said.

I smiled at her.

"Let's go, Cara."

The girl waved at me as they walked up the dock.

I peeked around the fisherman's boat that I had been using as cover to see if I could spot Jock, but he was gone. The old men sitting on the oil barrels were gone too. I frowned. What could Jock have meant when he said that it wouldn't be long until other people cleaned his boats? And was that comment related to the conversation that I'd overheard Jock have with the man in tweed?

I shook my head, not knowing what to think as I left the harbor and headed in the direction of Croft and Beckleberry.

After a short walk away from the harbor and back through

the village, I made the turn onto St. Charles Street, where the stone houses gave way to bright townhomes like Alastair's. I continued walking down the street, my eyes open and unblinking. I didn't want to miss anything. At this point, I wouldn't have been surprised if Bigfoot had jumped out in front of me, not that Bigfoot lived in Scotland—at least not as far as I knew. And if he did, I doubted that "Bigfoot" was his name.

The rest of the walk to the law office was uneventful, and I didn't bother knocking on the outer door that led into the building.

Outside the office, I knocked on the inner door, but there was no answer. I tried the doorknob, and it turned easily in my hand. I stepped into the waiting room, where I had been speaking with Cally just a few short hours ago. Cally was nowhere to be found, but Ivanhoe lounged on the settee. As soon as he saw me, he jumped from the seat to the back of the sofa and pranced back and forth. I knew from the many barn cats that lived on my parents' farm, he wanted some attention, so I walked over to him and held out my hand. He butted my palm with his soft head.

"Do you know where Cally is?" I asked the cat.

He looked at up me and butted his cheek into my palm. He really was the sweetest cat I'd ever come across. I couldn't help but wonder what would become of him if I returned to the States. Surely, someone in the village would be willing to take him in, but then thinking how much they disliked Alastair, maybe not. I told myself that I shouldn't get attached, but I knew it was a losing battle to even try to fight liking this cat with the darling pushed-in face and folded-over ears.

"I told you I can't discuss this right now. Alastair's body

isn't even cold yet. I need a little time." Cally's voice floated into the room through the crack in the door that separated the waiting room from the rest of the house. "No, I have not had enough time. We could have moved forward if Alastair was alive, but he is not." There was a pause. "It may not be your problem, but it most certainly is mine." Her voice was razor sharp.

I glanced down at Ivanhoe again as if to ask him what to do. He head-butted me in the arm. I wasn't getting any eavesdropping advice from him, but why should that surprise me? Cats are the very best eavesdroppers of all.

Before I could make up my mind as to what to do, Cally came through the door, tapping her phone's screen. She dropped it on the end table as if she couldn't stand even holding it in her hand any longer. That's when she saw me in the door. She jumped. "What are you doing here?"

Chapter
Twenty-Five

I nodded at Ivanhoe. "I came for the cat like you asked."
Mention of the cat reminded her that she was allergic, and she sneezed.

Ivanhoe gave me a look as if to ask me, "Can you believe this?"

Cally regained her composure. "I'm so sorry. Of course. I'm so sorry if it looked like I'd forgotten. It's just been an awful day."

"I can understand that," I said, excusing her. "You must be under terrible strain."

"That's putting it mildly. The last few months while Alastair has been working on this land deal have been a nightmare, and now . . . and now . . ." She couldn't complete her thought.

"And now that Alastair is dead," I finished for her, "it's all your problem?"

"Precisely." She nodded. "Would you like something to drink? I need something to drink, and tea is not going to cut it."

I hesitated. It was after five in the afternoon, but I wasn't much of a drinker. However, this might be my one chance to get some information out of Cally about the land deal. I was almost certain that the deal was what had led to Alastair's death. "Sure. I would love a drink."

She stood up and walked to a bar cart on the other side of the room. It was the first time I had noticed the cart, and it looked to be very well stocked.

She glanced over her shoulder at me. "What will you have?"

There were so many bottles on the cart, I didn't know how I could answer that question, so I didn't. "I'll have whatever you're drinking."

She lifted a dusty bottle of dark amber–colored liquid from the back of the cart. "Scotch it is. You're in Scotland after all. You might as well make the most of it."

Cally poured two healthy portions of Scotch into two glass tumblers. To me it looked like enough Scotch to floor a bear. I didn't stand a chance if I drank all of that.

Holding the two tumblers, she walked over to the seating area and held a glass out to me. I accepted it and took a sip. Then I sputtered and coughed. The alcohol burned the inside of my mouth and all the way down my throat. "It tastes like lighter fluid!"

She sipped from her tumbler of Scotch with no visible reaction.

She nodded. "It's from the Highlands. They say it can take the paint off a car."

"And why are we drinking it?" I massaged my scorched throat with my hand.

She held up her tumbler. "Because sometimes the burn reminds you what it is like to feel."

"I feel raw inside." I coughed again.

She nodded. "That works too. I think that is the exact word I would use to describe how I'm feeling today. Raw." She examined her tumbler. "This scotch cost two hundred pounds a bottle. Alastair was saving it for someday, but his someday never came.

"I think that is what his death has taught me the most: don't count on someday because someday will never come. Too many people put off fighting for what they want until what they think will be a better time—after they're married, after the kids are grown, after retirement—but the truth is, there is never a better time for anything.

"Time is the most unreliable thing to bank your life on. I'm guilty of it myself. I kept thinking that Alastair would come to his senses about me after I moved to Bellewick to become his partner, after the law office was established and doing well, after the land deal was done, but the joke is on me, maybe even more than it was on Alastair. There is no *after* those times, just those times alone. I wasted a good portion of my life waiting for *after* when I could have been living the life that I had been given in the moment." She took a sip from her tumbler.

I had a feeling this wasn't he first sip of Scotch Cally had had that afternoon. She was certainly more talkative than she had been that morning. I perched on the sofa across from her. "You were in love with him." I said it as a statement of fact, not a question.

She nodded and stared at her folded hands on her lap. "Even though I'm embarrassed to admit it, but now that he's out of my life, there is a void."

"I can understand that," I said, thinking of my own recent heartbreak. The difference was, Ethan was alive. What she was going through must be ten times worse. Alastair was permanently and forever out of her life. Alastair being out of her life might be the best thing for her, but the finality of it was heavy.

"I know others don't see the good that was in Alastair," she said. "But under his hard, all-business exterior, he was a very thoughtful man, or at least he was when we were in school together." She sipped her Scotch. "That was then. Alastair changed, and I didn't see it, or maybe I didn't want to see it. I wanted him to be the boy who I fell in love with back in school, the one who became a lawyer because he wanted to make a difference in the world, and in Aberdeenshire in particular. That's why he came back here. He returned to Bellewick because he wanted to help his village. Before Alastair opened his office here, the closest attorney was in Aberdeen, and many of the people in the village didn't want to or couldn't trust someone from outside the village to help them. You might have noticed that it is a very tight-knit community."

I smiled. "I did notice that. It seems like a lovely place, though."

"It is, but like every place else on the planet, Bellewick has its problems. I think Bellewick's problems are why Alastair lost his way. He wasn't finding a way into helping people like he wanted to, so he went another route entirely. Greed seduced him. This land deal was the greatest proof of that. No one wants those big, grand condominiums to block the village's view of the sea. Alastair didn't even want that, but it was a chance to make more money than he could imagine."

"You were talking on the phone with someone when I arrived." I held up my hand when her frown deepened. "I wasn't listening."

"It doesn't matter if you were listening or not. I have nothing to hide. The developer who wanted to buy the property just wanted to make sure that they could move on with the project."

"Clyde Blackwell?" I asked.

She raised her eyebrows. "Have you really only been in the country for a couple of days? Well, there's no point in denying it. Yes, it was Blackwell. They want me to move forward with it."

"Will you?" I asked.

"I do have an obligation to do something, since the law firm is the executor of the estate. Even so, I asked them for a little time so I could get caught up on the case and so I could bury Alastair." She stared into her drink.

"You're planning his funeral?" I asked.

She nodded. "I have to. There is no one else to do it."

"What about his sister?"

She laughed, but her laughter was devoid of humor. "His sister only wants to know how much money her brother left her. She had no interest in him when he was alive, and it is certain she will have no interest in him now that he is dead."

"But she's here," I said.

She stared at me. "Aileen in the village? Already?" She jumped out of her seat.

"Chief Inspector Craig said that he told her about her brother's death, and she came here because of it."

Cally started to pace. "This is bad—this is so bad."

"Aileen didn't strike me as the most likable woman on the planet, but why is it so bad?"

She stopped and clutched her glass so hard, I was afraid that it might break. "Because she can't be here—not yet. I haven't had time to go over her brother's will or make any of the arrangements for his funeral between his death and then the natural gas leak at his home." She shook her head. "I haven't had the time. I wanted everything settled before she arrived. I can't deal with that woman."

"I want to help if I can." I set my barely touched drink on the end table next to my seat.

Cally looked at me as if seeing me for the first time. "You're already helping by taking the cat. Let me just go get his things, and you can be on your way."

I wanted to argue with her. I didn't want to be pushed out of the law office. I really did want to help with the funeral or by playing interference to Aileen, if I could.

Cally returned a moment later, juggling a soft-sided cat carrier, a box of kitty litter, a bag of food, and a tote bag that looked like it was stuffed to the brim with cat toys. She shoved all of these things into my arm. "He likes his wet food more than the dry."

"Umm," I said.

"Oh right." She took the carrier from my arms, which only lightened my load a little. "Let me help you." She opened the carrier and set it on the floor next to Ivanhoe. The gray and white striped cat stared up at her as if to say, "You've got to be kidding, right?"

She pointed into the small carrier. "Time to go. Fiona is your new mummy now." She slurred the words.

"Umm, I didn't sign up to be anyone's mummy," I said. "I am only taking care of him until you can find a better place."

Cally pretended that she didn't hear my comment.

Ivanhoe pawed at the door as though he were trying to tell us that he was ready to go.

"Looks to me like he wants out," I said.

"He may want to go back to Alastair's townhouse, and he can't go back there. It's very likely the cat will never go back there." She looked down sadly at Ivanhoe, and he looked back at her as if to ask her what she was waiting for and to open the door.

Cally looked at me, and I shrugged. The most contact I'd had with cats was on my parents' farm. Those felines were strictly barn cats that never came inside the house, so it didn't seem the least bit odd to me that Ivanhoe wanted to go outside.

When I didn't say anything, Cally opened the door, and the cat went out. Ivanhoe headed right down the stairs that led him out of the building. Then he stopped and stared at me as if to remind me it was time to go. It seemed to me that he was going to be a bossy cat.

"Is this all from Alastair's house? How did you get it?" I asked, looking down at all the cat paraphernalia in my arms.

She shook her head. "I didn't know what he would need, and since I didn't know how long it would be before I can get into Alastair's house, I went to the market and bought them out of everything I could find that was even remotely cat-related. I'm sad that I can't keep Ivanhoe; he is such a sweet animal." She sneezed three times in a row and then ran a tissue under her nose. "As you can see, that would never work."

"I'll take good care of him," I promised her.

"I know. You are Ian MacCallister's goddaughter. Of course, you can take care of anything. Ian was the kindest man I've ever known and the first to welcome me into the village right after I arrived." She nodded at the door at the foot of the stairs, where Ivanhoe stood looking at me expectantly. "Let's get him into the carrier."

Cally went down the stairs, leaving me to gather up all of Ivanhoe's new belongings. The cat moved into Duncreigan with more luggage than I'd had.

Chapter
Twenty-Six

Ivanhoe never climbed inside the cat carrier; he much preferred to ride shotgun in my rental car. On the short ride from the village to Duncreigan, he sat in the passenger seat in the rental car like he took car rides every day of his life. I glanced over at the cat. "You're not phased at all by this," I said.

He languidly blinked his eyes at me. I interpreted that as cat-speak for "How could anything intimidate me when it's clear that I am far superior?"

I chuckled. "Well, I'll be happy for the company, but you have to promise that you won't chase Duncan, the squirrel. I know that he can be very annoying, but he's important to Hamish. Since he's important to Hamish, we have to play nice."

Another long cat eye blink was all that I received in return. I didn't want to know what that one meant, but it did not bode well for Duncreigan's resident squirrel.

I drove the rental up the hill to Duncreigan. As the cottage came into view with its centuries' old stone walls and black slate roof, I could appreciate it that afternoon more than when I'd first arrived, when I had still been groggy by the transatlantic flight—oh, and then finding the dead body shortly thereafter.

Hamish pruned the bushes on either side of the cottage's front door with a large set of garden clippers while Duncan perched on his shoulder, apparently supervising. I rolled my car to a stop just short of the house.

I opened the door to the car, and before I could stop him, Ivanhoe vaulted over my lap and out the driver-side door like his tail had caught fire. He made a beeline for the squirrel. Duncan chittered, leaped from his master's shoulder, and scaled to the very top of the fir tree to the south of the cottage. The tree had been planted there decades ago by my godfather's grandfather, with the hope that it would break the wind that travels over the cold, rocky fields around the property.

Duncan stood on his hind legs at the tree's peak and chittered angrily. It was clear that his choice words were directed at the cat.

Ivanhoe wasn't having it and began to stalk the tree with the same concentration as a lion set on taking down a wildebeest on the savannah.

I jumped out of the car and scooped up the cat before he lunged at the tree. I wasn't going to let him climb up the tree after the squirrel. I had seen enough firemen cat rescues while living in Nashville. I didn't think the Aberdeen firemen would like to make a stop at Duncreigan on their way back to Aberdeen, after spending the morning at Alastair's house with the natural gas leak.

Hamish stared at me with his mouth open. "What is *that*?"

I looked down at Ivanhoe and back up at Hamish. "It's a cat. He needed a place to stay, so I brought him here."

"What on earth are you doing bringing a hell cat to Duncreigan, lass? We don't have a place for a creature of that sort." Hamish scrunched up his round nose.

I cradled Ivanhoe in my arms, and he hissed softly to himself as he stared at the tree. So much for my pep talk on the drive here about leaving the squirrel alone. That clearly had not had any effect on Ivanhoe's behavior.

"He's not a hell cat," I said. "And it's only temporary." I was grateful that the cat, although obviously upset, didn't dig his claws into my skin.

Hamish held his clippers at his side and rubbed the back of his head with his free hand. "How can a hell cat be temporary? You must find the animal another home. Where is he from?" Hamish lifted the clippers and pointed at the cat with him.

Ivanhoe hissed in his direction. I could already tell that this arrangement wasn't going to work out well. "It's Alastair's cat."

"Then get that animal out of here," Hamish said, waving the clippers. "We don't want anything Alastair Croft ever had. That includes his hell cat."

I sighed. "He's not a hell cat. He's a very sweet cat, and he can't help it if he was Alastair's pet."

Hamish looked as if he wanted to argue with me on that point.

I shook my head. "Let me take him inside, and I can tell you everything. Can you at least bring his food and litter box from the car while I do that?"

Hamish grunted, but, to my relief, he leaned the clippers against the bushes and shuffled in the direction of the car. He popped the trunk and removed the cat paraphernalia that Cally had given me.

Still holding the cat, I held the door open for Hamish, and he unceremoniously dropped Ivanhoe's things just inside. I sighed again. "It will just take a few minutes to get him settled."

Hamish grunted and went back out.

I set the cat on the couch, and he immediately jumped to the floor. Then, while I set up his food and water in the kitchen, and his litter box in the tiny broom closet off the kitchen, he circled the area. Apparently satisfied with what he found, he stood by the fireplace, where Hamish must have started a fire while I was in the village. I was grateful to see it. The nights in Scotland were far colder than any I had lived through in Nashville, even in the middle of winter.

Ivanhoe walked to the pile of cat supplies, where Hamish had dropped them by the front door. The cat pawed at the new cat bed that Cally had bought him and then walked back to the same spot where he had been standing, by the fireplace.

I frowned.

Ivanhoe blinked at me, and when I didn't move, he repeated his action. He pawed the cat bed that Hamish had dumped with the cat's other things by the front door and then walked back to the same place next to the fireplace.

"You want your cat bed right there?" I asked.

He blinked at me again.

This time, I interpreted this for cat-speak meaning "Duh!"

I picked up the cat bed. Ivanhoe waited as I placed it in

the precise spot he wanted it, and then I stepped back. He hopped into the bed, circled twice, and lay down, closing his eyes. He, like me, had had quite a day. Also, he was doing a stellar job at training me to be his human servant. I couldn't help but wonder if his relationship with Alastair had been like this. I couldn't see Ivanhoe expecting anything else, and the idea of the unlikeable attorney doting on a cat's every whim made me like Alastair a bit more.

With Ivanhoe settled, I went back out of the cottage. Hamish was no longer pruning the bushes. I didn't see him or Duncan anywhere. In my gut, I knew they were over the hill in the garden. I stared at the rise in the earth that blocked my view of the gated garden from the cottage. I wished I could see over it, just for a peek to determine whether they were there, but the only way to know for sure was to walk over the hill and take in the garden. I knew that if I made it that far, the pull of the garden would draw me in.

I shook off my hesitation and walked over the hill. The ivy on the garden walls that had been greening since the moment I had arrived at Duncreigan was full and lush again. It was so alive, it was almost like it was growing before my very eyes.

There was no sign of Hamish, so I supposed that he was inside the garden. When I entered the gate, my breath caught in my throat. It was like night and day from what I'd seen earlier that day. The willow tree in the corner was laced with delicate flowers and the beginnings of bright green leaves. The grass was green, and it seemed that everywhere I looked, bulbs were shooting up from the rich, dark earth. The earth itself seemed to be a brighter shade. Buds appeared on bushes and seemed that they might open before my eyes. I was so distracted by what I saw around me that it took me a moment to realize Hamish wasn't in the front part of the garden. That could only mean that he was on the other side of the hedge, which is exactly where the chief inspector didn't want anyone to go.

I shook my head in wonder at how the garden had come back to life. Hamish would have told me that it was because I was there, but it was impossible to believe. Then again, the garden had been dead when I arrived, and now it was alive again. That couldn't possibly be because of me, could it? I have never thought of myself as a particularly special person. I felt I was average in all ways that you could be average, but maybe the garden disagreed. I shook the crazy thoughts from my head. I was letting the mystique of Scotland color my mind.

I walked deeper into the garden and stepped around the edge of the hedge. The climbing rose that wound its way around the standing stone was in full bloom now, but that wasn't all I saw when I peeked around the hedge. The most surprising thing was to find Hamish on all fours on the grass. Clearly, he was looking for something.

Was he looking for the key? I let my hand drop to my side and brushed my jacket pocket. The skeleton key that I'd found that morning was still there. I had completely forgotten about it in all the commotion that was going on in the village that day.

Hamish rubbed his calloused palm back and forth over the now plush grass and scowled as he did this in a sort of grid pattern. It looked like he was determined that he wouldn't miss a single spot in his search.

The key felt heavy in my pocket.

Duncan perched in a low Japanese maple tree just to the left of the hedge line. The squirrel began chittering. This caused Hamish to look up from his task and see me for the first time. The caretaker jumped to his feet much more quickly than a man half his age would have been able to do. "Lass, why didn't you tell me you were there?"

"Why are you on the ground?" I countered. "And don't tell me it's because you lost a contact, because you don't wear them."

"I was just checking the earth, lass," he said easily. "I am a gardener after all. The garden is much transformed since you arrive."

"Checking the earth?" I was doubtful.

"Aye," he said. "Now, what have you done with the hell cat?"

"He's not a hell cat," I said. I had a feeling this would be an ongoing argument if Ivanhoe lived at Duncreigan.

Duncan chittered in the tree again. Apparently, he didn't agree with my assessment of Ivanhoe.

Hamish leaned back and stretched his back. "Now that you have returned home, lass, Duncan and I should be on our way home as well. We have much to do to prepare our home for spring. It is the most delightful time of the year. You will be in awe when you see how the land that appeared to be sleeping for all this time comes alive and is reborn."

I waved my arms around, encompassing the entire garden. "I am already amazed."

He grinned so broadly, he showed off the missing molars in the back of his mouth. "This is only the beginning, lass, only the beginning. Soon you will learn what you are capable of. When you find the letter, all will be clear."

I sighed. What I wouldn't give to have Uncle Ian's letter in my hot little hand right at that moment. "Hamish, will you stay for dinner tonight? I can make you a nice dinner. I would really like to talk to you about Uncle Ian. You were the one who knew him the best."

He nodded. "Yes, I knew him the best, but you must know something about Master Ian. Even though I knew him well, I didn't really know him at all. He was a very reserved and private person. He was kind, but he didn't reveal much of himself to anyone, even me.

"I still would like to talk to you more about him. I had planned to do that when I arrived, but then, well, you know what happened." My eyes trailed over to the yellow crime scene tape that cordoned off the area directly beside the standing stone.

"Aye, I do know." He rubbed the day-old beard just beginning to show on the bottom of his chin. "But is there anything to eat in the cottage? The last time I looked, the cottage pantry was mighty bare."

"I picked up a few things while I was in the village, to tide me over until I have time to really make a list and go grocery shopping. Things didn't go exactly as I planned when I was in the village today."

Hamish didn't ask how my plan went awry, and I didn't tell him. It seemed to me that we were both keeping secrets from each other. His secrets had something to do with the ground around the standing stone, and mine had to do with what had happened in the village that day. We didn't know each other well enough to trust each other yet. I was hoping that would change. If I was going to stay in Scotland permanently, I needed to find people I trusted and who trusted me.

"Can you cook?" Hamish asked. "I thought American girls couldn't cook. They can never cook on the sitcoms that you send over here."

"You watch American sitcoms, Hamish?" I grinned at the thought of Hamish and Duncan sitting in front of a decades-old episode of *Friends*.

He scowled in return. "I may have seen a few when nothing else was on," he noted.

"Rest assured," I said. "I can cook. I'm actually a decent cook. At least, I've never gotten many complaints. It won't be anything fancy tonight, but I promise to make my famous spaghetti sauce next time you stay for dinner. You will love that. After the day we've both had, tonight's meal will be something much simpler."

He nodded. "Simple is good as long as it doesn't include food poisoning."

"Agreed," I said.

Chapter Twenty-Seven

Duncan catapulted from the tree onto Hamish's shoulder, causing me to jump. I had only known the squirrel for a day, and I still wasn't used to his gymnastics.

I stumbled back, and the heel of my boot caught on a tree root. That sent me crashing into the crime scene tape, which snapped under my weight. In the nick of time, I caught the edge of the menhir. My hand crushed the leaves of the yellow climbing rose that entwined the stone, and a sharp pain shot through my index finger. I jerked my hand away to find a pinprick of blood gathering there. The wound quickly went from a pinprick to a steady flow of blood. I held the hand above my chest to lessen the bleeding.

Hamish reached up and patted Duncan's side. "You should not scare the lass so," he lightly chided the red squirrel.

Duncan chittered in reply. I assumed he was saying, "She started it by bringing a cat home!"

My finger was bleeding badly, much worse than a prick from a thorn should have caused. Blood pooled on my fingertip and then spilled over the side, falling to the grass below. I grimaced. The last thing I needed was my blood at the crime scene of a murder. I knew that Craig and his team had already processed the scene, but I'd much rather not have my DNA this close to where a murdered man had been discovered. "You and Duncan come up to the cottage for dinner as soon as you can. I'm heading back home to treat this."

"There's nothing you can do to treat that mark." Hamish said this in the all-knowing voice that he had used a few times before. "The mark is a good thing," he added. "A very good thing. It's a tie, a connection."

"What are you talking about?" I asked. It seemed to me that Hamish either spoke in riddles or spoke about his squirrel. There was little else. I could barely follow the conversation.

He shook his head.

Duncan jumped from his master's shoulder and ran in a circle in the grass around the standing stone. His action caused me to shiver, but I wrote it off as typical squirrel behavior. I hoped that I was right.

I studied the blood pooling on the tip of my finger, and the image of me passing out in the middle of the garden, like Sleeping Beauty after she pricked her finger on the spinning wheel, came to mind. I felt lightheaded, but I told myself that the woozy feeling coming over me had more to do with the stress of the day and jet lag than the rose's thorn.

Hamish nodded, and I was grateful when he didn't argue with me and say something vaguely ominous again. He held out his arm like a falconer calling a hawk back to him. Duncan circled the standing stone one final time and then took a flying leap from the ground to Hamish's arm. "We are both ready for dinner. We will come with you."

I nodded, not exactly sure how Ivanhoe would react to

the squirrel dinner guest since he had already more than claimed the cottage as his home.

The walk back to the cottage was quiet. Hamish and I were both caught up in our own thoughts. I held my bleeding finger up but tried not to focus on how much it throbbed. It was surprising that such a tiny little thorn could cause so much pain.

When we entered the cottage, Ivanhoe, who was still on his bed in front of the hearth, lifted his head. The moment he realized Duncan was there, he leaped up, alighting on the back of the couch. The cat walked back and forth along the back of the couch, making a cooing sound that somehow sounded both endearing and menacing at the same time.

It seemed to me that Duncan only heard "menacing" as he chittered angrily on his master's shoulder. Hamish walked over to the fireplace to stoke the fire, which had gotten low while we had been outside. As he bent over, the squirrel jumped from his arm onto the mantle. Then, Duncan turned around and chittered directly at Ivanhoe, who crouched low on the back of the sofa and growled deep in his throat.

I eyed the mantle. It didn't look to me like there was enough space up there for the cat to land, should he decide that he wanted to jump up there, but I would have to keep an eye on Ivanhoe, to be safe.

In the tiny kitchen, I ran my throbbing finger under cold water. The blood swirled in the white porcelain sink and slid down the drain in a pink streak. In the bathroom, I found an ancient box of bandages. I wrapped one around my injured finger and went back to my guests.

When I returned to the cottage's main room, I found

Hamish sitting on an easy chair on the other side of the fireplace from the sofa. It had been my godfather's favorite chair, and for the briefest of moments I had this urge to ask the older man to move. I stopped myself. There was no reason Hamish couldn't sit in that chair, even if in my mind it would always belong to my godfather.

"How does a grilled cheese sandwich and tomato soup sound?" I asked Hamish.

"I can't say that I have ever had it. Is this an American dinner?" He rubbed his chin.

"Very," I said as I pulled the can of tomato soup out of the small bag of groceries that I had been able to grab at the market. It wasn't the same brand that I would have used back in the Tennessee, but it would do.

I poured the soup into a saucepan that I had found in the cupboard, then added water. I hadn't thought to buy any milk for the soup to make it extra creamy. For the sandwiches, I had, however, bought fresh baked bread, local cheese, and butter from the market.

As I cut the bread and cheese, I kept an eye on Duncan and Ivanhoe. The cat had settled on the back of the couch and no longer looked to be in attack position, but by the way his tail twitched, I didn't trust him. The moment Duncan decided to leave the mantle, it would be World War III in the middle of the cottage, but I knew better than to ask Hamish to have his beloved squirrel stay outside.

It didn't take long to make the two sandwiches, and the soup heated through quickly. Hamish folded his hands over his stomach. "That does smell nice. Can't say I smelled a meal just like that before. I'm impressed that you are an American girl who can cook."

I flipped the second sandwich onto the waiting plate, which was fine bone china. I assumed that my godfather had inherited the dishes. If I planned to stay at the cottage, I would have to find something else for everyday use. I was too much of a klutz to use such nice dishes for grilled cheese and cereal, which were my staples when it came to meals. I might be able to cook, but I was very much on the single-girl diet.

"Well, I would hardly call this cooking," I said. "But many American girls can cook. I would guess more can cook than can't. You shouldn't believe everything that you see on the sitcoms."

Hamish grunted. He wasn't buying it.

I set the bowls of soup and the sandwich plates on the old kitchen table that sat by one of the two front windows, the one farthest from the fireplace. I had asked my godfather once why his dining area was so far from the kitchen, when there was plenty of room to eat right there in the kitchen itself, and he'd said in reply that the kitchen was too close to the fireplace, and he couldn't eat when he was hot. This made me wonder how he'd eaten anything on his deployments overseas—many of which were to very hot places.

Hamish got up from my godfather's chair and joined me at the table.

As he settled into his seat, I said, "Thanks for staying."

He picked up his spoon. "Let us see what an American dinner is like."

I held my breath as he sipped from the soupspoon, set it

down, and then picked up the grilled cheese. He bit into it. His face was completely expressionless. I decided that must mean he hated it. I bit the inside of my lip.

"It's good," he said finally after he swallowed and took a sip of water from the glass next to his plate. "It's not as good as haggis, but it is good."

I beamed from ear to ear. "Thank you, Hamish. That really means a lot to me, and it's the first time any of my cooking had been compared to haggis."

He dunked a piece of his sandwich into the bowl of soup. "I would even eat it again if the offer came."

This made my smile grow by three watts, but feeding Hamish grilled cheese wasn't why I had asked him to stay for dinner. I had questions that needed answers, and I hoped that he would have at least some of those answers.

I reached into the pocket of my jeans and pulled out two identical skeleton keys. I set them on the table and slid them toward Hamish. "Are you going to tell me about these?"

All the color drained from the elderly caretaker's face.

Chapter Twenty-Eight

"Miss Fiona, where did you find that?" Hamish stared at the two keys on the table.

"In the garden, in the same spot where I saw you searching for it earlier. You knew that it would be there. How did you know?"

"I didn't know the key would be there—not for certain. But I thought that Alastair must have used the key to get into the garden, and if he had, it might still be there."

"So you knew about the second key." I folded my hands in my lap.

"There were always two keys. Master Ian had one; that is the key that I gave you. I had one as well. Of course, I would have one so that I could take care of the garden when Master Ian was away."

"Why did you tell me that there was only one key when I first arrived at Duncreigan, even before Alastair's body was discovered?"

Hamish made a move as if he were about to reach out and touch the keys, but then he changed his mind and let his hand fall back into his lap. "Because I had every intention of getting it back, and I didn't think it was worth upsetting you by telling you that one of the keys to the garden and cottage had been stolen. You were already skittish about living in the cottage to begin with."

"Stolen?" I shivered. "Stolen by whom?"

"Alastair."

"How?"

Hamish face turned a deeper shade of red. "It wasn't long after Master Ian died. I went to the Twisted Fox. I was distraught, and I had too much to drink. Alastair Croft was there." He still wouldn't meet my eyes. "He said some horrible things about Master Ian. He said that the garden's magic was false. I took the key out of my pocket and waved it at him. I said that I could prove to him that the magic was real and he had no right to speak about Master Ian in that way. He laughed in my face. I don't know when I had ever been so angry, Miss Fiona—I do not." His body shook as he spoke.

"Oh, Hamish." It was all I could say.

"When I returned to Duncreigan the next day, the key was no longer in my coat pocket where I had always kept it. I knew that Alastair Croft had taken it from me. So, when I saw Alastair Croft's body in the garden, I knew that he had gotten into the garden with the key that he had stolen from me. That's why you saw me looking for it. I hoped that it might still be there." He sighed. "And I suppose it was, since you found it."

"Did you ever go to Alastair and ask him to return the key?"

He nodded. "I did. I went to his law office. He came outside to meet me because he said that he had some important men meeting with him at the time. When I asked him, he denied it. I knew he was lying."

"Who were the men?" I asked.

"I don't know who they all were, but Clyde Blackwell was among them. I saw his face in the window on the second floor of the townhouse."

It didn't mean anything. Everyone in the village knew that Blackwell and Alastair were working on the land deal together. Even so, it made me even more suspicious of the developer. "Do you think Blackwell knew that Alastair had taken your key?"

Hamish wouldn't meet my gaze, and I had a nagging feeling that he was still holding something back from me. "Was that all you need to tell me, Hamish?"

He said nothing.

"It just seems odd to me that Alastair would be mocking the garden's magic when he was Uncle Ian's attorney. Something I have learned from almost everyone I talked to about Alastair is that he cared about money more than anything. Whatever his opinion about the garden, it wouldn't impact the money that he made from settling my godfather's estate. Why would he antagonize someone related to the estate?"

A single tear rolled down the old man's cheek.

"Hamish, what's wrong?" I asked.

"Alastair stole from me, but I have stolen from you and Master Ian."

I blinked at him. It was the very last thing that I had expected him to say. Hamish had always been so loyal to my godfather and the entire MacCallister family. I couldn't imagine him stealing from my godfather or from me. "How?"

Gruffly, he brushed the tear away from his cheek. "It was not for me, lass. It was for my great nephew."

"Seth?" I asked.

To my right, the fire was beginning to die down. I would have to put more wood on it soon unless I wanted to start all over again with building a fire from scratch.

"How did you know?" He stared at me in amazement.

"I met him in the village earlier today."

Hamish frowned. "It's not often he comes to the village. He is going to medical school in Aberdeen."

I bit my lip to stop myself from telling Hamish that Seth wasn't in medical school at the moment. The young protestor had told me not to tell his great-uncle. And although I had not promised that I wouldn't tell, I wanted to hear what Hamish had to say before I said anything about Seth.

Hamish shook his head as if the matter was of no consequence. "Seth is my late brother's grandson, and I promised my brother before he died that I would keep an eye on Seth. Seth told me several months ago that he would not be able to continue with school because he was out of money. I sent him all the money that I could spare. Although Master Ian paid me well, I wasn't able to send much." He dropped his gaze to his hands. "Seth said that it wasn't enough. He said he needed much more money and told me to borrow the money from Master Ian. It is well known in the village that the MacCallisters have money."

"So you asked my godfather for help?" I pushed my plate away. I had lost my appetite.

"No," he said, still staring at his hands. "I knew that Master Ian was in some harsh fighting overseas. I didn't want to trouble him with my nephew's financial burdens. I always knew that Master Ian would be deployed, fighting with the army for several months. I *borrowed* the money without asking, with the idea that I would pay it back before Master Ian returned from his tour."

My heart sank because I knew, as I suspected Hamish did, that Uncle Ian would have gladly given him the money if he had only asked. Also, this made me wonder about Seth. The young man seemed to be very sincere in his goal of helping Raj and the twins protect the coastline, but he had been lying to his great-uncle about being in medical school. What else had the young activist lied about? He had even told Hamish to get the money from Uncle Ian. And if Hamish had a motive to kill Alastair that was related to this money, Seth would have the very same motive.

Hamish sat across from me, still staring at his hands, with his shoulders slumped. He seemed to have aged a decade since he started to make his confession. "I will pay every penny back, Miss Fiona—I promise."

"I know you will, Hamish."

He looked up and met my gaze for the first time since he'd started talking. "Thank you. And my nephew will make a fine doctor. You will see."

I didn't reply to that. I didn't want to be the one to tell Hamish that Seth had been lying to him about going to school. If Seth wasn't using the money that Hamish sent him for his school bills, what was he using it for?

"Did Alastair know about you taking money from Uncle Ian?"

"Yes," Hamish said. "He was the executor of the estate,

and he was going over the affairs to settle things. He saw the money that I withdrew and realized what I was doing. Alastair Croft was many things, and among them, a smart man. That night in the pub, he wasn't saying anything against your uncle's garden. He told me that he knew about the money that I took from Master Ian. I had not done a good job of hiding that I took the money because I was certain that I would have it all paid back before Master Ian returned. He threatened to tell you."

"But the key," I said.

"I showed him the key to the garden to prove to him that I did nothing wrong and that Master Ian trusted me. I might have been trying to prove I was in the right, even though I wasn't."

"Did anyone overhear your argument?"

He shook his head. "We were at the Twisted Fox. Anyone could have heard us, but I suppose not. Wouldn't that person have come forward by now or gone to the police about what I did?"

I would have thought so too, but there was a chance that someone, the killer even, overheard and was keeping this knowledge to him- or herself for some reason. What exactly that reason was, I didn't know. "And you still believe that Alastair took the key."

He nodded. "I do."

"Even if he had the key, I still don't think he voluntarily went into the garden. The police believe that Alastair died in his townhouse and his body was moved to the garden."

"What are you talking about?"

That was right—Hamish didn't know about the events of

my day or the gas leak at Alastair's townhouse. I quickly filled him in about the gas leak, taking care not to mention Seth or anything about the protest. I wasn't sure how to break it to Hamish that his grandnephew had been lying to him. This wasn't the time.

"So someone stole the key from Alastair," Hamish mused.

"Or took it from her after he was dead."

Hamish nodded. "But it is no matter for me, Miss Fiona. I am in just as much trouble as ever because I have a motive for murdering Alastair, a very strong motive indeed." He paused. "Or at least that is what Neil Craig will believe when he learns the truth."

I didn't try to comfort him or tell him that he was wrong because we would both know that I would be lying.

A loud knock came at the front door of the cottage. Both Ivanhoe and Duncan jumped in place. The cat hissed, and the squirrel stood on his hind legs, putting up his tiny fists in a fighting stance.

Hamish and I made eye contact over the table. We both knew who was at the door.

Chapter
Twenty-Nine

The knock came again. "Fiona! It's Neil Craig!" Craig's deep voice came through the door.

"Answer the door, lass. It's time that I face what I have done," Hamish said.

I wanted to argue with him, but Craig's yelling and pounding became more insistent. "Fiona!"

With a shake of my head, I got up from the dining table and opened the door against the wind.

"Fiona," Craig said. "Have you seen Ha—"

He stopped mid-sentence as Hamish rose from his seat at the table. "I know why you are here, Chief Inspector."

Craig's thick, dark brows shot up. "You do?"

"You've come to arrest me."

Craig glanced at me to check whether I was following this conversation.

"Don't be afraid to say anything in front of Fiona. I've told her everything about me stealing from her godfather and how Alastair found out."

"We found evidence of it on Alastair's computer that we confiscated from his office."

Hamish nodded. "I knew this would happen. I should have told everyone the truth when Alastair's body was first discovered. I was too cowardly to face my actions then, but I can now."

Craig removed handcuffs from the inner pocket of his sport coat. "Hamish MacGregor, you are charged with the premeditated murder of Alastair Croft. I am here to—"

"Wait!" I grabbed Craig's arm. "You can't arrest him. I know that he didn't do this."

"Fiona, please, stay out of this. It doesn't involve you."

"It involves me. Of course, it involves me. Hamish is like family to me. Please, Neil."

Craig's eyebrows shot up when I called him by his first name. I think it was the first time that I had ever said it, and it sounded odd coming out of my mouth.

I still had my hand on his arm. "Just let me talk to you for a few minutes to tell you what I've learned. Please. If, after that, you still want to arrest Hamish, I can't really stop you, can I?"

The chief inspector stroked the end of his beard. "Five minutes, Fiona. Five minutes."

"I'll take it." I opened the cottage door against the wind and stepped through. As soon as I was outside, I regretted my decision because I shivered in the wind.

Craig came out of the cottage. "What are you doing out here?"

"I wanted to talk to you somewhere in private, where Hamish can't overhear us."

Craig frowned. "I thought you believed he's innocent."

"I do," I said into the wind.

"Well, we can't talk here. You'll be blown away in the

215

wind if you don't freeze first. Let's talk in my jeep." He put a hand on the small of my back and guided me to his jeep. Craig opened the passenger door for me, and I climbed in.

"I can open my own car doors, you know." My teeth chattered.

"I know that you can, but my mother always taught me to treat a lady right."

"I'm a lady now?" I asked. "I thought I was a murder suspect."

"You haven't been a suspect since I spoke to the airline." He shut my door before I could reply with a smart remark.

I shivered in the front seat while he walked around the car. He opened the driver's side door and was climbing into the jeep; then he stopped himself. "Wait a second." Craig hopped out of the jeep and went around to the back, where he removed something, closing the back door with a slam. A few seconds later, he jumped back inside the jeep and placed a red tartan blanket on my lap.

I held up a corner of the blanket. "What's this for?"

"You're cold," he said. He turned on the car and pointed two of the heating vents in my direction too.

"Is this part of the 'treating a lady right' thing?" I asked as he spread the blanket across my lap and tucked my arms underneath it.

Craig shook his head. "I should have never told you that. Now, why did you want to talk to me without Hamish?"

"Because I need to convince you not to arrest him."

"Fiona, the evidence—"

I pulled my arms out from under the blanket. "There are other suspects," I said, breaking in on him.

He folded his arms. "Like who?"

"Clyde Blackwell, to start. Maybe Alastair was thinking of backing out of the land sale because the village was so against it." Before he could interrupt, I said, "And there is Cally Beckleberry, his partner, who would get his business. Or his sister, Aileen, who gets some sort of inheritance." I began ticking the suspects off on my fingers.

Craig winced when I said Aileen's name. I decided to keep going and not get caught up in talking about his ex-wife when there were so many other suspects. "There's Raj Kapoor, who is so against the land deal, and his sister, Presha, who could be involved. Maybe she killed Alastair to protect her brother." I hated adding to my list Presha and Raj, both of whom I had instantly liked, but I had to make Craig understand that Hamish wasn't the only suspect. "And then there is Seth MacGregor."

"Hamish's nephew?"

I nodded. "Hamish stole that money so that he could give it to his nephew, who claimed that he needed it for medical school, but Seth lied. He's not going to medical school. What is he doing with all that money? Why did he lie to his uncle?" I bit my lip. "Don't tell Hamish about that. He doesn't know. I want to tell him . . ."—I paused—"when things calm down."

He nodded.

"But my number-one suspect is Jock." I went on to tell him what I had overheard before about Jock and the man in tweed. "Playing both sides might refer to something related to the land deal. What else can it be?"

"You make some valid points, but I do have a problem with all this."

I turned in my seat, clutching the blanket. "What's that?"

"You should not be following suspects or asking questions."

I opened my mouth to protest, but Craig held up his hand. "Let me finish. You shouldn't be doing those things because you should let the police handle it. Let me handle it."

"I can help." I dropped my hands to my lap.

"I'm not questioning your abilities. I don't want you getting hurt. Whoever killed Alastair planned his murder. He or she put a lot of time into thinking out how to take another person's life. The killer poisoned Alastair with natural gas. The coroner confirmed that today."

"If the killer had left the body in Alastair's townhouse, then it could have been mistaken for an accident or even suicide," I said.

He nodded. "He or she moving the body makes it a murder case. This is a person with malicious intention. That's not a person you want to meet. He or she also spent a lot of time, if your assumption is right, framing Hamish. Again, that is not a person you want to meet. If this person killed a very prominent villager, do you think there would be any hesitation in murdering you, an outsider?"

I swallowed. I hadn't thought of it that way, and I knew he was right. But at the same time, I had to do this for Hamish and, in a way, for Uncle Ian too. He'd loved Hamish dearly and trusted him, so I couldn't help but love and trust the old caretaker too.

"Two days. That's all I ask," I said to the chief inspector. "Give it two more days before you arrest Hamish. Investigate for two more days."

The sun had completely set at this point, and the only light to see by was the dim light from the cottage reflecting off the jeep's rearview mirror. Craig studied me in that light and said nothing.

"Two days is not too much to ask," I insisted. "Hamish is an old man who has spent his entire life in County Aberdeen, and most of that in Duncreigan. Where else does he have to go? He's not a flight risk. He would have willingly gone with you tonight if I hadn't stopped him."

Craig scratched at the whiskers on his right cheek and sighed. "All right, Fiona. You win. I will wait two days, but if nothing comes to light in that time from my investigation, I'll have to arrest him. I will have no other choice."

I put my hand on his arm. "Thank you! Thank you so much!"

He covered my hand with his and squeezed it for the briefest moment.

I pulled my hand back under the blanket, out of his reach. "Thank you," I repeated.

He nodded and opened the door to the jeep.

I hopped out my side before he could come around and open the door for me. As I did, I couldn't help but think that my ex-fiancé had never opened a car door for me in all the time that we were together. I wondered what his mother had taught him.

Craig walked me to the door of the cottage. "Tell Hamish that I'll drop by tomorrow to ask him a few more questions. And tell him not to leave the county."

"I will," I promised.

Craig nodded. "Good night, Fiona Knox. Hamish is very

lucky to have a friend as fierce as you." With that, he turned and went back to his jeep.

Without another word, I stepped into the cottage and found Hamish waiting for me.

"Where is Neil?" Hamish asked. "Is he taking me to the police station?"

I shook my head and repeated the instructions that Craig had told me to relay to the caretaker.

"You have done this for me, Miss Fiona. Thank you." Hamish stood by the door. "Please forgive me for what I have done."

I took his wrinkled hands into mine. "There's nothing to forgive, but I do forgive you. I'll help you get through this, Hamish. I promise." I held onto the old man's hands.

Gently he removed his hands from my grasp. "It is time for me to go. I am an 'early to bed, early to rise' sort. It is best to garden in the morning when the earth is still fresh with dew. It is when the ground is more welcoming to new life. To do that, I must sleep because I do not know how much longer I will have a chance to breathe the fresh and free Scottish air." He walked to the door with Duncan on his shoulder. The squirrel gave Ivanhoe a final flick of his bushy tail. If a squirrel could thumb his nose, I bet he would have.

The Scottish Fold cat growled deep in his throat. If I were Duncan, I wouldn't taunt the predator.

Hamish opened the door, and the sharp Scottish wind whipped across the high rocky land of Duncreigan. "Thank you for forgiving me, lass. That in and of itself is a gift."

The cottage door slammed shut after him.

I cleaned up the dishes from dinner and walked around

the cottage, looking at my godfather's photos. I stopped in front of the portrait of Baird MacCallister and stared at it long and hard. At this point, if the figure in the portrait had opened his mouth and spoken to me, I wouldn't have been the least bit surprised.

It was close to nine in the evening then, but I was wide awake. After the first night, when I'd passed out from sheer exhaustion from traveling and then finding a dead body upon my arrival at Duncreigan, I found that this night, I wasn't feeling the least bit tired. It was little wonder why. I was still on Nashville time, and it was still the middle of the afternoon there.

I decided that reading would be the best way to make me tired. I walked to the bookshelves and found an old, tattered copy of *Ivanhoe*. I waved it at the cat, who was back on his cat pillow by the fire. "Look what I found!"

He purred his approval.

I curled up on the sofa and wrapped a tartan blanket that I had found in the closet around me. The wool was scratchy against my skin, but warm.

Before I opened the book, I shot a text message to my sister back in Tennessee, asking her to go to the family farm and look for my letter from Uncle Ian. The letter would make everything clear. That is what Hamish had said at least, and since I had no other options, I chose to believe him.

There was nothing more that I could do to retrieve the letter from where it currently was. I tried to push the worries of mystical gardens and murder from my mind. I opened the book and began to read until dreams overtook me.

Chapter Thirty

The cold salt spray hit my face like a barrage of tiny darts, and the harsh wind burned my skin until it was dry and chapped. My footing was unsure on the slick black rock, but I pressed on. With my stomach flattened against the sharp rocks and their jagged edges digging through the fabric of my jacket, I threw my right arm out and grappled for the next handhold. I found it. As secure as I could be with the handhold, I threw out my right foot. For the briefest of seconds, it hovered in space seeking any kind of traction. There was none. Below, it felt like the sea was calling me to let go and fall in. It would be easier. But then my foot found the rock's edge, and the rest of my body followed as I flew to it.

Behind me another person pursued me, placing his own hands and feet in the places where mine had been. He was following me, but I wasn't afraid. I expected him to be there.

"We really shouldn't be doing this," the man shouted into the wind. "Do you know how many people fall to their deaths from these cliffs? We should go back and find some professional rock climbers to look into this, preferably when it's not pouring rain."

I looked over my shoulder but couldn't see the man who spoke to me. Even though I didn't know for sure who was there, I wasn't afraid. "We can't turn back now. I can almost see it." As I said the words, I had a sense that what I was looking for was up ahead of me, but I didn't know what it was. Again, I was unconcerned with this.

"It's not safe," the man said. "I would never be dumb enough to climb down here if I weren't following you."

I looked back at the faceless man and pressed my right cheek into the rock, staring hard. I still couldn't see who it was. "I never asked you to follow me."

"I'm not letting you die on my watch."

I turned my head again, taking care not to scrape my face on the rocks. Then, I saw what I was looking for. It was an indentation in the side of the cliff. A wave came in just then, and water splashed my side. I was drenched, and the cold Scottish air blowing off the North Sea chilled me to the marrow of my bones.

"Fiona!" the man behind me yelled. "Are you all right?"

I turned to yell back at him that I was fine. I opened my mouth and turned, and suddenly I heard a ringing sound. I did it again, and the ringing came again.

My cell phone rang for a third time, and I fell off the sofa onto the cottage's cold hardwood floor. The fire in the hearth had long died down because I had neglected to stoke it before falling asleep. The cottage was chilled through and through. Ivanhoe walked over to me and touched his damp nose to the side of my face.

I blinked a few times as my eyes adjusted to the odd moonlit shapes around the room. I was not anywhere close to my cozy apartment back in Nashville. No, I was in Scotland in my deceased godfather's cottage, a cottage that I'd inherited along with a mysterious garden that was tied to my destiny, and a murder victim's cat.

The ringing stopped. I had left my phone charging in my godfather's bedroom. I untangled myself from the tartan blanket just as the phone started ringing again. I scrambled to my feet and ran into the bedroom for the phone, which was plugged into a power converter that was in turn plugged into the outlet.

I didn't have time to waste on looking at the screen. "Hello?" The greeting came out like a croak. It was the best I could do in my sleepy state.

"Oopsies! You were asleep, weren't you?" my baby sister, Isla, asked.

"I was," I agreed. I wasn't about to deny that Isla had woke me from a dead sleep.

"I forgot about the time-difference thing," my sister said on the other end of the call. "You can still talk to me, right? What time is it there? Midnight?"

I fell back onto the bed, clutching my phone. "More like two in the morning."

"Oopsies," she repeated.

I held the phone to my ear as I threw back the duvet that covered the bed. I slipped underneath it, and my back settled against the headboard. "It's fine, Isla. I'm glad that you called. Did you get my text?"

"Yeah, that's why I was calling. You want me to go to the farm and get some letter. Why don't you just text Mom or Dad and ask them to get it for you?"

It was a good question. My parents were already at the farm and might have already seen the letter, but I didn't want to answer their hundreds of prying questions. I knew my parents: if they didn't like my answers, they would be on the next plane to Scotland. "Can you do it for me? I will owe you one."

She sighed. "Fine. But you know if I go to the farm tomorrow, Mom will trap me. She will make me eat pie."

"Sounds like a hardship indeed," I said.

"It is if you're trying to lose weight. I have graduation coming up. I can't roll across the stage."

I closed my eyes for a moment. My sister was curvy, but I would never call her overweight. She didn't need to lose an ounce, but since she didn't look like all the stick-thin fashion models on the covers of all the magazines she subscribed to, she felt like she was huge. Nothing could be further from the truth.

"Plus, it's cruel and unusual punishment for me to be faced with pie this week. It's finals. Who can turn pie down during finals? And what if it's strawberry pie? I'm doomed," she moaned.

Our mother's strawberry pie was amazing. If that was the pie cooling in my mother's country kitchen, Isla really was doomed. "Just think of it as doing a good deed for your favorite sister."

"You're my only sister."

"Who taught you to ride a bike? Who taught you to tie your shoes and multiply fractions?"

"You did," she grumbled. "Okay, fine, I'll do it, but you are going to owe me."

"I'm not holding a gun to your head, making you eat our mother's pie."

"You might as well be," she groused.

I sighed. "What do I owe you?"

"I don't know yet," she said. "But I'm thinking that it will be some sort of expensive graduation present. I like jewelry."

I groaned.

"You are coming back home for my graduation, aren't you?" she asked.

"I am," I said, hoping that I was telling the truth. I had been worried that Chief Inspector Craig was holding my passport, making it impossible to leave the United Kingdom. I would need to leave the country very soon in order to attend my sister's college graduation. As long as he had my passport, that was impossible. However, Isla didn't need to worry about any of this. She had finals and a fattening strawberry pie to contend with. I wasn't going to add anything to her list of concerns. Even so, I asked, "When is graduation again?"

She sighed with the force that only someone under the age of twenty-five could muster. "In two weeks, on the twentieth of May. I've told you that, like, four times."

"Sorry. I have a lot going on," I said.

She sighed again. "Are you planning to go back to Scotland after graduation?"

"I don't know," I said honestly.

"But I want you to come home." I could hear the hurt in her voice.

"I know, and I miss you," I said, meaning it because it was true despite how annoying my little sister could be. I missed her when I was halfway across the world from her.

"I want you to come home for good." There was a pout in her voice. "When will you know?"

"I'll have a better idea what my plans are when I come for your graduation."

"I wish you wouldn't go back to Scotland, but if you do, maybe I can come live with you for the summer. I'm not having any luck finding a job, and wouldn't it be fun if we lived with each other again like when we were kids?"

Fun? It sounded like a nightmare. We would kill each other. I was the neat and orderly one, and Isla was a slob. I shivered to think about the condition she would leave the cottage's tiny bathroom in. "Umm . . ." I trailed off.

"I don't know why you had to drop everything and go to Scotland in the first place," my sister said, completely missing the pause indicating my reluctance on the living-together thing.

"You know why I'm here. It's because Uncle Ian left me this cottage."

"Uncle Ian didn't leave me anything." There was the pout again in her voice.

"He was my godfather, not yours," I said.

"True, but he left you everything. Don't you think that's a little extreme for a goddaughter? Would it have killed him to include me?"

I grimaced.

"Sorry," she said, "that was a poor choice of words, considering he died. I just think he should have included all of us—you, Mom and Dad, and me—in his will, not just you. It's not fair. He didn't even leave anything to Dad, and he was Ian's best friend."

I didn't like where this conversation was going, so I decided to get things back on their original track. "I really do appreciate you going over there tomorrow and looking for the letter. When you find it, can you open it, take a picture of it with your phone, and text it to me?"

"Fine, but I don't know when I can get over there tomorrow. I have a lot going on too. If you asked Mom, you could get it a lot sooner."

"I can wait," I said.

"You can be stubborn," she complained.

"Look who's talking," I replied.

She blew out a breath, and I could see her frustrated expression in my mind's eye. "I still think you should just sell Duncreigan, take the money, and come home."

"I could never sell Duncreigan," I said. In fact, the idea had never occurred to me. Even when I'd learned about the inheritance and had still believed that I would be married to Ethan in a month's time, I'd never thought of selling my godfather's ancestral home. I knew Ethan and I would never live there, but I couldn't sell it. Ever. It had been in the Mac-Callister family for hundreds of years, and it had been so important to my godfather. "Besides I have nothing to come home to. My business is closed and . . ." I trailed off.

"OMG, Fi! That is the most ridiculous thing I have ever heard. You have Mom and Dad and me. Don't we count for something?"

I sighed, not bothering to hide it any longer. "Yes, yes, of course, you're all very important to me, but Mom and Dad have the farm. I can't go back there."

"Understood," she said.

"And," I said, "you're graduating from college in a few short weeks and about to start your own life. I can't get in the way of that."

"What you don't understand, Fi," she said, sounding much older that her twenty-two years, "is that you always think you cause trouble, you always think that you are in the way, but you never are. If anything, the opposite is true."

I wished I believed her.

Chapter Thirty-One

After I got off the phone with my sister, I tried to go back to sleep, but the dream about the cliff pestered me all night long. Every time I was about to see who was behind me or what was inside the indentation on the side of the cliff, I would wake up. Finally, at five in the morning, when it was starting to grow light out, I gave up and got out of bed.

By six, I was outside, walking in the direction of the garden. I had to see it again, and I needed to see it alone, without the police, without Chief Inspector Craig, and without Hamish. I pushed through the garden door.

Part of me was relieved to see the garden the same as I had left it the evening before, and the other part of me, albeit the smaller part, was disappointed. The buds that were gathering on the bushes were still there, and the hundreds of daffodils that were on the edge of blooming had not bloomed yet. The last time I'd entered the garden, there had been such a transformation that I couldn't help but believe Hamish, who claimed there was some type of magic there and that I was tied to it somehow. But that morning, it looked like any other garden at the beginning of spring. If I hadn't seen how dead the garden had been a few days ago, I never would have believed the garden's caretaker.

I came around the side of the hedge to the spot were Alastair had died. The fox was there. He was sniffing and pawing the ground around the standing stone.

"Are you looking for something?" I asked.

He stared up at me, and not for the first time, I felt like I was looking into eyes that I knew, but I couldn't place how I knew them. I expected him to run away, but instead he sat in the middle of the ring of crime scene tape and pawed at the rich earth again. All the time, he kept his gaze firmly focused on me.

"Are you looking for the key to the garden?" I asked. "Did you put that key in the garden?"

He sat up when I asked this, like a dog would when a treat was offered to him. I had the fox's full attention. I pushed back the alarm bells that were going off in my head, the ones that were telling me I was talking to a fox and thinking that he could understand what I was saying. I knew that was impossible. Even so, I reached into my coat pocket and removed the key I'd found. I'd left it in my pocket the night before, after Hamish and I had returned to the cottage and he'd told me the legend of Baird MacCallister.

"Hamish was looking for it too," I said. As I said this, I knew it was true. "Should I believe him that he didn't kill Alastair? I told Craig that I did, but even I have to admit, that it does not look good for my godfather's caretaker. Craig won't put off making an arrest for long."

The fox just stared at me without blinking and then turned and ran deeper into the garden. After a moment's hesitation, I ran after him.

He jumped from an old tree stump to a branch and then over the garden wall. At least one mystery at Duncreigan was solved. I now knew how the fox got in and out of the garden. At this point, with all the questions that I had swirling around in my mind, it was good to know something at least.

Shaking my head, I walked back through the garden, taking in all the plants that were about to bloom and all the work that would have to be done to get the garden into the shape that it had been in when my godfather had cared for it. Yes, Hamish was the caretaker of the garden, but I could see places that could use sprucing up. The question was, Could I afford to do it? My godfather had left me a handsome inheritance, but I couldn't live on that forever. It was not only impractical; it was impossible. I would have to find work, and the closest place for that was the village of Bellewick.

Perhaps I could get a job from Presha or her brother, Raj, until I figured out what my plans were. I could make tea, and I was reasonably good at laundry, as long as Raj didn't expect me to iron. This thought reminded me that I needed to return to the cottage before Raj got there. He was going to take me to the cliff where the land was in dispute between the Croft and Beckleberry law firm and the village of Bellewick.

By the time I crested the hill that gave me a clear view of the cottage, Raj was there. His olive-green hatchback looked as if it had been built before I was born. He smiled at me, and his white teeth gleamed in the morning sunlight. "Were you out for an early morning walk?"

I simply nodded. In actuality, I wasn't an early morning person. I'd had to be for my flower shop. Fresh flower deliveries had always been in the early morning, but it hadn't come naturally to me to get up that early. However, I wasn't going to tell Raj or anyone about my strange dreams. They were only dreams, and they didn't mean anything.

"I remember Ian liked to walk through the countryside in the morning as well when he was home. He was a brooder," Raj said.

I raised my eyebrows. "A brooder?"

He nodded. "He was quiet and seemed to be in his own thoughts quite a lot. I've been told that all the MacCallister men were like that." He walked around to the back of his car and opened the trunk. "I have your sheets right here in the boot, freshly laundered and pressed for you." He handed me the basket.

I held the basket again my hip. "Thanks so much for doing that for me. I'll set these inside and get my bag, and we can go."

He nodded. "I'll be right here waiting for you."

I hurried into the cottage and dropped the basket of sheets by the sofa. Ivanhoe was sitting on the windowsill, looking out in the direction of Hamish's home. I wondered if the cat knew where Hamish lived, and if he did, was he planning the squirrel's demise? I decided I'd rather not think about it.

I grabbed my bag and headed back out the door. Raj was already in the car, waiting. As I climbed into his tiny hatchback, I caught sight of a bit of red running across the field. I knew that it was the fox, and I had a strong desire to follow it.

"Fiona? Are you ready to go?" Raj asked when I sat there

with the car door open, looking after the fox for just a moment too long.

I closed the car door. "Yes, of course," I said. I told myself to forget about the fox and worry about the issue at hand.

As we drove down the hill, leaving Duncreigan and cresting another hilltop, I asked Raj, "What more can you tell me about this land deal?

Raj gripped the steering wheel a little more tightly, and the knuckles of his brown hands turned white. "It makes me furious to even think about it." He loosened his grip on the steering wheel. "But you are here to learn about it, so I will start at the beginning." He took a breath. "You know Bellewick is only thirty minutes south of Aberdeen. Aberdeen is the last good-sized city before you are in the middle of the highlands. Bellewick is just on the border of the highlands and the midlands, and sits along one of the prettiest stretches of the coast. Dunnottar Castle isn't too far from here either. Have you been there?"

I nodded. "I've been a couple of times with my godfather on past trips. The stairway to reach the castle is a killer."

He laughed. "That it is. But the view is breathtaking."

I couldn't argue with him about that. The view of the castle ruins was wondrous indeed.

"The land around the castle is protected, as it should be. Most of it is parkland to protect the seabirds, but the land on the North Sea just east of Bellewick is not. That is all private land and has always been so. It once belonged to the earl of Aberdeenshire. When the earl died with no heirs, the village hoped that the land would be bequeathed as a park or added to the public lands along the coast. We never expected that a money-sucking lawyer would grab hold of it and try to sell it to the highest bidder."

"I'm not that surprised. It's a valuable piece of real estate."

"You say that because you are American. You people would sell your kidneys to the highest bidders, if you could."

I pursed my lip, thinking that was a harsh judgment on an entire country, but since I still needed information from Raj, I decided not to pursue it. "Why is the land so important to the village?"

"Other than the busy harbor, it has been the village's access to the sea for hundreds of years. True, it never actually belonged to Bellewick or to any of the villagers, but it has always been the tradition that the villagers could use it. If a bunch of fancy condominiums are built there, the village's access to the coast will be blocked." He glanced over at me. "You, in particular, should hope that doesn't happen."

"Me? Why me?"

"Because even though you are not a MacCallister by birth, as Ian's sole heiress, you are connected to the MacCallister line, and the MacCallister line is connected to the particular spot along the coast where Baird MacCallister shipwrecked." Then he proceeded to tell me the same story I'd heard before about Baird, the shipwreck, and the standing stone.

Perhaps, Hamish had been telling the truth when he'd said that all the villagers knew the story of Baird and the menhir.

However, Raj's story took a different turn from Hamish's at the end. "Part of the ship was found about a mile off the coast from here. Divers were called in to review the wreckage."

This news took me by surprise. I'd have thought that I

would have heard from Uncle Ian or my parents if the wreckage of Uncle Ian's ancestor's boat had been found.

"What did they find?" I asked.

"The anchor," he said. "They were able to prove it was from the very ship that Baird was on. They also found some other metals scattered along the seafloor."

"Were any valuables found? Was there anything of value in the wreckage?"

He glanced away from the road, just for a moment, to look at me. "You mean treasure lost at sea?"

I nodded. "I guess." Images of swashbuckling pirates danced in my head.

"There were supposed to be five hundred pounds in Queen Anne five guineas on the ship. They were never found. Most likely buried under the ocean floor, and they could be scattered for miles."

"How much would that be worth today?" I braced myself for some astronomical number.

"It's hard to guess. Just one of the coins is worth fifty-five thousand pounds, if not more, to a dealer, and there were hundreds of them."

My mouth fell open as I did some quick calculations in my head. Although I had braced myself for the number, I'd never expected it to be anything close to the sum Raj was indicating. "I'm surprised that whoever found the wreck didn't make a stronger effort to search for the coins."

"They did. They spent two years at it but never found a single clue."

"You seem to know a lot of about Scottish history." I couldn't keep the surprise out of my voice.

Raj smiled. "This surprises you because I'm Indian?"

I felt my face grow hot. "No, I didn't mean it that way."

He grinned. "I am only giving you a hard time because I can. I am a student of history. I went to school to be a history teacher, you see. When my sister and I moved to Scotland, it was important to me that I learn everything I could about the country. Over time, it's become a bit more of an obsession than a passing interest."

"Why did you give up teaching if it was so important to you?"

He shook his head. "I didn't give it up. The requirements that I reached to be a teacher in India were much different from what they are in Scotland. I can't get my license to teach here."

I frowned, wondering if there was something more to it than that. "Couldn't you take a test or something to prove you could teach here? What about the University? Couldn't you have gone there and gotten the right credentials? That doesn't seem fair that you have to give up on your dream like that," I said.

A cloud passed over his face. "The time for that has come and gone. I am very proud that I have my own business that affords me a lot of time to read and learn more history. Besides, at my age, I no longer have a desire to be trapped in a room with two dozen teenagers. If I were teaching, I wouldn't have time for other pursuits like fighting this land deal."

"You are protesting on behalf of the villagers so they have access to the sea?"

He shook his head. "That is a side effect of my protest."

Again, my eyebrows rose.

"I want to save the coast. It's a fragile ecosystem and should be preserved for generations. True, this stretch doesn't have the nesting sea birds that it does closer to Dunnottar, but it's still important. Coastal erosion is a real problem across the world. I don't want this beautiful place to fall victim to human progress, like much of my home country of India has. When I think of how the coast and jungles there have been ravaged, it makes me ill."

"And Alastair didn't agree with you?"

He gripped the steering wheel. "Who knows what Alastair thought about this or any other environmental issue? All he cared about was making money, and that meant selling the land to the highest bidder."

I held onto my seat belt. "Do you think that belief got him killed?"

"It would be a reason for me to kill him."

I tightened my hold on my seat belt. Was Raj just about to confess to murdering Alastair while I was alone in his car with him?

"But before you ask, I did not kill him. I value life too much, even Alastair Croft's."

"If you didn't kill him, who do you think did?"

He glanced at me, and a strange look passed over his face. After a beat, he said, "I have no idea."

Why did I think he was lying?

"Does anyone else have a reason to get Alastair out of the way?"

"It's not for me to say." He clamped his mouth shut after that and didn't say another word. I'd gotten all the information that I could out of Raj, for the time being at least.

I stared out the window as we drove along the coast. Hundreds of feet below, the North Sea crashed into the sheer black rock, which was half-covered with low-grounding succulents and lichens. The drop was at least a hundred feet. I wished I could get a closer look at the plants so I could try to identify them. I've always been interested in growing things, and I credited my godfather for that.

When I was a child, he would take me for long walks through the wilds of Scotland and taught me to love plant life. It was the flowers that I was always drawn to. I adored flowers and always had. It was why I'd become a florist. I'd gone to college and studied business and horticulture so I could do just that. I'd always known what I wanted to do and what I wanted in life.

Low bushes of bright yellow gorse lined either side of the road. They were beautiful, but I knew if I even grazed them, I would be sorry. I noticed the bushes at the same time that I realized that Raj was still talking. I had been so lost in my own thoughts about my life that I had tuned him out.

"It would be a great loss if the environment was effected by this development," I said, hoping that I could get Raj to warm up to me again after my questions about Alastair's murder turned him cold.

"So, you care about the environment too?" he asked.

"Of course," I answered, relieved that I was able to jump seamlessly back into the conversation. "From what I've heard, I am against the development on the coast as well."

Raj smiled at me. "Ian would have been pleased to know that."

Before I could respond, he said, "Here we are."

Up ahead, I saw a breathtaking view of the North Sea and the cliff. The sky was bright blue, the same shade I had marveled at earlier. I knew that could change at a moment's notice along the sea, going from blue to pitch black in an instant.

A large pickup truck was parked near the edge of the cliff. This surprised me. Trucks like that were common back in Nashville, but I had yet to see one in Scotland. European-made compact cars were more the norm here. A large Ford truck certainly stuck out. I was about to comment on it, when Raj swore and shifted the car into park. He jumped out of the car when it seemed to be still settling on the gravel-covered earth.

I got out of the car too, just as soon as I could get my seat belt off. The buckle was on the other side than what I was used to in the States, so I was disoriented for a moment. In that time, Raj had charged the truck. A short British man climbed out of the pickup's cab. He wore a tweed jacket that I suspected cost as much as my wedding dress, languishing now in the bridal salon back in Tennessee. When the man came around the side of the truck and I could see his face, I realized that it was the same man in tweed who I had seen talking to Jock when I was on my way to Croft and Beckleberry to collect Ivanhoe.

Chapter Thirty-Two

As I made my way toward the two men, I stumbled on the ground, which was covered with uneven stones and low-growing plants.

"You have no right to be here. You shouldn't be here!" Raj yelled at the man.

"I have more right to be here than you do or your pathetic band of followers." The man pointed at a beat-up VW bug that was bouncing its way along the winding dirt road to reach the cliff. The car came to a stop next to Raj's car, and the three students from the University of Aberdeen—the ones I'd had met in the village the day before—piled out of the car.

"Look who's here," Seth said. "We got here just in time to show Blackwell we aren't going to let him ruin our coast!"

I stared at the man in tweed. Blackwell? This was the developer who I had been hearing so much about. This made me even more convinced that Jock had a tie to Alastair's death if he'd been talking to the developer so soon after it happened.

Cara and Kay jabbed their fists into the air in a sign of solidarity.

Blackwell ignored them and continued to focus on Raj alone. "None of us has a right to be here, but here we all are. I assume for the same reasons."

"We are not here for the same reason. They"—he pointed at the three young arrivals—"and I are here to protect this land. You are here to destroy it."

"We are all here," Blackwell said coolly, "because we want this land. Motive is irrelevant."

"Motive is never irrelevant," Raj snapped. "Our motives are pure. Yours are for greed."

Blackwell shrugged as if this was the least of his concerns.

"We don't want the likes of you, Blackwell, in Bellewick!" one of the twins shouted.

"Or anywhere close to it," the other agreed.

Cara, I think, removed a placard from the trunk of their car and waved it back and forth like the national flag bearer at the Olympic opening ceremonies. It read, "Save the Coast! No More Development!" in big, bold, black letters.

"This is private land," Blackwell said. "You can't protest here."

"Villagers have the right to let their voices be heard," Raj said. "Bellewick has had access to this land for centuries. You just can't take it away."

"That's just tradition," Blackwell scoffed. "That doesn't make it legal. I'm not taking anything away because the village didn't have anything to take."

The students began to chant. "Save the coast! Save the coast!"

Blackwell's eyes narrowed to mere slits as the students became increasingly louder with each chant.

"You should be ashamed of yourself for even thinking of ruining this beautiful place with your ugly buildings," Raj told Blackwell over the din of the shouting students.

Blackwell bristled. What Raj had said must have hit home, because he looked like he was ready to deck the Indian man in the jaw. Thankfully, common sense prevailed, and all Blackwell did was ball his fists at his sides. "My buildings are not ugly. Far from it. They will improve this barren place."

"Barren? How can you even use that word to describe this place? There are many signs of life—the plants, the animals, the birds, and the sea itself. Why can't you see it?" Raj too balled his fists at his sides as if it took everything in him not to punch Blackwell in the mouth—or maybe even push him off the cliff.

Blackwell's chin jutted up. "What are you still doing here? Alastair promised me that he would get rid of you once and for all, but you are still here."

I perked up when I heard this. Could Alastair have threatened Raj's life, and then Raj retaliated by killing him? I would have believed it if Alastair had been killed in a fit of passion like being pushed off this cliff, but Alastair had been poisoned. I couldn't see Raj doing that. It took too much thought.

Raj clenched his fists tighter. "Yes, I'm still here, and Croft isn't. Maybe you should think more carefully about what side you're on. Now that Croft is dead, the deal will fall apart."

Blackwell laughed. "Doubtful. I'm working with his partner, Cally Beckleberry, to get this deal done. The project might be delayed ever so slightly, but rest assured, it is most certainly proceeding as planned. Cally Beckleberry will see to it for me, and from there I can start hiring contractors and working on the plans."

Raj shook his head. "Cally will never go through with making the deal with you. She cares too much about Bellewick and its villagers."

"She already has," Blackwell said.

Raj paled.

I found myself frowning. Hadn't Cally told me that she was against the deal? Why was she working with the developer? Someone was lying.

"You can't stop progress," Blackwell said. "You always fail. Money is the great incentive. You have to remember, the great majority of people don't much care for anyone but themselves, and if they can make money by crawling over someone else to get ahead, they'll do it."

Raj's face and neck turned an alarming shade of red. "I refuse to believe that."

Blackwell laughed. "And that's why you will always be on the losing team."

"I don't believe that either," I spoke up. "There are a lot of people who want to do the right thing, even if it costs them something personally."

Blackwell turned to me. "Who's this?"

I straightened my shoulders. "I'm Fiona Knox of Duncreigan."

Blackwell quirked his eyebrow at Raj. "Another one of your naïve environmentalist students?"

"Hardly," Raj said. "She's Ian MacCallister's American goddaughter."

Blackwell studied me with interest. "And do you find this place to be beautiful, Miss Knox?" Again Blackwell's eyebrows went up.

"I do," I said. "I much prefer it condo-free."

He shrugged as if my opinion was of no concern. "Mr. Kapoor," he said, turning back to Raj, "you and your merry little band of protestors can stay here all day and all night and freeze to death. It makes little difference to me, but I am telling you, when this deal finally does go through—and it will—you will never set foot on this coast again."

Raj opened and closed his mouth.

Blackwell smiled as if he knew that he had finally gotten the best of his rival and enjoyed the victory immensely. He nodded at me. "Welcome to Scotland, Miss Knox."

Despite myself, I shivered at his icy tone. If he had been a snake, his tongue would have flicked out of his mouth at me.

"Tyrant!" one of the twins shouted after him as he walked back to his giant pickup truck. "Tyrant!" she repeated, and this time her comrades joined in.

Raj said nothing. It appeared that he was still absorbing the shock of the encounter even after Blackwell had driven away.

I touched Raj's arm. "Raj, are you all right?"

He blinked at me, and then with a frown deeply etched on his face, he nodded. "Yes, I'm fine. I can't let Blackwell boss me around. He might have money on his side, but I have conviction. I also have right on my side."

The three students came over to us.

"Are you joining our protest?" Seth asked.

"I wanted to see this place while I still could."

"Hopefully, you will be able to see it for years to come," one of the twins said.

While I spoke with the students, Raj walked to the cliff's edge and looked out. "Fiona," he shouted over his shoulder. "Come here and look at what's at stake."

I followed him to the edge of the cliff. The students were on my heels. As I walked, the spongy ground gave some under my step. More spiny gorse clung to the edge of the cliff, holding the soil in place and stopping the ever-threatening risk of erosion.

A weathered bench overlooked the sea, but none of us made a move to sit on it.

Waves crashed into the cliff, leaving a thin layer of foamy, white bubbles in their wake. The bubbles soon dissipated just in time for the next wave to hit. The scent of salt water, seaweed, and fish attacked my nose.

Seabirds flew in and around the cliffs and squawked at one another. Most of them were seagulls, but I spotted the stilted flight of a puffin that was making its way home from fishing in the sea. I watched the puffin until it flew out of sight. My uncle had told me that those birds would fly for hundreds of miles in search of fish to feed the chicks that they left behind on the cliffs, and that the mother and father puffin always took turns feeding the chick until it was old enough to leave its rocky nest. It seemed impossible to me that the little bird could make such a journey with its awkward little wings. At this time of year, the birds were returning to the Scottish cliff to nest. Perhaps there weren't any nests on this very cliff, but I couldn't help wondering what impact this new development would have on the puffins and other birds who traveled by this place on their long journey home.

The salt spray misted my face as another large wave crashed against the cliff. To my right, I had a clear view of the harbor. However, from this vantage point, the fishing vessels looked like children's bath toys bobbing in the water.

Below me the black rock was jagged. It looked climbable, but only a fool would try it with the waves coming with such force. As I looked down, pieces of my dream came back to me. I felt the jagged rock against my palms as I grappled for a foothold on the slick surface, and the faceless man behind me was there.

A strong hand grabbed my arm. "Hey, careful there," Seth said. "You almost went over the cliff. I know you want to get a good look at it, but you should be more careful. That's the second time one of us had to catch you and stop you from falling in the water, and trust me, falling from this height onto those rocks would be a much worse fate than taking a cold dip in the harbor." He pulled me away from the edge.

I was breathing heavily, and my heart felt like it was beating a mile a minute. I placed a hand to my chest. Raj and the students all stared at me.

Cara cocked her head. "Are you okay? You're not going to be sick, are you?"

I shook my head, doing my best to regain control over my breathing. "I'm fine. This place is so beautiful. I guess I was overwhelmed by idea that the village will no longer be able to take in this view."

The students nodded at my answer, and I knew that I had said the right thing to distract them.

"We all feel the same way," Raj said. "I have an idea. Let's return to the village and regroup. I could go for a bite of breakfast at the pub."

"I can always eat," Seth said.

The girls agreed.

Raj and the trio headed to their cars, but before I followed them, I peered over the edge of the cliff once more, half-expecting the memory of my dream to crash over me again like waves against the rock. It did not.

Chapter Thirty-Three

The students spoke excitedly about what they would eat at the Twisted Fox. It sounded to me like Seth planned to eat everything Lee MacGill had on his menu.

We walked into the pub, and all the usual suspects were there. Lee was at the bar, taking orders. Popeye and his cronies were beside the large hearth, sharing tales, with grouchy Jock perched on a barstool.

In addition to these fixtures, the dining area of the pub was packed with villagers who were there for a hearty Scottish breakfast. Two young waitresses wove around the tables, carrying trays of tea and scones as well as beans, roasted tomatoes, and black pudding. This last was a sausage made with animal fat, pork blood, and oatmeal. I had never worked up the nerve to try it, and I hoped that I would stay a coward in this case.

"There's a table," Cara said, and she pointed at the corner of the room not too far from where Jock sat at the end of the bar. I inwardly groaned. Of course, the only available table in the place would be right next to him. Jock glared at me as Raj, the students, and I settled in our seats.

Lee walked over to our table and smiled at me. "I see you're making new friends, Fiona."

I smiled in return, feeling more at ease now that Lee was there. Jock could shoot daggered looks at me all he wanted. I wasn't going to let it bother me, or so I told myself.

"I took Fiona out to see the land that Alastair was trying to sell," Raj said.

Lee's brows knit together. "Oh really?"

"Have you been out there to see it?" I asked the bartender.

Lee looked down at me. "I've been there, sure. I bet everyone in this room has. It's a good place to visit in the village, and a common place for teenage couples to get away for some alone time." He waggled his eyebrows at me.

"I bet," I said, rolling my eyes.

"But I don't go out there much anymore. Haven't been in years. I much prefer to be here inside my pub. This is my spot. I may be a Scotsman, but I much prefer the indoors, with a fresh pint of beer and a warm fire. Not that I have the luxury of enjoying either very much while trying to keep this place up and running." He removed a small notebook and a pencil from the back pocket of his jeans. "What can I get you?"

"Tea and a scone for me," I said.

"No black pudding?" he asked.

I shook my head.

He grinned. "We will turn you into a real Scot yet. When you eat black pudding, you will earn that title."

I wasn't sure the title was worth it, but I didn't voice this opinion.

Raj and the three students placed their orders with Lee. I noted that none of them had ordered black pudding either.

Seth stood up. "I've got to hit the loo." He got up from the table and went to the left, around the bar.

The twins wrinkled their matching noses.

Raj and the girls chatted about the posters they planned to make for the protest, and I stood up. "I'll be right back." I didn't wait for them to reply, and I went in the direction that Seth had gone.

The pub was much larger than I had at first thought. The main room was an L-shape. I followed the ell to a doorway in the back, over which a sign read "Toilets," and just in case I was uncertain what the word meant, a picture of a toilet accompanied the words on the sign. I went through the door into a narrow and dark hallway, which I doubted looked much different from when it had been built in the very late eighteenth century, with the exception of one electric light, a naked bulb that hung form a loose fixture in the ceiling.

When my eyes adjusted to the dim light, I spotted another sign directing me to where the toilets were. Rounding a corner, I heard a trill of laughter come down the hallway. I followed it and found a narrow doorway that led into the pub's kitchen.

I peeked inside the kitchen. A man stood at the stove, stirring something that looked like porridge. I grimaced. I had never taken to Scottish porridge. My father loved it and said that it reminded him of his childhood. Growing up, my sister and I had teased him that he'd been raised like Oliver Twist, always begging for more.

Another sign pointed me in the direction of the toilets around yet another corner. I was starting to wonder if I should have left Reese's Pieces to mark my path like E.T. did in the movie.

I practically bumped into Seth as he was coming out of the restroom.

He pulled up short. "Oh, sorry."

He made a move to step around me, but I blocked his path in the narrow hallway. "I need to talk to you."

His brows knit together. "About the protest?"

"No." I shook my head. "It's about your great-uncle, Hamish, and how you have been lying to him."

Seth paled. "Did you tell him I dropped out of medical school?"

"Not yet. What are you doing with all that money?"

He pressed his thin lips into a line. "That's none of your business."

"Then you give me no choice but to tell Hamish that you have been lying to him this entire time."

He leaned toward me. "Are you threatening me?"

I crossed my arms. "Maybe."

"You can't do that."

I shrugged. "You can either tell me or Chief Inspector Craig."

"Craig? Why would I tell Craig?"

"Because all of this is related to Alastair's murder. Craig almost arrested your great-uncle last night for the murder of Alastair Croft, over the money that he gave you. The chief inspector would have arrested him too, if I hadn't stopped him."

"That's unbelievable. Uncle Hamish would never hurt anyone." His mouth fell open.

"You and I both know that, but the police don't. If you didn't use it for medical school, what did you do with the money, Seth? You have to tell me."

He leaned against the cool stone wall, and his face was flushed. "I had some debts that needed to be paid."

"What kind of debts?"

"I started playing cards while I was at university, and it got worse in medical school. I sort of lost control of it."

"You're a gambler," I said.

"Not anymore!" he cried. "I realized what I was doing was meaningless, and I found Raj and this protest. I've given up cards and put all my energy into the protest." He paused. "But I still have to pay back the people I owe, or bad things could happen."

"Who do you have to pay back?"

"I'm not answering that." He glared at me. "Will you tell my great-uncle?"

I shook my head. "I don't know, but I have to tell Craig."

He stared at me angrily. "You promised that you wouldn't."

I shook my head. "I never did."

"You're just like every other liar that I've ever met. You're just like . . ."

"Just like who?" I asked.

He didn't answer and instead pushed past me, hurrying down the narrow corridor.

After Seth stomped away, I must have made a wrong turn, because I couldn't find the kitchen, which was my marker to return to the main room of the pub. Instead, I found myself in another hallway. At the end of the hallway was a door. I was about to hurry toward it, when it opened. Jock stepped out. He scowled at the ground. I jumped back into the hallway from where I'd come and pressed myself against the wall. I moved out of his line of sight just in time, because he stomped down the hallway away from me. I let out a sigh of relief when he didn't turn down the hallway where I was hiding, but kept going straight.

After a minute of listening to my heart beat out of my chest, I peeked back down the hallway. There was no sign of Jock or anyone else. I debated heading in the direction that Jock had gone because I assumed that it would lead me back to the pub, but curiosity got the best of me, and I went back to the doorway where he had appeared.

I opened the door and was disappointed when I found myself peering into a storage closet, a rather large one. The shelves of the closet were lined with dozens upon dozens of bottles of alcohol, many of which I didn't recognize at all. However, I did see on the shelf a bottle of the Scotch that Cally had given me the day before. I decided that, after my disastrous sip of it back at the law office, I'd give the Scotch a wide berth.

Something bright yellow caught my eye. It was sticking out from under one of the shelves.

I picked up a bright yellow piece of sticker. It said, "Refill date: 20 April" and ended with the year.

Refill? I wondered. *Refill of what?* It could be anything. Lee was running a pub, for goodness sakes. He probably had to order and reorder supplies constantly. I took a closer look at the little scrap of label, and read "Tan" on it. I didn't know if *Tan* was the whole word or the beginning of another word.

"What are you doing back here?" a male voice asked from behind me.

I jumped a foot into the air and bumped into one of the shelves holding the liquor. Thankfully, I caught the bottle of gin before it hit the floor. With my heart in my throat, I set it back on the shelf and turned to see who was behind me.

Lee stood in the doorway of the storage closet, staring at me. He took a step back as I stumbled out of the closet, shoving the scrap of label into the pocket of my jacket. "Oh, I'm sorry. I got turned around when I was coming out of the restroom."

He frowned. "If you're trying to find your way back to the pub, you should have turned right out of the toilets, not left."

I gave him an apologetic smile. "I've never had a great sense of direction."

He seemed to relax and smiled in return. He stepped into the storage closet and moved to a bottle of whiskey. "Let me just grab these, and I can lead you out."

"Thanks, Lee," I said. "It seems that you're always saving me."

He grinned. "It's a bartender's duty to make sure that the customers can make it back to the bar safely. That's how we make our money." He grabbed a bottle of tonic as well, and holding the three bottles in the crook of his left arm, he stepped out of the storage closet. He removed a key from the right hip pocket of his jeans and locked the door.

When he caught me staring at him, he said, "This door is supposed to always be locked because it's where all the alcohol is stored, some of which is very expensive. You have seen some of my clientele. I wouldn't put it past Jock, for example, to come back here and help himself to a bottle or two if he was so inclined. One of the waitresses must have left it unlocked. I'll have to remind them to remember to lock it."

The mention of Jock put me on edge, but I didn't think

he'd been in the storage room to steal liquor. There had been nothing in his hands when he'd left. I considered mentioning what I had seen to Lee, but thought better of it.

With his hands full, Lee told me which direction we were headed with a nod of his head before making his way down the hallway in the direction Jock had gone just a few minutes earlier.

I followed Lee through yet another hallway, and we popped out on the other side of the bar from where Raj and the students were eating breakfast.

"We have to do something. We have a killer in our midst!" a voice shouted just as soon as Lee and I stepped through the doorway.

Kipling stood in front of the bar in his volunteer police uniform, waving his arms, and by the looks of it, very few were paying him a second thought.

Chapter Thirty-Four

"Neil Craig and the Aberdeen force aren't taking the murder of Alastair Croft seriously enough. If I had overseen the case, the murder would have been solved by now, but Neil and his colleagues are doing everything that they can to thwart my part in the investigation."

I glanced around the pub as Kipling built his case against Craig and the entire Aberdeen police force. Only half of the crowded room was listening, with bemused expressions on their faces. The other half was ignoring Kipling completely and tucking into their large Scottish breakfasts. That made me think of my own scone, which I was certain must be cold by now.

Lee groaned and carried the bottles behind the bar. He handed them to a waitress who was standing there, before coming back around the bar. "Kipling, it's far too early in the morning for shouting about revolution."

Kipling spun around to face Lee. "Lee, you cannot let your friendship with Neil cloud your judgment. He's not doing his utmost to catch the culprit of this crime."

Lee shook his head. "I'm certain that he is. Neil Craig is a good cop, and it will serve you well to remember that he is one of our own."

Kipling looked as if he wanted to argue, when a female voice chimed in. "Oh, I know for certain that Neil Craig can do no wrong in this village."

I turned my attention away from Lee and Kipling and spotted Aileen Croft standing in front of the door.

"It was very clear who the village was going to side with when I filed for divorce from him all those years ago, which is exactly why I had to leave Bellewick forever. I wouldn't have even come back now if I hadn't been forced to by these unfortunate circumstances. But my brother would have wanted me to return and collect my rightful inheritance after he died. I know he would."

"Are you admitting why you came back, Aileen—for the inheritance? Is that the only reason?" This question came from Jock at the bar. His lip curled in disgust. For some reason, his obvious dislike of Aileen made me feel better. It told me that his animosity wasn't just reserved for me. It was also possible that the pub regular just hated women, especially strong women, as a rule.

"Did you kill your brother for that money?" Jock asked.

A gasp rushed across the room. Everyone seemed to be shocked that Jock would just ask her outright like that whether she'd killed her brother. Everyone was shocked except for Aileen herself. She simply laughed. "I know that's what you all would like to be true. I never was the village darling."

"You were other things to the village," a male voice muttered.

Aileen's eyes narrowed, and she scanned the room, looking

for the source of the comment. When no one made eye contact with her, she went on: "I will have you know that Neil has cleared me of any wrongdoing. I was at work at my job in Wales when my brother was killed. Neil called my employer and confirmed this. As much as all of you would like me to be the killer, it is impossible. I was nowhere near Bellewick when Alastair died."

Inwardly, I sighed. On the one hand, I was glad that Craig had proven Aileen to be innocent of the crime because that narrowed down the list of suspects, but on the other, I was disappointed for the same reason. I hadn't had much of a list of murder suspects to begin with. In my mind, the most likely killer, because he had the strongest motive, was Raj, and I didn't want Raj to be the killer. I liked him.

I glanced over to where the Indian man sat with the three students. The four of them had their heads together as if they were planning their next strategy to stop Blackwell from buying the land.

Another prime suspect for me was Jock McBride, but as far as I knew, he didn't have a motive, although I found his conversation with Blackwell highly suspicious. I wanted him to be the killer just because I didn't like him. I knew that it wasn't fair or kind, but there it was.

The door to the pub opened again, and Chief Inspector Neil Craig filled the doorway. My heart skipped a beat for a moment as the sun backlit his reddish-brown hair, making it look like it was ablaze. The chief inspector scanned the room quickly in a practiced move. His eyes stopped on me, and I had to remind myself to keep breathing.

"Just the man we've been speaking about," Aileen said in

mock cheer. "Neil, will you tell these kind villagers that I have been exonerated in my brother's murder."

"You aren't guilty of your brother's murder," he said in a clipped voice. He stepped all the way inside the pub.

She gave him a cold smile. "It seems to me that you are implying that I might be guilty of something else, dearest, and this to a woman you once claimed to love. You should really give up your bitterness."

Craig scowled in return. He walked through the pub and stopped in front of me. I could feel the eyes of everyone in the pub on us.

"Fiona," the chief inspector began, "I'm glad that you are here. Can I speak to you outside for a moment?"

I nodded and tried not to let it bother me that everyone in the pub was watching as he led me out of the pub. When we were outside, Craig took a few steps away from the door.

I followed him. "I'm glad you pulled me out. I have something to tell you." I told him what Seth had revealed to me about his gambling debts.

He ran a hand through his thick brown hair. "What did I tell you about not getting involved?"

"I was just asking a question," I said.

"Please stop asking questions, for your own safety and for my blood pressure."

I scowled.

The chief inspector shook his head. "What you found out about Seth is interesting, and I will follow up. But first, I want to visit Duncreigan to look at the garden again. You mentioned that you wanted to be there."

When he said this, I realized that he'd promised to visit the garden the day before but had never shown. "Why didn't you go there last night when you came to the cottage to . . . ?" I trailed off because I had almost said "to arrest Hamish." I stopped myself in the nick of time. The fewer villagers who knew that Hamish was being considered for arrest, the better.

He glanced at the pub. "It was too dark, and as you know, other things came up."

I nodded. "I would like to be there. I rode into the village with Raj," I said. "If you don't mind giving me a ride, I'll come with you."

He nodded.

"Let me just go tell Raj that I'm leaving." I said.

He nodded again.

I hurried back inside the pub to Raj and the university students. I left several pounds on the table, covering the cost of my scone and tea, and took the scone with me. Seth refused to look at me when I told them that I was leaving. Raj and the twins were so focused on their conversation about protest strategy, they hardly noticed that I had gone.

When I returned to Craig, he was speaking with Lee.

"I don't think you have anything to worry about. Kipling is all bluster," Lee told the police officer.

"I'm not worried," Craig said.

Kipling turned red in the face. "I will have you know that I am keeping a close eye on this investigation. If you make one false step, I will call you out on it."

"You do that, Kip," Craig said, seemingly unconcerned.

I removed again from my pocket the tag I'd found in the

storage room. *I should just throw it away,* I thought. It was just a piece of a sticker—a sticker to exactly what, I had no idea.

"Fiona, are you ready?" Craig asked.

I looked up from the sticker, hidden in the palm of my hand, and dipped my head in assent.

Craig nodded at Lee before heading for the pub's front door.

Instead of tossing it, I tucked the scrap of paper back into my pocket and followed Craig out the door.

Chapter Thirty-Five

Craig eyed the scone in my hand as he started his police jeep. "Try not to get too many crumbs on my upholstery, please." He winked at me to let me know that he was teasing.

I held the pastry out to him. "Would you like half?"

He shook his head.

I broke off a piece of scone and popped it in my mouth. Even though it was cold, the pillowy pastry melted on my tongue.

During the short drive to Duncreigan, I peppered Craig with questions about the investigation into Alastair's death, but he ignored or deflected each one of them. Finally, when we were within a mile of the cottage, I gave up entirely.

Craig parked his jeep next to my rental car, just short of the cottage. As the jeep's tires settled in the gravel driveway, Hamish, with Duncan on his shoulder, came around the side of the cottage.

I opened the passenger side door and got out. Hamish stood in front of me and wrung his wrinkled hands. "Have you come to arrest me again?"

"No, Hamish," Craig said.

"The chief inspector needs to take another look at the garden," I said.

I could have been wrong, but I thought I saw Hamish pale ever so slightly. It was hard to tell since his skin was so weather-beaten by the wind and sun.

Hamish nodded. "Very well."

I felt Hamish's eyes on our backs, all the way up and over the hill toward the garden, until we were out of his line of sight.

When the walls of the garden came into view, I marveled at the fact that I could no longer see the stone walls through the ivy. The door was completely hidden.

"Where's the door?" Craig asked.

I grinned up at him. "Let me lead the way, Chief Inspector."

He chuckled. "Fine, Miss Knox, lead on."

With assurance, I stopped at the place along the wall where I knew the door would be. I slid my hand through the tangle of vines and waxy leaves to the door handle. At the chief inspector's direction, I had been leaving the garden unlocked, so I didn't bother removing from my pocket either of the skeletons keys, mine or the one I had discovered in the garden the day before.

I pushed down on the door latched and stepped through the entrance. When I was inside the garden, I turned and put my hand back through the open door and gestured for Craig to come through.

To my surprise, I felt Craig take hold of my hand and allow me to pull him into the garden.

When the chief inspector had safely cleared the door, he gave my hand a small squeeze before letting it go.

I stepped away from Craig on the pretense of checking the garden's progress. It wasn't much of a pretense. The progress was amazing. There was no mistake about it. The garden was alive again. Bright yellow and iridescent white daffodils, which had been mere buds earlier that morning, were in full bloom. An English robin twittered and hopped from branch to branch in the willow tree, which was also in full bloom.

"I'm no expert on plants," Craig said, taking in the lovely scene, "but something very strange is going on here."

"Hamish says it's me." I squatted next to a hyacinth and inhaled its perfume.

The chief inspector's head snapped in my direction. "You're doing this?"

I stood up, regretting that I had even mentioned it, but it was too late to take back my words now. "Hamish claims that I'm the one who brought the garden back to life. He says it began to grow again because I'm in here at Duncreigan."

"The rumor about this garden being magical is true?" he asked. "I always thought that it might be."

"Is that why you and Alastair tried to steal the menhir?"

He ran his hand through his hair. "Maybe. It was a stupid idea, and it was far too big for us to move. I would have forgotten about the attempted prank long ago if Hamish didn't remind me now and again. That man can hold a grudge."

I thought about that a minute. "Do you think he had a grudge against Alastair because of the money and killed him?"

"It's possible."

I shook my head. "No. It's impossible for me to believe that kind, old man could hurt anyone, and he certainly wouldn't move a body from the murder scene to my godfather's garden, only to incriminate himself even more."

"You have a point there. The moving of the body is problematic," Craig admitted. "I know that Hamish cares about this garden. It does seem odd that he would move the body here. We know Alastair died in his home." He paused. "I can tell you care about the garden too, but how are you connected to it?"

"I don't know how I'm related to this garden or how I am connected to it," I replied. "I know that the garden was dead when I arrived, and this is my third day in Scotland, and it is like this. That's all I know."

Craig stared at me for a long moment. I stared back. His deep brown eyes seemed to scrutinize every corner of my face as if he were looking for some evidence that I was lying. I wasn't, so he didn't find anything. Finally, he dropped his gaze, and a small part of me felt victorious for the first time since I had met him.

"I need to go back to where the body was found." He started toward the hedge.

As we came around the side of the hedge, I half-expected to see the fox with the blue eyes there, perhaps with another clue in his mouth, but he was nowhere to be seen.

Craig stopped in front of the menhir and tilted his head to the side. The crime scene tape was askew and clearly mangled.

"Before you go thinking someone tampered with the crime scene, I need to tell you something," I said.

He glanced over his shoulder at me. "What's that?"

"That was me."

He turned all the way around. "What was you?"

"The mangled crime scene. I kinda sorta fell on the standing stone." I did my best to sound sheepish.

He pressed his lips together as if he was trying to hide the urge to laugh. "You 'kinda sorta fell on the standing stone'?"

"Okay, fine." I held my hands aloft. "I fell on the standing stone. It was an accident. If it makes you feel better I was justly punished for my clumsiness." I showed him the wound on my finger. "One of the rose thorns got me."

Craig took my right hand in his and inspected my finger. The mark where the thorn had dug into my flesh was barely visible. I doubted that anyone would know it was there if I didn't mention it. I doubted I'd know it was there if I didn't feel it throb every so often.

The chief inspector lifted my hand to his mouth and kissed the tip of my finger where the thorn had pierced it. His bristly whiskers tickled my skin. A shiver ran all the way down my spine.

He released my hand. "It doesn't make me feel better that you were hurt in any way, but my diagnosis is that you'll live."

I swallowed. It might be true that I would survive the thorn attack. The kiss was a completely different story.

"I have something for you," Craig said and took a step closer to me.

I braced myself and looked up at him. Was the chief inspector going to kiss me? Did I want him to kiss me? I took a step back. No, I didn't. No, I didn't think I wanted him to. I was pretty sure that I didn't. Maybe.

Craig put his hand in the breast pocket of his sport coat. He came out with an American passport. "This is for you."

I blinked at him. Of all the things that the chief inspector could have given me at that moment, my passport hadn't even been a possibility. For some reason, I felt disappointed.

He held the passport out to me. "Don't you want it? Because I can keep it if you don't."

I took the passport from his outstretched hand, taking care not to touch him as I retrieved it. I opened the passport and looked at the photo to confirm that it was mine. It really was a horrible picture. I knew that all passport photos, just like driver's license photos, were, as a rule, bad, but I hated the thought of the chief inspector looking at this particularly terrible photograph of me. "You're giving this back to me. I thought you meant to keep it until the end of the investigation."

"I had no reason to keep it any longer. You aren't a suspect. You never really were because you were nowhere close to here when Alastair died." He shrugged and then his face broke into a grin. "I'll turn around if you have to stick it back inside your bra or wherever you keep it."

I frowned at him. "It was in my money belt that I wore while traveling through the airports," I said as my face grew blazing hot. I shoved the passport into the back pocket of my jeans. "Thank you for returning this. I really needed it. I have to go home in two weeks."

"Oh?" he said, sounding as if he was doing his best to sound disinterested in my travel plans. "You're leaving Scotland?"

"For a little while at least. My sister is graduating from

college, and I have to go back to Tennessee for her graduation. If I miss graduation, Isla will run me up the nearest flagpole."

He laughed. "She sounds tough."

"You don't know the half of it."

"Tough women must run in your family," he said.

"I wouldn't call myself a tough woman," I argued.

"I would," he said, as if his opinion on the issue was all that was needed to make it true.

My phone beeped. I checked the screen. The text was from Isla.

"What is it?" he asked.

"My sister sent me a text." I didn't look up from the small screen.

"The threatening one?" he asked with a bit of teasing in his voice.

"I only have one sister, so yes, the threatening one." I tapped the screen to open the text message. It contained a photo.

It read, "I found the letter." That was all.

Chapter Thirty-Six

There were no exclamation points, acronyms, or emojis in my sister's text, which were usually the majority of my sister's messages. When I got full, correctly spelled words from Isla, I knew that she was upset. The photo would tell me why.

Instinctively, I stepped away from Craig, not that he could read my phone's screen from where he stood, but I wasn't taking any chances.

> *My dearest Fiona,*
>
> *If you are reading this letter, it means something happened to me on the battlefield. I am sorry to leave you, my dearest, but I have always felt the deepest need to serve my Queen and Country.*

I felt my throat begin to close up as I read my godfather's words. It was the letter, the letter that Uncle Ian promised Hamish he would send me. It was real. I took a deep, shuddering breath and continued reading.

I don't regret this happening. I died for a purpose, and so many others don't get that chance. My only regret is leaving you without telling you everything you need to know. The cottage and the garden are yours now. This is both a gift and, my dear one, a responsibility. Your most important work now will be caring for the garden at Duncreigan. It is the work that you were born to do. I knew this from the moment that you were born. However, it became even more apparent to me when you were a small child and had an immediate love for plants and growing things. As you grew, so did your love of gardening and flowers. It was more evidence for me that you would naturally be the person that I would select to be the Keeper of the Garden after I was gone.

The first Keeper was my ancestor Baird MacCallister, whom I have told you about, and his portrait hangs over the fireplace in the cottage. Hamish will tell you the story of Baird, but please know that the magic he discovered in this place is real. It comes from the land, from the menhir, and from the rose. Now, it will also come from you.

My hands shook as I read the last line. The magic would come from me? Was that even possible, and what did that really mean? None of this was making sense, just like nothing had made any sense since I'd arrived in Duncreigan.

Dear one, I do wish that I could have been with you longer to tell you and make things clearer. Just know that this is important work, very important work, and you are a successor of a long line of proud and talented gardeners who have cared for Duncreigan before. Hamish knew my grandfather, my father, and me. He will be the one you should turn to when you are unsure about something in the garden, but remember, the garden needs you to tend it, not Hamish. He can give you advice, but the garden will only thrive if you give it the attention it deserves.

You are gifted in caring for plants, but this garden is unlike any that you have ever cared for. As the Keeper, there are rules you must follow that my father told me about, just as his father told him, going all the way back to Baird. Follow those rules, and the garden will bestow a gift on you.

"Fiona?" Craig touched my arm, and I jumped two feet into the air. "What's wrong? You look like you've seen a ghost."

Seen a ghost? No. Heard from one? Maybe.

Craig stepped over to my side. "Is everything all right? Did your sister have some type of graduation emergency?"

I stared at him.

"Why are you crying?" he asked. The teasing sound left his voice. "Is it bad news? Is your sister all right? Did something bad happen at home?"

I touched my cheek, and it felt damp. I hadn't known that I had been crying. I blinked, and tears spilled over and slid down my pale cheeks. I wiped the tears away. "My sister is fine." I walked away from him toward the willow tree and continued to read.

Rule #1: It's important that you and the garden stay connected. You must visit it as much as possible in your early days. In time, you will be able to leave it for longer periods, as I did.

Rule #2: The garden should be cared for and treated like any other garden. You must water, weed, and feed it. The better cared for the garden is, the stronger your connection with it will grow. Hamish will help you as he helped me.

Rule #3: The menhir and the rose are the heart of the garden and the source of the magic. They were there first, and everything else grew up around them. They are your true connection to the magic. To know what the garden wants you to know, you must touch the stone. Do not approach this task lightly. You will see things that you may not want to see.

These are all the rules, dear one. Three simple but important rules, and remember, you cannot bend the garden to your will. It will only reveal to you what it wants you to see.

In time, you will learn how to use the garden to its full extent. The visions that it bestows are different for every Keeper.

Whatever the garden reveals to you, you must use that knowledge for good to help others. That is the deal that Baird struck with the sea, and the one that we must uphold at all costs.

Please know, dear Fiona, that I am proud of you for taking on this burden, but also know that I am sorry to

*give it to you as well. I know what a weight this can be.
I joined Her Majesty's army to escape it, but I could never
truly break free from the pull of the garden, even when I
was on the other side of the world. I wish that your life
could be freer, but for now until the end of it, you will be
tied to Duncreigan and the garden and this responsibility.
I know you will succeed. I have great faith in you.*

Love always, Uncle Ian

"Fiona?" Craig's voice was much gentler than before. "What is it?"

I blinked at him. "It's from my godfather."

"Ian is dead. How could he send you a text message?"

I blushed again, and not for the first time in front of the handsome police officer. "After he died, Uncle Ian instructed the army to mail two letters for him. One was sent to Hamish, and the other was sent to me. I never got my letter because I had left for Scotland before it arrived at my home in the United States. After I left Nashville, I had my American mail forwarded to my parents' farm out in the country. I asked my sister to go there and look for the letter. She found it and texted me a photo of it so that I could see what it says."

"And what does it say?" he asked.

"That all the rumors about this place are true. It is magical," I said, not even knowing why I was telling him this, but knowing that I had to tell someone. Because if I did, it would sound less crazy in my head, or at least that is what I hoped would happen. "This garden is magical, and I have the magical gift to care for it just like Hamish said I did. Hamish was right."

"Do you believe it?" He studied me.

Ignoring Craig, I walked over to the standing stone and tore the crime scene tape from it. For the first time, I took a very close look at it. At first sight, it appeared to be a plain piece of granite, but on closer examination I could see faded carvings in the stone. There was just one carving, a three-prong spiral that was repeated over and over again. I recognized it as an ancient Celtic symbol.

During one of my visits, I think when I was about eleven or twelve, Uncle Ian had made a game up in order to teach me the Celtic symbols that were engraved in ancient stones and painted in caves throughout what is now Great Britain and Ireland. I remembered that he called this one a triple spiral, or a triskele. They were more common in Ireland than they were in Scotland. I wracked my brain, searching for whatever Uncle Ian had told me about them.

When Christianity had come to Scotland, the triple spiral had come to represent the trinity, but before that, it always represented three elements like birth, life, and death—or creation, preservation, and destruction.

"Fiona, what is going on?" Craig asked.

Still ignoring him, I stared at the stone, and the urge to touch it was overpowering. Finally, I gave in and placed my hand on the stone, which threw me back into my dream.

Chapter Thirty-Seven

"Fiona! Fiona!" I was on the cliff again, and Chief Inspector Craig was yelling at me. I turned back to look at him, and a strong hand shook me awake.

I was back in the garden once more, and Craig's face was just inches from mine. I could see the creases in his lips, he was so close.

"What the hell just happened?" he demanded. "Where did you go?"

"I have to go back to the cliff," I said.

"The cliff? What are you talking about?"

I turned and hurried around the hedge to the garden exit. Craig grabbed me by my wrist before I could get very far. His stride was more than twice mine, and I would never be able to beat the man in a footrace. "Tell me what is going on."

"I had a vision when I touched the stone. I guess that's the best way to describe it."

"A vision of what?"

"Of a dream that I've been having. It's always the same. I'm on the cliff."

"What cliff?" he asked, sounding increasingly more bewildered by my vague responses.

"The cliff Alastair was trying to sell. His death is tied to that place. Somehow I know that it's the motive for his murder."

"It is the most likely motive," Craig agreed. "There is a lot at stake if the land deal goes through. So many people will be upset either way the decision finally is made. If the deal goes through, it will hurt the village financially, as well as obscure its view of the sea."

"It's more than that," I said. "His death has something to do with the land itself. I have to go there and see for myself."

"I don't think that's such a good idea," the chief inspector said.

"It may not be, but I'm still going."

"I'm going with you." His tone left no room for argument.

"Of course, you're coming with me. You are part of this too." I didn't tell him that he was part of this because I had seen him in the vision. I broke free from his grasp and ran for the garden's door.

· In the time that it took us to run back to the cottage, the weather had changed dramatically. The blue sky and fluffy clouds were gone, and the sky grew darker by the second. To the east, it appeared that a storm raged somewhere over the North Sea. I knew that Craig must have taken note of the change in the weather, and I was grateful when he didn't try to talk me out of going to the cliff.

"I'm driving," Craig said, marching to his jeep.

"Good," I said and followed him.

The ride to the cliff was short, and when we arrived, unlike that morning, there was no one there. The sky was almost black when I opened the door and exited the jeep. The wind threw me back against the car door. I fought against it to shut the door.

Pieces of yellow grouse that had been torn from the low-growing bushes flew around me, and the seabirds that had been there in the morning were all gone. Unlike me, the gulls and puffins knew better than to linger along the jagged coast with a storm coming.

I headed for the cliff and the place where I had seen some semblance of a trail earlier in the day.

"What are you doing?" Craig shouted into the wind as I took my first step from the grassy edge onto the bare black rock.

"I have to see what's there. The dream is telling me to look," I shouted back in order to be heard. Then I kept going.

"You can't go down there," he protested.

"I have to," I argued. "That was part of the vision."

"You have to be insane."

I didn't bother to argue with him because I was afraid that he might be right. I was a little ways down the cliff when I heard Craig follow me.

"This is a bad idea," he shouted. "The sky is going to open up at any moment."

Before he could even finish his sentence, the rain came, not in a sprinkle or a drizzle, but in sheets. At this point, the edge of the cliff that we had left was fifteen feet above my head.

And then it was just like the dream.

The cold salt spray hit my face like a barrage of tiny darts, and the harsh wind burned my skin until it was dry and chapped. My footing was unsure on the slick black rock, but I pressed on. With my stomach flattened against the sharp rocks and their jagged edges digging through the fabric of my jacket, I threw my right arm out and grappled for the next handhold. I found it. As secure as I could be with the handhold, I threw out my right foot. For the briefest of moments, it hovered in space, seeking any kind of traction. There was none. Below, it felt like the sea was calling me to let go and fall in. It would be easier. But then my foot found the rock edge, and the rest of my body followed as I slid along, pressing myself up against the rock.

Behind me Craig followed my lead, placing his own hands and feet in the places where mine had been. "We really shouldn't be doing this," he shouted into the wind. "Do you know how many people fall to their deaths from these cliffs? We should go back and find some professional rock climbers to look into this, preferably when it's not pouring rain."

I looked over my shoulder but couldn't see his face. "We can't turn back now. I can almost see it." As I said the words, I had a sense that what I was looking for was up ahead of me, just as it had been in the dream.

"It's not safe," Craig said. "I would never be dumb enough to climb down here if I weren't following you."

I looked back at him and pressed my right cheek into the rock, staring hard. "I never asked you to follow me."

"I'm not letting you die on my watch."

I turned my head again, taking care not to scrape my face

on the rocks. Then, I saw what I was looking for. It was an indentation in the side of the cliff, just like in my dream. A wave came in then, and water splashed my side. I was drenched, and the cold air coming off the North Sea chilled me to the marrow of my bones.

"Fiona!" Craig yelled. "Are you all right?"

I turned to yell back to him that I was fine just as I disappeared from his sight into the indentation in between the rocks.

I found myself in a cave, protected from the wind and rain. The only light to guide me was the dim beam that the storm permitted through the crevice in the rock I had just slid through.

I removed my cell phone from the inner pocket of my jacket and shone it on the cave floor, which was made of the same black rock that dotted the eastern coast of Scotland. It seemed that everything in the room was black. I ran the light back and forth along the floor, and to my surprise, it reflected off something metal. Whatever it was, it was small, and I had to run my weak beam over the same area three times before the glint of metal appeared again. When it did, I kept the beam trained onto it until I was able to reach it.

It was a coin, or I thought it was a coin. I bent over and picked it up. It was most definitely a coin, and a very old one at that. I rubbed dirt and grime away from the surface of the coin and found the weathered face.

Craig squeezed through the crack in the rocks. I shoved the coin into the inner pocket of my jacket. I needed to understand what I had discovered before I showed it to him.

"You could have told me that you found a cave," he yelled, his voice echoing off the walls.

"I'm so sorry." I walked over to him. "I guess I just got carried away with my discovery. Are you all right?"

He stared down at me, but I couldn't make out his expression because of the lack of light. "I am now that I know you're not dead."

"Sorry," I mumbled and stepped back from him. I realized that I was far too close for my own comfort, although the chief inspector wasn't complaining about it.

Craig pulled a pocket-sized flashlight from his coat pocket. Even though the flashlight could fit in the palm of his hand, the beam was powerful and gave off ten times the light that my phone's flashlight app did. I turned the app off and tucked the phone back into my pocket.

"You have a flashlight on you?" I asked.

He held it under his chin, Halloween style. "Yes, I have a flashlight. I'm a cop."

"Can you shine the light around, so we can see what we're dealing with?"

Craig did as I asked and shone the light around the cave in a systematic way. I was sure he did it exactly as he had been trained by the police force. Craig was a by-the-book sort of guy, which I found both frustrating and appealing, and which pretty much summed up how I felt about Craig altogether.

His beam moved into the north corner of the small cave and fell on a bright yellow cylinder. Craig kept the beam on the yellow cylinder as he walked toward it.

"What's that?" I asked.

"It's a tank for scuba diving, I think," he replied.

He crouched in front of it. "And it looks fairly new. I don't see the date on it for when it was last serviced."

"Do you scuba dive?" I asked.

He laughed. "No. But Aberdeen has a lot of scuba divers who work on the docks. Service men to boats, underwater welders—that sort of job. I've had some cases that involved them, so I know scuba equipment. I'll never actually do it, though."

I considered this.

"Why would a welder from Aberdeen leave his scuba gear here?"

He laughed. "I'm sure it doesn't belong to a welder. My guess is the gear was left here by a treasure seeker. Since it looks like new, I'd have to guess that they will be back. This equipment isn't cheap."

"A treasure seeker?"

He nodded. "Someone who dives for buried treasure. You know, the daredevil sort who jumps into the ocean in search of shipwrecks and the like."

"Like Baird's shipwreck?" I said quietly. The coin felt heavy in my pocket. I should tell Craig. I knew that I should tell him. I just couldn't bring myself to do it. I decided that I wanted to verify that it was a coin from Baird's ship before I told Craig. It would only require a short Internet search to confirm, and then I promised myself I would tell the chief inspector what I had found.

"Exactly like Baird's shipwreck," he replied. Craig shone the light on the tank and stopped the beam directly on a bright yellow sticker that was half torn away. The torn sticker looked like the matching half to the one in my pocket, which I had found at the Twisted Fox earlier in the day. Something nagged at the back of my mind about that torn sticker and that tank. I knew whatever it was, it was important. I just hoped that I would remember what it was in time.

Chapter Thirty-Eight

When the chief inspector and I returned to Duncreigan, we looked like drowned rats and smelled worse. I, however, was not going to mention that. Apparently, the chief inspector didn't have the same qualms because he said, "You smell awful."

"You're not a bed full of roses yourself," I remarked as I unlocked the cottage door.

He threw back his head and laughed, and I found myself smiling at him again. I wished that I would stop doing that, but it was become increasingly difficult.

Ivanhoe looked up from his spot by the low fire. When he saw that Duncan wasn't with us, he settled back into his nap. It seemed that the red squirrel was the only thing that could motivate the cat to move from his cozy bed.

There had been no sign of Hamish and Duncan in or outside the cottage when Craig and I returned from our cliff adventure. I guessed that they had gone to Hamish's cottage long before the rain began to fall.

"He looks like he's made himself right at home," Craig said.

"I'm starting to think that this is more his home than mine," I said. "I suspect that's just how he likes it too."

"I'm sure of it," the chief inspector agreed.

My teeth chattered. "I let the fire die down again." I rubbed my eyes. "I should have called the gas company this morning to turn the gas back on, so I can more easily heat the cottage. I keep forgetting."

"I have a pellet burner at my house in Aberdeen. It heats the entire house, and the pellets feed the fire on a timer. It's less expensive than natural gas, if you're trying to save money. If you purchased one, I could show you how it works," he offered.

I stared at him. "Would that be official police duties?"

"After what we have been through today, I think we are beyond official police duties, don't you?"

"Scaling a cliff in a storm was a bonding experience?" I asked.

"You could say that." He smiled at me.

I took a step back. "I'm going to go change. I'm sure Uncle Ian has something that you can wear."

He gave me a look. "Ian wasn't six five."

"True," I admitted. "But give me a moment, and I'll go see what I can find."

The chief inspector nodded and stared building up the fire again to warm the cottage. Something about the image made me smile, and I had to turn away. But I wasn't fast enough. I know that he saw the look on my face.

I hurried into my godfather's bedroom and changed quickly out of my wet clothing into yoga pants and an oversized sweater that fell to the middle of my thighs. Then, I began sorting thought my godfather's clothes, looking for something for Craig to wear that I thought had at least a chance of fitting the much larger man. Finally, I found an extra-large T-shirt and a pair of sweatpants in the back of one my godfather's dresser drawers. I carried them with me out of the bedroom.

"Here you go," I said and handed the clothes to the chief inspector.

Craig arched one of his red eyebrows. "And you think these are going to fit?"

"They are the best I have," I said as I shooed him into the bedroom.

In a minute, there was a crash inside the bedroom, and Craig swore.

"Everything okay in there?" I called through the door.

No response. However, I could hear Craig flailing around the room as he struggled to get dressed. Ivanhoe and I shared a look.

A moment later, Craig came out of my godfather's bedroom, wearing Uncle Ian's clothes. The sweat pants were about four inches too short for him, and the T-shirt looked like it had been painted on his body. I did my best not to stare. I failed. I covered my mouth to hold back the laughter.

He held out his arms and spun around, so that I got a full view of his outfit. "Go ahead and laugh about it."

I choked, unable to hold back the giggles that bubbled up in the back of my throat. "You look ridiculous!"

"I know I do, and if I hear that you told anyone about this, I will have you arrested." He dropped his arms.

"On what charge?" I wanted to know.

"Defamation of a police officer," he said, not missing a beat.

"Is it defamation even if it's true?"

"In my case, yes. You have to remember that I'm a very good cop."

"Oh, I've known that from the moment I met you," I said, holding his gaze perhaps a moment too long.

A strange expression crossed the chief inspector's face, and I looked away. I cleared my throat. "If I had a dryer, I would pop your clothes into it and dry them out, but I don't. It's on the long list of upgrades that I plan to make to the cottage if I stay."

"When will you make your decision?" he asked.

"I haven't decided," I said, chuckling at what I thought was my own witty answer.

Craig wasn't laughing with me. "For what it is worth, I think you should stay." His brown eyes held mine.

I stepped back and pretended to check the fire that Craig had expertly replenished while I was changing in my godfather's bedroom.

"Would you like something to eat?" I asked.

He smiled as if he understood that I wasn't ready for wherever this conversation could lead us. "No. It's getting late, and I should head back to Aberdeen. I have several reports that I have to file with the department before I call it a night."

"Oh," I said, surprised to find I was disappointed with his response. Never mind that all I had to offer him was the same that I had fed Hamish the night before: grilled cheese sandwiches and tomato soup. I shook off the feeling. "Let me get you a bag to put your wet things in." I went to the kitchen and came up with a shopping bag. I folded Craig's clothes and tucked them inside. "There," I said, as if I had accomplished something of great importance. I handed the bag to him.

He took it from me and put his soggy shoes back on his bare feet. There was nothing that I could do about the shoes. Uncle Ian hadn't left anything behind that would come even close to fitting his enormous feet.

Neil walked to the door and turned. "You are an interesting woman, Fiona Knox. I've never met anyone quite like you."

"I've never met anyone quite like you either, Chief Inspector Craig," I said in reply.

He smiled. "For what it's worth, your fiancé is an idiot. He doesn't know what he has lost."

My heart constricted. "Thank you," I said barely above a whisper. "I should have left him first. I would have been much happier if I had."

"I am guilty of this too," he said sadly.

"Aileen?" I asked.

He nodded.

The fire crackled in the fireplace.

"The truth is," Craig said, "most people show you who they are from the very start, but we can't see it because we're blinded by who we wish them to be."

His words burrowed into my heart and poked at the wound there. "I saw what wasn't there," I whispered.

He shook his head. "No, you saw what could be, what you wanted to be. You saw a dream. There is nothing wrong with dreaming." He walked toward me until he was standing just inches away. Then he leaned forward and kissed the top of my head. "Next time, find the man who matches the dream."

I swallowed and whispered, "Okay."

I watched Craig climb into his jeep and drive away in the dwindling rain. A dark form moved behind the single fir tree beside the driveway, and I jumped. "Who's there?"

There was no answer.

My heart felt like it was lodged inside my throat. "Show yourself." I could barely get out the words.

Just when I was about to slam the door and run back into the cottage to call Craig to ask him to come back, a voice said, "It's just me, lass."

I placed a hand on my chest. "Hamish, you nearly gave me a heart attack. What are you doing hiding out there in the rain?"

He stepped around the tree and walked to the cottage, taking what shelter he could under the small overhang above the cottage's front door. "I just came to check on you, lass. To make sure you were all right." He paused. "But I saw that you were not alone . . ." he trailed off.

"The chief inspector was here as part of the investigation into Alastair Croft's murder," I said. "We were discussing the case."

"He was wearing Master Ian's clothes," he said.

A blush ran up my neck, across my face, and into my hairline, but I refused to explain why the chief inspector had borrowed my godfather's clothing. "Where's Duncan?" I asked when I noticed the squirrel wasn't in his usual spot on Hamish's shoulder.

"He decided to stay home. He doesn't care for the rain."

Hamish smiled slightly. "He doesn't like to get his fur wet. His red coat is his pride and joy." He cleared his throat.

I stepped back in the doorway. "Why don't you come in from the rain?"

He shook his head. "Now that I have seen with my own eyes that you are all right, I should head back and check on Duncan. He doesn't like me to leave him for very long. I will check on the garden before I go back."

"I was just there. The garden is fine."

Hamish studied me for a moment. "I will always check the garden. Even though I'm not the Keeper like you are, I'm forever connected to it too and will protect it at all costs."

"But you would never kill for it," I protested. "I could never kill for it."

He took a step back into the rain. "You would be surprised by what we are both capable of doing if we can justify it in our own minds." With that, he tipped his hat at me and disappeared into the dark rain.

Was Hamish right? I thought about the key to the garden and the coin in my pocket. In my mind, I justified not showing those items to Craig. I closed the door, unsure if I was more afraid by what Hamish had revealed about himself or by what his words had revealed to me about myself.

Chapter Thirty-Nine

The next morning, I woke bright and early and was out the door, heading toward the village in my rental car before Hamish even arrived to do the morning gardening. I needed the Internet because I wanted to do some research to see if my hunch was right. I wanted to know if I'd found one of the lost Queen Anne five guinea coins from Baird Mac-Callister's shipwreck that had happened all those centuries ago.

I didn't have Cally Beckleberry's phone number or the number for the law office. I wanted to know if what Blackwell had said was true, and she was helping him secure that land. I still felt that Alastair's death was tied somehow to the sale of the coast. All I'd had was Alastair's private cell number, and I wasn't going to call that. Since I couldn't call her in advance, I decided to take a chance that Cally would be at the law office early, trying to catch up on all the work that her law partner had left behind.

When I reached the street the law office was on, my hunch paid off, because I could see a light on in the second-floor window where I knew the waiting room for Croft and Beckleberry was.

The outer door to the office was open like it always had been. I went inside and up the steps to the inner office door, which was locked. I knocked on the door.

Nothing happened. I waited for another full minute before I knocked again.

After a beat, I heard the deadbolt turn in the door, and it opened. Cally stood on the other side of the door, but she wasn't the Cally that I remembered. Her stylish hair was standing up straight on the top her head. However, the most shocking thing was that she was wearing a tracksuit. I had never pegged Cally as a tracksuit person.

"It's you," she said. "You might as well come in."

I hadn't expected Cally to give me a hug, but her reception was less than inviting. The waiting room of the law office was an absolute mess, so much so that I assumed that Cally had been robbed. There were files and papers all over the floor in makeshift piles.

"What happened in here?" I asked, alarmed.

"It's nothing. I'm just trying to get a handle on all the cases. I found out that Alastair was working on some cases that I knew nothing about." She rubbed her eyes, and what was left of what I assumed was yesterday's eye makeup smeared into her eyebrows.

"What cases are those?" I asked.

"More things to do about real estate. Nothing as serious as the land deal on the coast, but I didn't know about them. It was pretty tough to discover that Alastair didn't always tell me what he was working on. We were business partners. I had a right to know what cases my law firm was involved with." She blinked at me. "Why are you here? Is something wrong with the cat?" she asked, sounding worried.

I held up my hand as if that alone with ward off her panic. "Ivanhoe is fine. In fact, he's made himself right at home at the cottage."

She sighed. "That's a relief. I don't think I can take any more bad news at the moment."

"Have you heard from Blackwell that he wants to go forward with the land sale?"

She blinked at me. "How do you know about Blackwell?"

"I met him yesterday morning. Raj Kapoor took me to the location on the coast." I didn't add that I went back later to the same spot with Craig and found a secret cave with a coin that was potentially worth tens of thousands of pounds.

She frowned. "I know how the Kapoor twins and the entire village feel about the land deal. I feel the same way. Just between you and me, I have been looking for a way to stop it."

"You have?"

She nodded. "I think that Raj is right, and we can make a case for environmental protection. Raj wasn't getting very far with that tactic, but he owns a laundromat. I'm an attorney. I know what to say and who to say it to. I've already spoken to a couple of people in government. They say I have a strong case."

"But you stand to lose so much money," I said as I sat on the same sofa I'd sat on the first day that I had met her.

"I don't want it. The cost to the coast and the village is too high. I've struck a deal that I can donate the money that the law firm earned to the same charities the earl wanted to donate the money from his estate to. All other monies from the sale, even if it is sold to the government, will go to them too."

I folded my hands on my lap. "That's very admirable of you."

"The money isn't important," she said. "Not all attorneys are in this business to make money. Some of us want to do good in the world. It was why I went to law school, and I thought it was Alastair's motivation for being a barrister too. I think it was, once upon a time, until greed took over," she said sadly. She cleared her throat as if she was tamping down some type of emotion that threatened to boil over the surface. "Did you come here to ask me questions about the land deal? Because I am tired of answering them."

"Actually, no. Can I use your Wi-Fi?" I asked. "There's no Internet at the cottage, and if I use my American cell phone data, I'll be paying off my cell phone bill until well after I retire."

She frowned.

"Please. I just have check to something online. I'll be off in a second."

She shrugged. She came back a moment later with a slip of paper. "Here's the password. Check what you need to, and then please leave. I have a lot of work to do."

I read the paper. " 'Ivanhoe Rocks'?"

She sighed. "Alastair set it up. He really loved that cat."

"I can tell." I punched the code into my phone and connected to her Internet. I went to my web browser and typed in "Queen Anne five guinea." Immediately, I had results that looked an awful lot like my golden coin. I flipped to the photo gallery on my phone to compare the image that I had found online with the coin that I'd discovered in the cave. The coin itself was hidden in the cottage and tucked in my makeup bag for safekeeping. I was done with carrying clues around in my pockets.

Toggling back and forth between the two photos left no doubt in my mind that they were identical coins. My cave coin wasn't as clean and polished as the one I'd found online, but it was clear that they were the same. My hands shook as I realized that I had a coin worth fifty-five thousand pounds in the same hot-pink makeup pouch as my mascara.

There was no putting it off any longer. I had to tell Craig what I'd discovered. I had a feeling that he wouldn't be pleased that I'd hidden it from him.

Cally sorted files, sitting cross-legged on the floor, while I did my coin research. Perhaps her organizing method explained the tracksuit.

Since Cally seemed to be preoccupied with her filing, I pulled my phone out again and dialed Craig's number. The call went directly to voicemail.

"Hi," I said, being purposely vague in case Cally was listening. "It's Fiona. I think I might have found something that would be of mutual interest to both of us. It's related to our adventure last evening. Call me back as soon as possible. Thanks."

While I was on my cell, another phone within the inner part of the office rang. Cally jumped to her feet and ran inside to answer it.

The ringing stopped, and I could hear her voice through the open door, although I didn't know what she was saying.

I walked over to the pile that she had been sorting while I was leaving a voicemail for the constable. Cally had attached a sticky note to the stack that read "Ongoing Foreclosures."

I raised my eyebrows. I didn't know that Croft and Beckleberry worked in foreclosure law, but as the only law office in the village, I supposed they did a little bit of everything.

Even though I knew it wasn't entirely ethical, I flipped through the file to see what the pending foreclosure cases were in the village. My hands froze when I came across a name I recognized.

It was a name I knew and had seen before. I left the law office before Cally finished her call.

Chapter Forty

By the time I arrived at the Twisted Fox, it was eight in the morning. The place was already full of breakfasters. I walked to the bar, and like always, Lee was there, polishing a glass.

"Fiona!" He smiled at me like he'd just won the lottery by seeing me. "What brings you away from your garden on this fine morning?"

I tried to keep my voice even like it was just any other day. "Just out early today, I guess. I think that my internal clock has finally set to Scottish time."

He grinned. "Scottish time is the best time."

"My godfather always thought so. He was very proud to be Scottish."

"As he should be. And as *you* should be," Lee said.

"I am," I said. "I especially like all the stories. It seems that the Scots have some of the best stories."

"That we do."

"My favorite are about the shipwreck along the coast. I could listen to my godfather's stories about those for hours. Did Uncle Ian ever tell you those stories?"

He stopped polishing the glass and looked at me. "Everyone in Bellewick knows those stories."

I folded my arms on the bar, feeling confident and unafraid because we were in an open space with so many people about. "Uncle Ian told me about his ancestor Baird MacCallister, for example. That was his favorite, but it wasn't until this week that I learned how much money was lost at sea with that shipwreck. It would be a fortune today. Just finding one of those coins would be like winning the lottery. What do you think about that?"

"I think you should stick to gardening," Lee said, leaning across the bar and glaring at me.

That was the moment I realized I had overplayed my hand. I was about to get up from the barstool and run away, when something pinched the back of my neck, and then everything went black.

When I woke up, I had no idea how much time had passed, and I was bouncing in the backseat of a car. It smelled like stale pizza and seawater, which was not an appealing combination, and nausea came at me like a wave against the cliff.

I tried to move, and that was when I realized that my hands were tied in front of me with a piece of wire. I supposed I should be grateful that they weren't tied behind me. I pulled on the wire as quietly as possible, and it bit into my wrists. That wasn't going to work.

I could tell that we were climbing in altitude. I didn't know if it would be better for me to sit up and face my captor or continue to play possum. Neither option seemed like it would do me much good.

"You should have let me kill the girl back at the pub,"

Jock said. "I could put her body in her garden just like I did with Alastair. It would be fitting."

Jock! Lee was working with that jerk, Jock? Then, the detail that I'd tried desperately to remember while I was in the cave with Craig the day before hit me. The first day that I had met Lee, he had told Jock to go clean the hull of a boat or he'd said something close to that. I knew that he'd said that the barnacles were waiting for Jock. Jock was a scuba diver. The gear in the cave was his. That's what my subconscious wanted me to remember. Unfortunately, the realization had come an hour too late.

"No more planting bodies in gardens," Lee chided, talking with his co-murderer. "If you hadn't made that mistake with Alastair, we wouldn't even be in this situation because the girl would never have been involved in the first place."

"How was I supposed to know that she would consider herself a Nancy Drew?" Jock said with a pout in his voice.

"You should have known. She's American, remember," Lee countered. "They never know when to leave well enough alone. And we wouldn't be in this situation if you hadn't decided to knock her out," he continued grumpily. "I was handling everything just fine in the pub."

"You heard the questions she was asking," Jock said. "The girl knew you were the killer. It was just a matter of time before she told Craig about it. Then, we'd both be sunk. I can't go back to prison. I've done my time. If knocking off this annoying American girl keeps me from spending another minute behind bars, I'm going to do it."

Lee sighed. Jock was trying his patience. "We don't have a choice now. We have to get rid of her, don't we?"

"I brought my gun," Jock said.

I shivered at the mention of a gun and felt like the entire car shook when I did. I froze. They didn't seem to feel the tremor from my visceral reaction.

"No shooting," Lee said. "Bullets are too easy to trace."

"It would be quicker. Please don't tell me you have some elaborate murder plan for her like you did with Alastair. That was way too complicated. In my mind, murder should be simple," Jock said. "Bang. You're dead. Move on."

"I hired you to help me with this, so I get to decide how we kill people, okay? You will be paid handsomely for your work. We've already found four coins, and that's just the tip of the iceberg of what could be down there. It will be more than enough to pay off my gambling debts and more than enough to save Twisted Fox from closing."

Gambling debts? I thought. I would bet anything that Lee was the person or one of the people that Seth was afraid of or maybe even owed money to.

"Twisted Fox wouldn't be in foreclosure if you hadn't mortgaged it so many times to pay for your gambling habit."

"Shut your mouth," Lee snapped. "I may have made some bad decisions in the past, but I love my pub and am going to save it any cost."

"Fine," Jock said in annoyance. "I need the money too, you know. I've got bills."

"You just have to be patient a little while longer for your cut. If Alastair had been willing to be patient instead of moving ahead with that land deal that would completely cut off our access to the dive point, he would have got his cut too, but he was too impatient. Now, he's dead," Lee said without an ounce of remorse.

I felt the car rock to a stop, and I braced myself so that I wouldn't roll off the seat.

"We're here," Lee said, as if announcing our arrival at grandma's house.

My stomach turned. I couldn't believe that I had thought this man was my friend at one point.

"Get the girl," Lee said.

While they were distracted with climbing out of the car, I rolled onto my back. Jock opened the back door behind the passenger seat, and my feet were pointed in that direction. When he leaned into the car to pull me out, I kicked him in the face.

He screamed in pain. Jock stumbled back and swore, calling me a string of terrible names. Even though I had been able to kick him, sitting up while my hands were tied was no easy feat and took a moment too long, which was just long enough for Lee to reach in and yank me from the car.

"I'm going to kill her!" Jock screamed, still holding his face. Blood poured through his fingers where his nose was. I hoped I'd broken it.

Lee jerked me toward the cliff's edge. I fought him with every step.

"Stop fighting me, Fiona!" he cried.

"So you can kill me?" I shouted back. "You've got to be kidding!"

Lee glared at me with those bright blue eyes. I couldn't believe that I had once thought they were welcoming. I had been wrong, so very wrong. His eyes were cold just like the rest of him.

"You shouldn't be angry at *me*," I said. "What about your partner?"

Jock glared at me. Blood dripped from his face. "Shut up!"

"Jock has been talking to Blackwell. He was playing both sides to ensure he would come out on top."

Lee stared at Jock. "Is this true?"

"She's lying," Jock spat.

"I saw him with Blackwell, and I've already told Chief Inspector Craig about it. He could be talking to Blackwell right now."

Lee let go of me, but before I could run away, Jock charged. I had nowhere to go, and he pushed me off the cliff.

I dropped fifteen feet, and my body crashed feet first onto a rock outcropping, but it was good fortune because that stopped me from falling all the way to the sea below. I crumpled to the rocky ledge and pain radiated from my ankles all the way up my back. I felt like someone had donkey-kicked me in the chest, but I didn't think anything was broken. I groaned. I didn't want to get up. Maybe they would leave me there and think I was dead.

A shot was fired, and rock splinted into a thousand pieces just above me. That was all the motivation I needed to move. I scrambled to my feet and made my way along the rocks just as I had the night before with the constable, just as I had in my dream. But this time I had to be even more careful and move even more slowly because my hands were tied. I wasn't sure I could do it with my hands tethered together like they were.

Another shot was fired. That one missed me by just a hair. I would have to try to make it to the cave. The only other choice would be to dive into the ocean, but with my hands bound and the North Sea so frigid, I didn't dare take my chances in the inky waters.

My fingers dug into the uneven cliff, and the sharp stone cut into my palms. I ignored the pain. Those rocks under my hands and feet were the only things holding me in place; they were the only things saving me.

More shots were fired. I used an outcropping of rocks to shield myself.

"If you can't hit her with a bullet, go down there after her," I heard Lee scream at Jock.

That made me move faster. Each handhold was precarious, as I had to use my hands together like one clumsy claw.

When the indentation in the rock, which I knew was the mouth of the cave, came into view, I whimpered in relief. Behind me, I heard Jock grunting as he made his way across the rocks while I slipped into the cave.

When I was inside, I let my eyes adjust enough to the dim light so that I could see where I knew the scuba tank would be.

I picked up the scuba tank and hoisted it into my bound hands. It was full and would make a good weapon. But it was also heavy and awkward. I knew that it would take all my strength to swing it, and I really would have only one chance.

I heard Jock before I saw him, so with the tank in hand, I moved to the mouth of the cave. When Jock's face appeared in the opening to the cave, I did not hesitate. I whacked him in the face with the scuba tank. He screamed and fell back from the edge into the sea below.

I dropped the tank on the cave floor, shaking from head to toe. I couldn't believe what I had just done, even if it had been in self-defense. I slipped to the cave floor. I don't know how long I sat there, when I heard movement outside the cave.

I scrambled to my feet and was about to pick up my scuba tank for a second time when I heard, "Fiona! Fiona!" It was Craig calling me.

But was it really him or was it a trap? It sounded like him. And even if it was a trap, I couldn't hide in this cave forever. I peeked my head out of the cave and saw Craig making his way across the narrow ledge.

"Craig! I'm here!" I blinked at him and held up my still-bound hands, standing in the narrow mouth of the cave.

"Thank God," he said. "You're alive." He quickened his pace to reach me.

"Where's Lee? He's behind everything," I said. I glanced up and down the cliff edge, looking for the corrupted bartender. "He was behind everything," I repeated brokenly.

"Don't worry about him," the constable said. "He's in the back of my jeep. I have two officers keeping a close eye on him."

I felt my body melt with relief. "Wait! How did you know where I was?"

"Seth."

"Seth? How?"

"He confessed that he was paying off gambling debts to Lee, and Lee needed the money to save his bar. He saw Lee and Jock put you in the car and followed their car here, then called us."

"Wow," I said, but I couldn't help thinking that Seth could have called the police while he was still in the village.

Craig reached into his jacket pocket and came out with a Swiss army knife.

"Yet another handy tool you have in your jacket," I said as he cut through the wire.

He smiled. "You bet. Now, can we get off this cliff for good."

"Happily," I said, meeting him on the ledge.

Epilogue

Three days later, I was in the garden, weeding around the bearded purple iris that had just come into bloom. Irises were one of my favorite flowers. They were so dramatic, but short-lived. The irises at Duncreigan were some of the most spectacular I had ever seen as their ruffled petals unfurled. Since I was learning that gardening in a magical garden was much different from gardening anywhere else, it remained to be seen if these beard irises at Duncreigan would be short-lived. The same could be said for the visions that the garden gave me. They were becoming more frequent the more the garden bloomed, but I had yet to mention this to anyone.

Ivanhoe snoozed next to me in the grass. I had learned that the cat would much prefer to be outside. So the Scottish Fold and I had struck a deal. He could be with me when I worked in the garden if he agreed not to kill any of the small creatures that lived there, including the birds and, most importantly, Duncan the Squirrel. So far, he had kept up his side of the bargain, but I knew, given the right opportunity, Duncan was in some serious trouble. I prayed that the red squirrel never let his guard down when it came to the cat.

Hamish and Duncan came into the garden then. Hamish pushed a wheelbarrow of mulch, and Duncan chirped from his perch on Hamish's shoulder.

Ivanhoe flicked his tail but gave no other indication that he noticed the new arrivals, although I was certain he knew where Duncan was at all times.

I looked up from my weeding. "Thank you for bringing that down, Hamish."

"Of course, Miss Fiona. I will do anything to help with the garden. You know that."

"I do," I agreed.

"I just came from the village. The Twisted Fox is closed until further notice. No one in the village knows where they will find their next meal. It is a real shame that Lee had to go and kill Alastair and ruin the pub for everyone." Hamish set the wheelbarrow down and placed a hand to his back as he straightened up. "And I will never forgive him for trying to kill you, Miss Fiona. If he wasn't already in prison, I would do much more than box that boy's ears."

I smiled up at him. "I appreciate that you want to defend me, Hamish, but I'm fine."

He studied me and then nodded, as if he had decided that I wasn't any worse for wear from my frightening encounter with Lee MacGill on the cliff edge. "But it still remains to be seen what will become of the Twisted Fox," he said. "Maybe someone in the village will buy it. It would be a shame if it was sold to any outsider."

"Maybe they will," I said, thinking of what Raj had told me the day before about his plans for the pub.

"So you mean to stay, Miss Fiona," Hamish said.

I stood up from where I was kneeling in the grass. "I do. I have all this now, and I have no one to go back to in Tennessee. I mean, I have my sister and parents, of course, but my flower shop is gone. And . . ." I trailed off. I was learning that it wasn't as easy to recover from a broken heart as I wished it to be. The murder had been a distraction for a time.

Hamish nodded as if he understood what I was unable to say. "There's nothing as bad in the single life as a bad marriage. Take it from me, lass." He said this in such a way that I wondered what Hamish's past was. As long as I had known him, he'd always been my godfather's bachelor caretaker.

"I still hurt, Hamish." I whispered it.

His wrinkled face folded into a sympathetic smile. "I know. You might always. Your heart does not have an on-and-off switch. It would be easier if it did, wouldn't it?"

I smiled.

"But," he went on. "If you married him, you wouldn't be here right now with your garden. You wouldn't be fulfilling your destiny. You would have half a life." He grinned, showing off his missing molars. "You would not have met Duncan."

I eyed the squirrel on the pile of mulch and laughed. My smiled faded.

"Aye, yes, the pain, lass . . . Time is the only healer I can offer ye. It's the only healer that any of us have to rest our heart upon. Hour by hour, day by day, it will get better. And then one day, you will wake up and not feel the sting any longer. Something will have shifted, and you won't even realize that it's happened. That's how time works, lass." He paused. "And someday you will be ready to find love again."

"But what if I don't find it again? What if this was my one

chance?" I asked the questions that plagued me and whose answers I feared most.

"Nothing in this life is certain, nothing in this life is promised, but I can tell you this: you can have a full and beautiful life, and having that depends on you and you alone."

I looked out over my garden and saw it coming to life. Trees budded and green shoots shot up from the ground. By midsummer, the garden would flourish with every color of the rainbow. It was full, beautiful, and alive. My life would be that too—unexpected, brand new, and one I had the opportunity to write on my own terms.

Hamish returned to his weeding, and I turned to my attention back to the bearded irises. With near-silent steps, the blue-eyed fox appeared in front of me. He stared at me, holding my gaze for what felt like an eternity, and where I had seen those eyes before finally clicked in my head.

With shaky hands, I removed my garden gloves. "Uncle Ian?" I whispered the question.

And the fox winked.

Acknowledgments

Memories have always been more important to me than possessions, so as a teenager, I promised myself that I would travel the world and make as many memories as possible while I could. Even as a young adult with very little money, I traveled, sleeping in luggage compartments of train cars and eating candy bars and potato chips because it was what I could afford. Many years later, I am so happy to share with all my dear readers one of favorite countries, Scotland, and bring that mystical place to life in a new and magical way.

This book wouldn't have happened if it had not been for the support of my super agent and beloved friend, Nicole Resciniti, who encouraged me to write about my travels. She particularly liked the idea of Scotland. Nicole, thank you always.

Thanks too to Crooked Lane Books and my editor, Anne Brewer, for giving *Flowers and Foul Play* a cozy home in your impressive list of mysteries. I'm so excited to be working with all of you, and I could not think of a better place for this book that is special to me.

Thanks to my friend, David Seymour, for his unfailing encouragement while I was writing this book. The chocolate helped a lot too.

Acknowledgments

Love and gratitude to my dearest friend, Mariellyn Grace, and her beloved daughter, Laurie. When I said that I had to return to Scotland to research this novel, Mariellyn did not hesitate, and we took little Laurie on her first of undoubtedly many Go-Go Girl adventures across the world. It was a perfect trip with two of my favorite people on this earth.

Love, as always, to my family, Andy, Nicole, Isabella, and Andrew, for cheering me on.

And to my mother, Rev. Pamela Flower, who is in heaven, thank you for raising me to be a fearless adventurer. I wanted to see the world because you saw it first, and you are with me everywhere I go.

And finally to my Heavenly Father, thank you for so many unexpected dreams come true. I am grateful that some of those dreams can include a hint magic too.